ONE THING AFTER ANOTHER

A passing log swept the boat out from under Maggie, and she dropped with a shocking splash into the river, the rope slipping agonizingly in her hands. Suddenly her body was tossing and turning with the torrent.

Then she felt Colin's arm about her waist. "Got you!" he yelled above the river, nearly breaking his own hold on the rope with the shock of her added weight. "Grab on now!" Flinging her arm wildly in his direction, she hooked her elbow about his neck, nearly throttling him.

When at last they reached shore, and Maggie had clambered out of the water onto the bank, she looked up to see a large green-and-turquoise dragon that murmured to herself: "Aha! Dinner is served."

Song of Sorcery

Elizabeth Scarborough

BANTAM BOOKS
TORONTO • NEW YORK • LONDON • SYDNEY • AUCKLAND

SONG OF SORCERY

A Bantam Book / February 1982
2nd printing .... May 1984

ISBN 0-553-24554-6

Published simultaneously in the United States and Canada

Bantam Books are published by Bantam Books, Inc. Its trade-
mark, consisting of the words "Bantam Books" and the por-
trayal of a rooster, is Registered in U.S. Patent and Trademark
Office and in other countries. Marca Registrada. Bantam
Books, Inc., 666 Fifth Avenue, New York, New York 10103.

PRINTED IN THE UNITED STATES OF AMERICA

H   11 10 9 8 7 6 5 4 3

For Betty, Don, Monte, and Gladys Scarborough and Richard Gridley Kacsur and the pets who are my family. And for Dr. Martha Kowalski, who checked her own laboratory work while her office nurse was fighting dragons. Also for Jeannie Jett, Marion Watts, Allen Damron and Dr. Jeff Trilling, who not only believe in fantastic beasties and awesome enchantments, but believe in me as well.

ACKNOWLEDGEMENT

The "song of sorcery" quoted by Colin (and added to by him) is a compilation of several different versions of "The Gypsie Laddie," "Whistling Gypsy O" or "Gypsy Davey," a popular folk ballad believed to date from the 1600's. I am deeply grateful to Dover Books for reprinting *The English and Scottish Popular Ballads* collection, edited by Francis James Child, from whom the lyrics I've used in *Song of Sorcery* have been gleaned, and also to the many wonderful performers of folk music whose artistic stewardship of these old songs has been a continuing source of inspiration. I owe particular thanks in this respect to my good friend Allen Damron and to Laurie, Rusty and Autumn of BANISH MISFORTUNE.

1

If if hadn't been for Maggie's magic, the eggs would have tumbled from the basket and shattered when the panting barmaid careened into her. The automatic gathering spell barely had time, as it was, to snatch the eggs into the container before they were spilled back out again as the distraught young woman began tugging at Maggie's sleeve.

"Come! Be quick now! Your old Granny's at it again!"

"Be careful!" Maggie scrambled to keep her eggs from breaking, trying at the same time to snatch her sleeve from the girl's grasp. "What do you mean?"

"Some poor young minstrel was singing a song, and just like that she starts ravin' and rantin' and changes him into a wee birdie, and commenced chasin' him and callin' on her great cat to come eat him up! Oooooh, I hears the cat now— do be quick!" This time she had no occasion to do further snatching at the sleeve, but slipped instead on the forgotten trail of egg mess left in Maggie's wake as she galloped across the barnyard and through the tavern's back door.

Wood clattered on stone and fist on flesh as the patrons of the tavern rudely competed for the front exit, tripping on overturned chairs and trampling table linens underfoot in their haste to be gone. Only three of the most dedicated customers remained at their table, placidly sipping their brew, watching the commotion with far less interest than they watched the level in their flagons.

Granny's braid was switching faster than the tail of a cow swatting blowflies as she ran back and forth. She showed surprising agility for one of her age, and for all her leaping about was not too out of breath to utter a constant stream of hearty and imaginative curses. With the grace of a girl she bounded over an upturned bench and then to the top of a

1

table, whacking the rafter above it with furious blows of her broom.

"Come down from there this instant, you squawking horror, and take what's coming to you!" Granny demanded, black eyes snapping, and body rocking with the fury of her attack. "Ching!" she hollered back over her shoulder. "Ching! Here, kitty. Come to breakfast!"

It was fortunate for the mockingbird that Maggie saw him dive under the table to escape the broom before the cat spotted him. Just as the cat gathered himself for a pounce on the low-flying bird, Maggie launched herself in a soaring leap and managed to catch the cat in mid-pounce, retaining her grip on him as they landed with a "whoof" just short of the table.

Struggling for the breath their abrupt landing knocked from her, Maggie clasped the cat tighter as he squirmed to escape. "Grandma, you stop that right now!" she panted with all the authority she could muster from her red-faced, spraddle-legged position on the floor.

"I will not!" the old lady snapped, taking another swing at the bird as it landed safely back in the rafter above the table. "No two-bit traveling tinhorn is going to gargle such filth in MY tavern about MY in-laws and get away with it." She jumped down from the table, looking for another vantage point from which to launch her attack.

"Whoever he is, Gran, change him back," Maggie insisted, setting the cat free now that the bird was out of reach on the rafter, quivering in its feathers at the slit-eyed looks it was receiving from both broom-wielding elderly matron and black-and-white-spotted cat.

The old lady glared at her granddaughter and primly adjusted her attire, tucking her braid back into its pin. "I most certainly will not."

"You most certainly will," Maggie insisted, noting with some consternation the set of her grandmother's chin and the anthracite glitter of her eyes. "Grandma, whatever he's done, it's for Dad to dispense justice—it just isn't the thing these days to go converting people into supper for one's cat just because they displease one. What will the neighbors think of us? It isn't respectable."

The old lady made a rude noise. "As if I cared about that. But alright, dear. Only wait until you hear what he did—wait

2

till your father hears! That birdbrain will wish Ching *had* made a meal of him before Sir William's done with him!"

"But I didn't *write* the tune," protested the man who materialized in place of the mockingbird as Gran snapped the release ritual from her fingers. His arms and legs clung to the rafter for dear life. "Please, somebody get me a ladder."

"It isn't that high," snorted Grandma contemptuously. "Ching can jump it from this table."

"One of you men come help me with this thing," Maggie said, taking hold of one end of a long bench. A member of the stalwart society who'd remained at their station during the melee, being between pints, sauntered over and lifted the opposite end of the bench, and together they stood it on the table so that the former mockingbird could use it to descend.

"Now then, sir." Maggie stood with hands on hips as the stranger dusted himself off. "You have upset my grandmother terribly, and I want to know how and why. What did you say to her?"

"*I* upset *her?*" he stammered, red deepening his already ruddy cheeks.

"What did he say to you?" Maggie whirled on the grandmother, who sat cross-legged on the floor, trying to calm her cat. The cat was attempting to maintain a seriously threatening hissing crouch while being dragged flat-eared and whip-tailed into the old lady's lap.

"Nothing much, dearie," replied the grandmother, pouring over her descendant a gaze of the purest molasses. "He can explain to your father. Chingachgook is a trifle upset. I'll be at my cottage if you need me." She dimpled her dried-apple cheeks at the stranger. "Do sing Sir William that delightful song, young man. Ta, Granddaughter!" A wave of her arm and a final whip of the cat's tail from the crook of her other arm, and she was off.

When Maggie looked back for the stranger, she found him by the hearth, inspecting a fiddle for damage, setting it to his shoulder and lightly drawing a bow across the strings. He had slung a guitar across his back.

"You're a minstrel, then?"

He had to try out several notes before answering. "I'd hardly be making myself so popular with my music and all if I were a stonemason, now would I?" He spoke flippantly and Maggie thought it was to conceal the tremble in his hands as,

3

apparently satisfied that his instruments were undamaged, he slipped fiddle and bow into a soft skin bag. "Who are you?" he asked, "besides the relative of that witch?"

"You might do better with a sweeter lyric, minstrel. The one you've used so far today hardly seems to please, now does it? I am also Sir William's relative, as a matter of fact. He's my father."

The minstrel blinked twice, rapidly, as if expecting the medium-sized dusky-colored girl to be transformed into his idea of a fair and lithesome noblewoman. She continued to stare at him frankly and without noticeable approval, giving at best, in her bare feet, coarse brown tunic and skirt, and dirty white apron an impression of pleasant ordinariness dealing with momentary unpleasantness. Remembering his manners, the minstrel bowed, briefly. "Colin Songsmith, Journeyman Minstrel, at your service, lady."

She had followed his inspection with one of her own as far as her own dirty feet, and now looked up from them to meet his gaze with shrewd brown eyes. "You're looking no great treat yourself. Wait a bit."

Watching her disappear through the back door, Colin sank down onto a bench that had miraculously remained upright and passed long, tired fingers over his eyes. Being changed from one thing to another, chased by witches and cats, and being changed back again was not the sort of thing his apprenticeship had prepared him for. He could make fair to middling instruments, write stirring epic sagas and set them to equally stirring and complimentary music, play lute, zither, harp, dulcimer, pipes, and drums competently, and fiddle and guitar splendidly, if he did say so. He was quite prepared to entertain at feasts and be feted, to immortalize adventures and be considered an adventurer by association, to record history, and to have all the ladies wooing him ever so prettily for songs immortalizing their own particular charms.

But no, he had decidedly not been prepared to be one moment singing the latest southern ballad to an appreciative audience, and the next to be regarding his fiddle from a bird's-eye view while the matronly sort who had served his cakes and ale batted at him with a broom, shrieking to her cat to come and eat him.

He had hardly been instructed in maintaining his aplomb while hanging onto rafters, getting splinters in his fingers and knees, while some brown-haired young woman argued with

4

her grey-and-brown-haired grandmother about the respectability of feeding him to the cat, the animal in question evidencing no doubt whatsoever as it lashed its wicked tail at him and licked its wicked chops.

His ruminations were interrupted by the return of the unlikely noblewoman, armed with a broom. Colin knocked over the bench he had been sitting on in his haste to escape.

"Don't be a goose," she said. "I'm only going to dust you off a bit. You're all over feathers and dust, and if you're going to see my dad you'll have to be somewhat more hygienic. He's been sick, and you reek of contamination." He managed to stand still while she broomed him with brutal briskness.

After five months in bed, no amount of twisting and turning and repositioning could make Sir William quite comfortable. It wasn't just his legs, injured when an arrow inexplicably found its way into his horse while he was hunting, causing the poor beast to rear and roll on him. Granny Brown claimed sickbed fever had prolonged his recovery far past the usual convalescent period, and lack of active use had caused his legs to weaken and his wounds to mortify, conditions she continued still to fight with her entire herbal arsenal.

What he wished was that Amberwine could come home— even for a short visit. Although she had no healing magic whatsoever, and cheerfully admitted incompetence at managing even the simplest aspects of household or estate affairs, her lighthearted faery gaiety and placid, accepting intelligence brought the dimples out from under Granny Brown's traditional witch scowls, and even slowed the brusque and practical Maggie down to something close to gentleness.

Ah well, he sighed to himself, arranging his bedclothes in a position suitable for the company whose footsteps he heard climbing the long spiral staircase to his tower chamber. He'd made her the best possible marriage to that southern lord—the fellow might even get to be king, they said, and she seemed to like him in the bargain. Where he'd find such a match for thorny Maggie was more than a sick man should contemplate. It was complicated arranging marriages for not-quite-born-in-wedlock children one acknowledged belatedly. The village witch's daughter who at the age of two years is declared to be the daughter of the Lord-High-Mayor-Knight-Protector-of-His-Majesty's-Northern-Territories (And Incorporated Villages) tends to remain the village witch's daughter. No amount

5

of equal education or advantage seemed to be able to make of a witchchild as refined a lady as her faery sister. For all of Amberwine's extra encouragement and coaching, Maggie remained neither fish nor fowl, her mother's line too base for nobles, her father's too noble for the base-born lads. Too bad she wasn't a son, so all he'd have to do would be to leave her the estate, which she managed most capably, and find her a wife. Worthy wives were bound to be more common commodities than worthy husbands, he felt sure.

To the poundings on his chamber door he called permission to enter, and a disheveled Maggie did so, followed by an only slightly less disheveled young man.

"Hullo, Dad." She dropped a kiss on his forehead.

"'Lo, Magpie. Who's this?" He made an attempt at hearty cheerfulness in the direction of the young man.

"I caught Granny trying to feed him to Ching," she replied. "She was in a dreadful huff."

Sir William narrowed his eyes at the young man. "What did you do to cause my mother-in-law to wish to make cat food of you, sir?"

"Your pardon, noble sir." The young man made him a low bow. "Colin Songsmith, Journeyman Minstrel, at your service. Noble sir, I don't know why the lady was so vexed with me. I only sang the latest southern ditty for her, practicing it, y'know, before presenting it to you."

"Present it to me then, dammit, and let's get to the bottom of this. Maggie, dear, do scratch my shoulder—ah, right there—good girl."

Since his fiddle rendition of the tune had met with such avian results, Colin unslung his guitar from his back and tuned it. The tuning gave him time to compose himself. Finally he tapped his fingers on the soundboard of the guitar and told them, "Not being from this district, or the one where the song originates, I can't understand the fuss over it. I learned it from Minstrel Giles. He said he always comes north this time of year to avoid the first blossom of some of the southern plants. Gives him ill humors of the nose and throat, he says, and, as you well may imagine that's an unhandy affliction for a troubadour." He paused to allow this professional confidence to sink in. Maggie nodded briskly that she was perfectly capable of understanding occupational hazards and the old man impatiently waved him to continue. "Ahem—yes, as I was saying, folk down south at least, find

6

this an entertaining tune. Giles says it's all the rage." He paused again for dramatic emphasis before striking the strings in a minor key. The guitar sent ripples of sobbing across the room once, twice, and once again.

The minstrel's features coarsened and his voice dropped to a lower register. The guitar was a stone fence he leaned upon as he confided ribald gossip to another peasant. The music galloped along in time to his voice.

"The gypsy Davey came riding along,
Singing so loud and gaily.
He sang so sweet and so complete,
Down come our faery lady . . . down come the faery maid.

"She come trippin' down the stairs
Her maids were all before her
As soon's he saw her pretty face
He cast some glamourie o'er her."

Sir William opened his eyes. A gypsy man had wreaked a great deal of havoc in the village two festival seasons ago by absconding simultaneously with two of the estate's dairy maids, sisters whose soiled state Sir William had had to launder with generous donations to their dowries so they could be safely wed before they whelped. If the fella'd charmed a faery he must be quite the charmer indeed—the faeries were so enchanting themselves, they generally saw through the "glamourie" of others.

The minstrel dropped the peasant role and became the gypsy, insinuating himself into the lady's romantic imagination. Casting Maggie as the lady, his passionate glances totally confused the expression of polite attention she had maintained. Trying to stare down the minstrel's false gypsy as she would her grandmother's cat, she found herself annoyed that she was unable to look away when she wished.

"Will you forsake your husband dear,
And all the wealth he gave ye?
Will you leave your house and lands
To follow Gypsy Davey—to ride with the Gypsy Dave?

Maggie flushed, her dark skin burgundy with befuddlement as the minstrel released her eyes to become narrator again.

7

"She dressed herself in her gay green cloak
And her boots of finest leather,
Then mounted on her pony fine,
And they rode off together.

"Late from huntin' came Lord Rowan,
Asking for his lady.
The one did cry and the other reply
'She's gone with the Gypsy Davey—rode away with the
Gypsy Dave.'"

Intricate minor patterns wove through the main theme,
invoking hoofbeats fading away from the lady's fine home
across the moors. The minstrel didn't look up from the guitar
again until the last keening notes quivered off his strings to die
in the stillness around him. Sir William's face was a most
alarmingly unhealthy eggplant color, and the resemblence
between Maggie and her grandmother was suddenly uncomfortably apparent.

"Well, Dad," she smiled around sharp white teeth, "What
d'you think? Boil him in oil, or flay him alive?"

What had Colin's masters taught him at the academy? In deal-
ings with aristocrats, when in doubt, grovel. He knelt so fast
he banged his knee on the floor. "Your pardon, m'lady, Sir
William. I only did as you asked. I meant no offense, and
can't think why the tune has given it. I'll never play it again
—ever." In your vicinity, at least, he added to himself, searching for an exit as Sir William's skin regained its former pallor.

"Perhaps you should choose less exotic material in the
future, lad," the old knight advised drily, "or not mention
names in your ditties. The Lord Rowan cuckolded in your
song, unless of course there's another one, is my son-in-law,
married to my younger daughter, the Lady Amberwine."

Colin gulped, his eyes darting furtively to the leaded glass
window and back to the long flight of stone steps they'd
mounted coming to the tower room.

"Who *was* this fellow with the stuffy nose who taught you
that song?" Maggie asked.

"Minstrel Giles, m'lady?"

"I was wondering if he'd like that nose removed?"

"Maggie!" snapped Sir William, "You're scaring the lad to
death, you little heathen. He said it wasn't his song." He
turned more kindly to the minstrel, who by now was perspir-

ing profusely. "Sorry, son." He jerked a thumb at his glowering daughter. "She's a terrific girl, really, just awfully fond of her sister, as we all are around here." He shook his head. "I don't understand this at all. Winnie—Lady Amberwine—is not at all your average running-off sort of girl. She's too considerate for that type of thing. To just leave without explanation! No letter to us! Even if she didn't like her husband, which I could have sworn she did, she'd hardly have placed her family in such an awkward spot without giving us fair warning—"

"Fine lady, indeed, noble sir," the minstrel agreed emphatically, "I'm sure she's a fine, *fine* lady."

"Too right, she is that." Sir William's hands tortured the bedclothes for a few moments before he turned his baffled and miserable face to Maggie.

She leaned down and hugged him. "Aw, Dad, of course she is. She wouldn't just go gallivanting off with the first passing gypsy—you know very well she can hardly decide which gown to wear to breakfast in the morning without consulting every servant in the house, and me and Gran besides. She certainly wouldn't be able to bolt altogether on the spur of the moment like that! It'd take her a week to pack!" She glared again at the cowering Colin. "Must have been one of His Lordship's enemies paid that Giles fellow to make up that awful song."

Colin gulped and waggled a tentative index finger for attention. "Begging your ladyship's pardon," he began, not really wishing to call notice to himself again but equally reluctant for Giles to suffer the consequences of his own silence. "Giles confessed that he only gave the tune a bit of a polish—it was actually a popular creation."

"Common gossip music, then, eh?" Sir William looked even older and sicker than he had looked when Colin came into the room, and he had appeared twenty hard years older than Maggie's grandmother then. "Maggie, what can be going on with the girl?"

Maggie looked down, shoving her fists deep into her apron pockets. "I don't know, Dad."

"You remember that nasty gypsy fella running off with Mullaly's daughters and nearly emptying my wallet trying to save their foolish reputations?"

"Yes, Dad, I remember. Betsy and Beatrice Mullaly are as bovine as their charges, though. Everybody knows that. Winnie's got more sense."

9

"I think so. I don't know. I wish I had my legs under me, so I could go see Rowan and talk to him myself." He made an impatient attempt to rise. Maggie gently pushed him back onto the bed.

"That's no good, and you know it. I'll go talk to Rowan."

The old man looked at her for a long time, then closed his eyes and sank back against his pillow. "Of course you will, lass. You're the only one who can, I suppose." Then opening one eye he looked at her again, more sharply. "You're not thinking of going alone, of course?"

She shrugged. "Why not? We can't have it all over the territories what I'm up to if there's nothing in it. I'll be alright. I've got my magic to protect me, after all."

He snorted. "Hearthcraft, hmph. All very well for running the castle or tavern, but what are you going to do if you meet a bear, girl?"

"Very well, then," she conceded, trying not to allow their disagreement to tire her father any further. "I'll take the mockingbird, here, with me."

The pronouncement came as a complete surprise to Colin.

Sir William peered closely at him. "Oh, then if a bear comes along HE sings the creature sweetly to sleep with a bloody lullabye, and you turn it into a great bloody hearthrug?" He ran a hand through his thinning hair, grayer since the accident. "Ah, well, he's responsible to his guild for his conduct, and if he's with you I can at least be quite sure he won't be spreading that song about. I suppose it wouldn't be wise to have any of the local guard go. I doubt any of them would purposely slander your sister, but people don't seem to be able to forego telling everything they know, nonetheless." He sighed once more, deeply, and capitulated. "He'll have to do, I guess."

"Good." She kissed her father's cheek again and rose to her feet. "I'll just go put binding spells on the cleaning I've already done, and enlarge the larder a bit, before I talk to Gran about handling anything that comes up while I'm gone."

"That should be exciting," Sir William mumbled to her back as she swept through the door ahead of Colin.

10

2

Maggie was unalarmed to hear the Territorial troops marching in close order drill, accompanied by professional mourners keening for the dead and wounded, as she entered her grandmother's cottage. She recognized the tromping of the marchers as her gran's heavy-handed double beat on the loom batten, which always sounded like an advancing army, complete with fife and drum corps, and the keening sound as the old lady chanted a song in the ancient tongue to make the work less tedious.

"Maggie, darlin'!" Her grandmother exclaimed, raising her legs past the edge of the loom bench and twirling around on her behind to face her granddaughter. "I'm so glad you're here! Now you can do this nettlesome chore and I can stir up that batch for Betsy Baker."

"Funny, I was just talking about her." She picked up a shuttle, changed the shed with a tromp on the foot treadle, then clucked her tongue at her grandmother. "Really, Gran, look at all these broken warps you've left hanging. It'll never hold up this way!"

Gran regarded her through the measuring glass she held at eye-level, slowly pouring a smoking yellow fluid into it. "You, my dear, are the home economist. *I* am the alchemist. I'll stick to my own field any day. All those itty-bitty threads—bah!"

"Well, I've yet to see you turn tin into gold," Maggie replied, her thumb and forefinger lightly spinning the broken ends together again. With the mending spell she was projecting from beneath her conversation, the warps should be stronger when she had respun them than they were originally.

Gran added an irridescent blue powder to the yellow fluid, and curls of green smoke interlaced with the yellow wafting toward the string-tied bundles of herbs that hung so thickly

11

from the ceiling that Maggie sometimes felt she was walking upside down in a meadow. "I have always considered that a very silly practice, Magdalene. Tin is much more useful." Gran always put on her most dignified air when practicing her craft. Maggie had received instructive lectures at these times, surrounded by noxious fumes and falling bits of materia medica from the ceiling, and was always addressed during these sermons as "Magdalene," her full name, which she particularly disliked.

Turning on the bench to face her grandmother's back, Maggie leaned against the front beam of the loom, her right foot swinging, rumpling the striped rug she'd woven for Gran's floor. She'd have to reweave another bald spot, she noted. Gran was always spilling something caustic and burning it, or the cat was kneading it bare. "I'm going down south, Gran."

"So Ching told me." She set the beaker of liquid down and faced her granddaughter. "Don't you think it's Amberwine's business who she chooses to go with?"

"I suppose so." Maggie frowned at her nails and tried to explain the uneasiness she had felt since hearing the minstrel's song. "But she's not like us, Gran. I mean, she was always having to remind me to stop and think how what I was doing was going to make other people feel—she never just DOES things."

"You think she was coerced?"

Maggie nodded. "Or something like that. Or Rowan's mistreated her—though I rather think she'd have been back home by now if that were the case. Anyhow, whatever she's doing, she won't mind a visit, will she? And I shall finally see somewhere besides this stupid village. Do you know, one of the guards who accompanied Rowan to the wedding told me the flowers are already out down there this time of year?"

"That's not all that's out, dearie." Gran regarded her severely. "Our climate may be inhospitable a great deal of the year, but it does serve to discourage a lot of the nonsense they put up with down south. I had a message from your Aunt Sybil only a month or so ago, that she had seen bandits from across the Brazorian border destroy a mountain village right near Rowan's territory. And there's dragons and werewolves and ogres and pirates out there as well," she sat down, wearied by the length and import of her list, "and lions and tigers . . ."

12

"Don't forget the bears," Maggie said drily.

"And bears. And don't you laugh at me, my girl. Even a unicorn can be very dangerous, if startled. Worst of all, though, are the people. Witches and wizards can be very territorial, so you'd best be a bit more polite to strange magicians than you are to your old granny. And men, of course. Speaking of which, Magdalene, I do not think your father very wise to send you off with that scandalmongering Songsmith character."

"Don't be silly, Gran. He's just a musician—he doesn't have any magic at all."

"Don't be silly yourself. You don't know if he has any magic or not, and he's a man, isn't he? How do you suppose there got to be more of them than there are of us, and why do you suppose our powers are getting weaker every generation?"

"Surely this is not MY Grandmother Brown getting all moralistic with me?" Maggie grinned.

Granny looked embarrassed. "Of course not, you impudent wench. But pairing off, if done at all, should be done only after your powers are fully developed and tested. Your poor mother never did amount to anything, witchwise, getting involved so young and all . . ."

"Now don't go blaming Dad . . ."

"I'm not. I'm hardly the bigot some folks are, but . . ."

A playful rapping at the door interrupted her, and there was no waiting for her to grant entry before the door opened and a round face topped by a thatch of white hair peeped around the door at them. The face leered, and a matching set of rosy fingers waggled at them. "Good day to you, Goodwitch Brown, Mistress Maggie. May I come in?"

"Appears to me you're already in, Hugo," Granny said. "What can I do for you?"

The man seated himself in Granny's only other chair, a rocker. He grinned, showing a collection of teeth in every known metal. "Well, I'm only just up to the north, Goodwitch, and I thought I'd pop in and get a bit of my usual." His watery blue eyes strayed to Maggie and overstayed a welcome they'd never had to begin with.

"To be sure," said Granny, climbing onto her narrow bed to reach a row of handmade jugs on the shelf above it. She had to sniff several before selecting one.

Hugo followed her movements for a moment before licking his lips and addressing Maggie.

"Well, Mistress Maggie, I understand you're taking a nice trip."

"News certainly travels fast."

"I suppose you're going south to visit your lovely sister?"

"Toads! Does the whole village know already?" Maggie was annoyed. Not only had she hoped to keep her mission a secret, but she particularly did not want a gossipy old goat like Hugo the Peddler to know her business.

"No, no, no. Never fear, dear lady. I won't tell a soul. You know I'm quiet as Medusa's boyfriend when it comes to a lady's private secrets, eh? But I was taking a new hammer over to the smith, and he told me you were journeying tomorrow, so naturally I just assumed . . ."

"Here you are, Hugo." Granny poured a little of the powder from the earthenware jug into a paper, folded the paper with great ceremony, and presented it to the peddler. "Six coppers, please."

"Six!" Hugo protested while unclasping a neat brocade coin purse he carried at his belt. "It's gone up, has it? I remember when it was two."

"Inflation," Granny said cheerfully, tucking the money in the pocket of her skirt. "The cost of practicing witchcraft these days! I couldn't begin to tell you how that drought last summer cut into my profit margin. Some of my most valuable plants were scorched, and probably won't even come up this year at all . . ."

Hugo was backing out the door, tipping an imaginary cap as he left. "Yes, well, goodbye, ladies."

Maggie let out a whoop of laughter. "Oh, Gran, how COULD you? Six coppers for that rubbish!"

"It's all part of the charm, dear. Good magic always is better if it costs something more than the client can comfortably afford."

"What's it for?"

"Impotence. You can come in now, darling." She cooed the last in a tender voice never heard by anyone in the village, including Maggie. Chingachgook, her black and white cat, leaped into the room from the windowsill, and onto her lap.

"Well, I may have need for some of those powders myself."

"I thought you might, so in my antique wisdom I have prepared a couple of things for you."

"Such as?" Maggie sat down abruptly on the weaving bench as Ching launched himself from Gran's lap to her

14

shoulder. Gran pulled her own braid forward and carefully extracted seven long hairs from it. "Here, you're the weaver, plait these into a chain, and wear it round your neck."

"In order to do what?" Maggie's fingers flew through the loops of hair, and she plaited the chain closed in an intricate invisible knot behind the curtain of her otter-brown hair.

"Make yourself more clearly understood, of course," purred Ching, bumping her cheek with his head.

Maggie started, but, seeing her grandmother's smirk of satisfaction, resigned herself. "I suppose having Ching along will help me talk with the larger non-human types. But I hope I won't have to hear the horse complain about his sore feet and the bad grass?"

"Not unless you ask Ching, dear. I should think that with no one but that maudlin minstrel along, you'd be happy for intelligent company."

"Yes, Gran."

"Speaking of intelligent company, you'd better stop and see Sybil on your way, or there'll be another rupture in the family tree."

Maggie wriggled with impatience that caused Ching to abandon her shoulder. "Gran, it may be urgent that I reach Winnie!"

"All the more reason that you see Sybil." She thrust a thonged leather bag at her. "Here's your medicine pouch. Now run along. I'm sure the estate will take care of itself."

"It'll have to," Ching muttered, settling his chin on his front paws and wrapping his tail around his nose.

3

Maggie was so anxious to get away from the village that she left Colin and the pack horse far behind in the first half hour on the road. After a long frozen winter at Fort Iceworm, it was a joy to splatter over the muddy tracks and splash through the pools left by melted snow from the last storm a month earlier. She scarcely noticed the nip at her ears as her mare created a wind for them, and the flopping tug of her woolen cape as it billowed out behind her made her want to sing from exhilaration. The smell of the new, tender grasses, the smell of anything at all after a sub-zero winter of buried vegetation and frozen noses, was sweeter by far than any of the perfume worn by the ladies at Winnie's wedding. Even under a dull gray sky, the colors of spring were dazzling after the stark blacks and endless expanses of everlasting white. Mostly there was green, of course, but there were also redbirds and bluebirds and an occasional brave blossom of yellow or purple.

Her neighbors, whom she did spare a glance as they leaped into drainage ditches to escape being galloped down as she sped past, were also colorful. After nine months of black and deep indigo and brown that they wore against the cold, it was good to see the dark coats finally exchanged for the women's costumes of red and gold skirts, blue or yellow blouses, and white embroidered aprons and kerchiefs. Most of the men dressed more soberly even now, a plow being less kind to white aprons than a butter churn, but Maggie knew that soon on market days they would be slipping over their smocked homespun shirts felted vests embroidered in the most outlandish scenes and hues their womenfolk could devise. The more fantastic the embroidery, the more fantastic the man, folk said, for what woman would ruin her eyes doing such work for a nincompoop?

16

It wasn't until she had to wait for a flock of sheep to dawdle across the road that the minstrel, panting and red-faced, galloped up on his mud-flecked buckskin horse. Ching, being jounced unmercifully in the basket he occupied atop the pack horse, yowled filthy feline curses.

Colin struggled to contain his ire as he reached the witch and her sweating chestnut mare. "Your pardon, milady, but if you try to maintain this pace, you'll kill your beast before we reach the next village."

As the thorough tonguelashing she was receiving from her grandmother's cat began to sink in, Maggie bit back the angry retort she'd meant for the minstrel, and instead nodded meekly and gently urged her horse forward as the last sheep passed.

Encouraged by this apparent acceptance of his authority, Colin added generously, in the grand language he'd been schooled to use with the aristocracy, "We troubadours are well versed in the ways of the road. Pray let me be your guide, milady."

"Oh, pray go soak your head," Maggie replied, unable to control her temper this time. "There's only this one bloody road south from here to the Troutroute River, according to Dad's map. What's there to know, anyway? Look," she pointed to a red bag tied in the fork of a tree. "The path is even protected with medicine bundles. Probably as exciting as a walk around the barnyard."

Colin didn't know what to say. How could *he* tell this pushy female, who even though she wasn't anywhere near being what he would call sweet and innocent, nonetheless seemed pretty naive, what the perils of the road were? Fresh from the Academy this spring, he truthfully hadn't experienced a great many of them himself. He was sure there were some, however, as his fellow students from parts of Argonia more exotic and sophisticated than East Headpenney, where he'd been raised, had told absolutely harrowing tales. And the history the masters gave in Lyric Appreciation classes, he felt sure, was not born of conflict, magical or unmagical, to be dispersed merely by hanging a medicine bundle in a tree fork. But go tell that to Mistress Know-it-all.

So they jogged along in silence for a long while; the dull clop of the horses' hooves and the occasional jangle of the strings on Colin's instruments as he shifted weight in the saddle were the only sounds. They had quite passed all the

17

farms that surrounded Fort Iceworm, and were negotiating the more rugged, unmaintained track that was the South Highway when Maggie, who had been sneaking an occasional guilty side-long glance at Colin's tight-lipped face, cleared her throat.

"Lovely day, isn't it?"

Colin's expression thawed just a bit. "Can't say as it is, really."

"No, beastly I suppose, actually, from your point of view." Having made herself an opening, she had very little idea how to proceed. Diplomacy, as had been frequently pointed out to her by loved ones who had occasion to know, was not Maggie's long suit. "See here, minstrel, you really mustn't be so bloody touchy about every little remark I make. A person makes a simple topographical observation and you get all huffy." She noted with increasing exasperation that her humble apology wasn't exactly producing instant rapport, but nevertheless plunged ahead. "I only meant that any fool should be able to find their way down a road that's the only one there IS . . . don't you think?" she ended in a voice rather smaller than the one she'd begun in.

Colin blew an angry breath out over clenched teeth. "And *I* only meant, *milady,* that I have perhaps had occasion to learn things about traveling that might prove instructive to a girl who's never been off her father's estate, that is, if she chose to listen instead of biting people's heads off all the time."

"Biting people's heads off? Did I bite anyone's head off? What do you think I am, an ogress, that I bite people's heads off?"

"Please stop chewing so loudly, witch," yawned Ching as he shifted to a more comfortable napping position in the basket. "Your dulcet tones are giving me a pain in the whiskers."

Maggie's shoulders drooped and finally she nodded. "Alright, maybe a little bite. But you met my Gran, and Dad, though he's a nice sort of fellow for one of the ruling class, cares more about hunting than managing things, and has a head to match those boar trophies on the walls at the tavern sometimes. Winnie, when she was home sort of kept things smoothed over and everyone peaceful. I'll be the first to admit those tactics can be very effective but, Toads, minstrel," she looked directly into his eyes now, a plea for understanding, "sweetness and light just don't get the

18

hearth laid or the sheep sheared. Someone has to see to it that things get done. And one can't forever be saying, Please, sir, I beg yer pardon, sir, would you kindly toss the slops out if it isn't too much trouble and you've nothing better to do?" He still didn't say anything. "It's alright, you know, if you want to turn back north. There's a little path that skirts round the village, so no one would know. I'll really be fine."

"I wouldn't be so fine, though, if something should happen to you while I'm supposed to be with you, and your father found me elsewhere. I'll accompany you, as arranged, milady."

"At least stop calling me 'milady', then. My sister is the lady in the family, whatever your songs say to the contrary. I was born into what you might call the unauthorized distaff branch of the family. Dad didn't marry my mother until I was two. Maggie Brown, apprentice witch, is my entire noble title. A simple 'Maggie' will suffice."

Colin grinned suddenly. Perhaps it wouldn't be such a long journey after all. He began to whistle softly and had gotten through four choruses before he caught Maggie's baleful eye and realized he was humming the very song that had caused him to sprout feathers. He offered a sheepish smile. "I know you don't like the words but it is a rather catchy tune, don't you think?"

"Definitely not," It was, though.

"Well, madam, I DO take requests."

Maggie stopped herself just in time from requesting silence. Instead she asked. "Do you know of a place up ahead, oh guide, where we could stop to eat?"

"No, but hum a few bars and I'll improvise." He almost fell off his horse laughing at his own cleverness.

"Forget it," Maggie groaned. "I just lost my appetite."

Though Colin's laughter could hardly have disturbed Ching, who was able to sleep through the numerous explosions resulting from Gran's arcane experiments, the cat nevertheless chose to open an eye and extend a black paw up the side of his basket. "*I* have not lost *my* appetite," he informed Maggie, aborting the stretch as he recalled his precarious position. "One hardly expects, when traveling with a hearthcrafter, to grow lean in the process."

"Too right, cat," Maggie apologized, feeling irritably at the same time that all the apologizing she was doing was getting to be a nasty habit, "Sorry if I was inconsiderate."

19

"Oh, that's alright," Colin replied, thinking she was addressing him, "Just having a bit of fun. There's a little knoll ahead that ought to be fairly dry and not too muddy."

They found the knoll and tied their horses to a tree at its base. Extracting a light lunch of cheese and dried apples, which Maggie reconstituted to fresh, and fresh bread from the horses' saddlebags, Maggie divided them between Colin and herself. She took out a packet of dried fish, expecting to find Ching at her heels, eager to devour it. Instead, she had to look all around the hill before she saw him, crouched at its base farthest from the road, switching his tail with concentration. "Chingachgook, here's your lunch."

"Not now, dammit," he hissed. "I'm trying to hear what he's saying."

"What who's saying?"

"Whoever's in there, of course."

Maggie started down the hill. "It's not polite to eavesdrop."

"Well, he sounds very upset about something and I only wanted to know what," Ching said, sitting up and giving her his best innocent-wide-eyed-kitten look, which was somewhat spoiled by his coloring, white chin and nose with eyes and ears a black, furry bandit's mask.

"What is it, Maggie?" Colin called through a bite of apple as he trotted down the hill to join them.

"Ching hears something in there. Look, there's a little doorway!" A semi-circular piece of sod quaked and cracked away from the rest of the knoll.

"Yes, and it's *opening*," Ching hissed, crouched and whisker twitching once more.

The wet-faced, red-eyed gnome who emerged was indignant. "Can't a fellow even mourn the fate of his best friend without you nosy mortals hollering on his rooftop?"

"I wonder what those taste like," Ching mused.

Maggie shoved him back. "Behave yourself, cat."

"We're sorry to intrude on your grief, sir," Colin said, removing his cap and leaning over a bit so the diminutive person would not have to look up so far to him. "It's obvious you're in some sort of trouble. We extend our condolences, and would do what we may, to alleviate your pain and atone for our rudeness." It was always extremely unwise to be anything but courtly to Little Folk, leprechauns, gnomes, brownies, and the like. Every reference Colin had ever heard made to them advised caution and courtesy even

20

beyond that ordinarily extended to human nobles, for the Little Folk were strange and touchy and alien. Being so very small, they had never, like merfolk, witches, faeries, or even ogres, intermarried with people of larger dimensions, and they remained shy and reclusive. Although this gnome was the first Colin had ever seen first-hand, close up, he had known a boy in East Headpenney, an unfortunate orphan whose parents had unwittingly destroyed the underground home of a gnome family.

"Ah, waly, waly, waly," cried the little man as he sat down on a toadstool, wringing his red pointed cap in his hands, "Alas, poor rabbit!"

Judging by his behavior, it seemed as though he had decided to take them into his confidence. Colin ventured a question. "Rabbit is the name of your friend, then?"

"Rabbit he's named, as rabbit he is!" nodded the gnome, sniffing and digging in the pockets of his green knickers. "He comes to my house to bowl with me every quarter moon and every half, without fail. When he didn't come as usual, I went looking for him."

"And you couldn't find him?" Maggie asked sympathetically.

The gnome took out a coin-sized handkerchief, blew his nose hard, and glared at her. "I f-found him alright. Caught in one of your horrid iron traps, his back leg nearly sundered, a-perishing of pain and fright."

Even Ching looked shocked and as compassionate as it was possible for him to look.

"I've tried all I know to free him," the gnome said. "But the power over iron is beyond my skill, and I've not the brute strength to spring it."

"You'd better show us where it is then," Colin said, "before whoever set that trap comes to check it."

If it hadn't been for Ching's hunting ability, they might have lost the gnome's track as he ran through the freshly green meadow and into the woods beyond. Not far from a deer path fairtly etched through the undergrowth, the rabbit lay panting out his life, his soft white fur speckled red on both sides of a cruel trap that bit his leg like the disembodied dentures of an ogre.

When Colin had released the trap, he started to pick the rabbit up, but Maggie stopped him. "His life is too fragile within him now for movement, minstrel. I've helped my Gran with a couple of cases like this, not on rabbits, of

21

course, but I know that glassy-eyed look. Best thing to do would be to splint the leg and give him something for the pain first, then let him rest a bit." She took off her kerchief and offered it to the gnome. "Spread this on him, sir, to keep him warm. I'll see if I can find an ice poppy to ease his pain, though it will be hard to locate them without the flowers."

"Failing that," said Colin, pleased to have an alternative to doing exactly as the witch directed, "perhaps I ought to go fetch MY medicine."

"YOUR medicine?" she asked. He was gratified to see how surprised she looked.

"You witches aren't the only ones prepared for this sort of thing, you know. All minstrels are supposed to keep with them while traveling no less than two ounces of strong apple brandy in case of emergency."

"I didn't see him whipping any of that out while he was flying around in the rafters," remarked Ching, licking a paw.

"Waly, waly, waly, waly," sobbed the gnome, who had wrapped the kerchief close around the rabbit's torso and had taken his friend's head on his lap and was rocking back and forth, stroking the long, soft ears.

"Waly, waly, to be sure," said Colin, sprinting back down the deer path, "Be back in a flash."

Maggie turned back to the gnome, hunkering down, as Colin had, to face him on a civil level where she would not be talking down to him. "Is there a nearby creek, Master Gnome? Ice poppies like the banks of creeks, and we ought to have water to cleanse the wound anyway."

"Through yon trees, maid. But hasten, do. His life force dwindles . . ."

Maggie picked up a wad of the hems of her cape and skirt in one hand and used the other to push away the wet willow wands that slapped at her face and clothing. Willows in such profusion made her uneasy with their sharp-tongued leaves and the way they had of making the path ahead or anything behind them hard to see. She was glad it was not later in the day, for Gran had told her that there were willows which actually uprooted themselves to follow travelers who stayed on the road past twilight. Of course, Gran had never said the trees did anything but follow, still—

She shivered. "Travel must not agree with me, cat. I'm jumpy as grease on a griddle. I have the oddest feeling we're being watched." When no teasing reply came from the cat, she looked around for him. He was crouched at her heels, fur glistening with dew from the grass and bristling, head turned to the left, ears ever so slightly rotating backwards and forwards, whiskers working. "Very reassuring, cat," said Maggie.

"You're the one with the big brown eyes, Witchy," growled the cat. "Find the damn pool and the damn posies, and cure the damn bunny, and let's get out of here." His fur had continued to rise while he talked, and he now appeared twice his normal size. "I've been in dog kennels I liked better."

"I know what you mean. I keep feeling there's something besides the gnome and the rabbit at our backs."

"Then *move*," said Ching.

"Alright, alright, only everything's so gray I can't really see very much either." She parted the branches of two willows which had originally grown on either side of the path, but whose drooping branches now completely obscured it. Slogging through the wet grass and soggy branches, they were both damp and cold by the time they came to the banks of the stream.

There was a different feeling there by the stream than there had been in the willows. Something about the place, some unidentifiable quality, poured over Maggie, so that, emerging from the trees to the grassy banks that held the blue waters, she took one soft step at a time until she stood absolutely still beside the gentle flow. It was the chilling, active blue of the killing crevasses of the great glacier that was its mother, but beautiful too. Around it, all about them, the air was mist-muffled and quiet, though there was the tinkle of the water, and once the song of a bird reached them, distinct and perfect. But here the sky did not seem dismal gray as before, but shone with the pearly transluscent silver-pink of the inside of a sea shell. The leaves, rustling without sound, glimmered in green pale, dark, and pale again like a jeweled gown winking in the light as its owner curtsied

"There's enchantment here," said Ching quietly. Though he himself was more or less impervious to most spells, he had defluffed and come out of his crouch to stand, ears up and tail waving a gentle J behind him, at Maggie's side.

"Yes," she said.

"It's across the stream, watching, in those trees."

Maggie let her eyes drift to the area he indicated. The cat's vision was not as precise as her own, but his sixth sense was far better developed.

Had it been a brighter day, she would, of course, have seen the unicorn immediately. As it was, his fog gray coat and opalescent horn blended so perfectly with the atmosphere in the woods that at first she mistook him for a bit of afternoon sky glowing through the boughs and branches. Only the amethyst eyes betrayed his presence, regarding her curiously across the icy blue water.

"He wants to know," Ching told her, "if you are a virgin maiden."

"That's certainly a personal question when we haven't even been properly introduced," she mumbled, a little taken aback. Then she stared back into the jeweled eyes and nodded, "Not tall, blonde, lily-like, or in any particular distress, but I believe I meet all the essential requirements."

Those requirements were apparently the unicorn's only criteria for making the acquaintance of female persons, for he waded gracefully across the stream to stand before her, carefully dipping his beautiful head, horn averted, naturally for his forelock to be petted.

"Really, chum," Maggie said fondly while administering the solicited attentions, "You ought to be a little more discriminating than THAT. I know any number of maidens whose virginity is the *only* thing they're at all scrupulous about. They wouldn't hesitate to sell you out to the constabulary for the price your horn would bring."

"Will you stop lecturing that horny creature and find out if there are any ice poppies around here, before the rabbit croaks and his pal puts a curse on us that won't quit?" asked Ching, impatient now that the unicorn's spell was no longer binding him, the unicorn having little or no interest in cats.

"Oh, of course," she replied dreamily, a large besotted smile warming her face as she stroked the unicorn's mane and fed him the core of her apple, which she had jammed in her pocket when Ching found the gnome's home. "Only with Moonshine here we don't need ice poppies. As soon as we take the bunny some of this water, after you've dipped your horn in it," she said, speaking to the unicorn, not the cat, "the little rabbit will be good as new." She lay her face against the pale, sleek neck of the enchanted beast, her arms a copper garland encircling him. "I never met a unicorn before. He really likes me."

"Will you get him to use his power so we can get back to

that rabbit?" the cat demanded, switching his tail. "I thought we were out for sisters on this jaunt, not horseflesh."

Reluctantly, Maggie released Moonshine, who nuzzled her hand again before performing the necessary magical service. There was no need to ask him aloud. Once her credentials were established, unspoken rapport linked them instantly, with no need for the cat to interpret. Her early admonitions had been absolutely useless, Moonshine told her. Regardless of her character, race, creed, color, or place of national origin, the first virgin maiden a unicorn met was it, the love of his life. He was only fortunate that HIS maiden, Maggie, was so kind, so understanding, so intelligent, so beautiful, so lovely in every possible way, far beyond his coltish dreams.

"I'll be back right away," she promised, stumbling over a dead log as she pushed back through the willows, trying to look over her shoulder at the same time.

"Watch it," Ching hissed, "you almost stepped on my tail!"

Maggie didn't even apologize, and stumbled twice more, almost spilling the precious fluid out of the cup of birch bark she had fashioned to hold it.

Colin was there when they got back to the gnome and rabbit. He stopped his sentry's march when he saw them, and knelt beside Maggie as she bathed the rabbit's leg with the healing water. "We have a problem," he told her, as she sluiced more water on the back of the injured leg; the front was already showing signs of improvement. The gnome wrung his hands, but had stopped saying "waly, waly" altogether. "Our horses and provisions are gone."

"What?" she stopped bathing the wound, and the gnome took the bark container from her hand into both his arms, setting it awkwardly beside him, and continued to dribble water on the rapidly healing leg.

"The horses, food, my musical instruments, everything, is gone."

"How can that be? The reins were tied well to that tree."

"Eureka!" cried the gnome. "He stirs! Rabbit, Rabbit, old friend, can you hear me?"

"I don't know, but they're gone."

With the aid of the gnome, the rabbit was soon sitting upright. At first he eyed Ching with distinct reservations, and regarded the humans warily as well, but when the gnome who introduced himself, now that he had the time, as Pop,

25

explained their role in his recovery, Rabbit declared himself boundlessly grateful and much in their debt.

"And to your kind friend, the unicorn, as well, missus," he added to Maggie. Having communicated for so long with Pop, who spoke Argonian, even if some of his expressions were a little dated, the rabbit was perfectly able to converse with Maggie and Colin without an interpreter. It was Ching, in fact, who needed a translator if he wished to address Rabbit, for he was unable to converse with any animals who might normally provide him a meal. Although he could converse with any non-human animal of his own or greater stature, mostly by understanding their thoughts and making his own wishes known without benefit of vocalization or gestures, his particular familiar's magic was mindful enough of his sensitivities to free him from the necessity of making dinner conversation with any who might normally be his prey.

Reassured about the rabbit's recovery, they fell to brooding on their horseless state, Colin resuming his pacing off the deer path, Maggie nibbling her knuckles, Ching attacking and retreating from various leaves and twigs. "It's too bad unicorns don't care for anyone but maidens," Maggie said, "or Moonshine could take us to Rowan's estates, I'm sure, or at least as far as Aunt Sybil's cottage."

"Even if he would," Colin reminded her, "we could hardly embark on such a long journey with no provisions and only one mount. Besides, I'd like to get my hands on whoever's made off with my fiddle and guitar!" He slapped one fist angrily into the palm of the other hand and looked very fierce for one of a normally cherubic appearance.

"Perhaps," suggested Rabbit, "it was the trap-setter."

"You *know* who set the trap, Rabbit?" Pop asked.

Rabbit twiddled his front paws somewhat diffidently before answering, "Well, I suspect it was the same bowman who shot the horse of the great knight after the first snowfall. He has been lurking about since; my cousins who dwell close to the castle have been made nervous by his lurkings and comings hither and yon."

"The Great Knight?" Colin asked, "Do you mean Maggie's father, Sir William? He was crippled up for some reason or other . . ."

"Thanks, Colin," Maggie said, wincing at what a rabbit's opinion would be of her father, to whom hunting was an occupation done with more regularity than breathing, "I

26

hadn't really thought I'd mention the relationship at this point—"

"Do not fret yourself, maiden," said Pop, "'tis well known the sins of the father are visited on the son, not the daughter."

"With a little work, that could be a rhyme," Colin said.

Rabbit thumped gently the paw which had been injured and was now soft and glossy as new. "The Great Knight is not the killer of our kind that this bowman is. My cousins warned me of snares, but I thought not to look for such an engine of destruction as this." His eyes showed a little more white as he sniffed the trap, involuntarily taking a half a hop back.

"We don't see iron used like this often," Maggie agreed. "It's too difficult to get, and expensive. Even wolves are usually killed with deadfall or arrow or lance. Except for horse's shoes, and kettles and pokers the peddler brings, I hardly see an iron implement this far north from one season to the next."

Colin snorted and said with some bitterness, for he was sorely injured by the loss of his instruments, the best of his efforts as a luthier, "I suppose there's some satisfaction in knowing that we were probably all harmed by the same party."

Pop interrupted him by leaping to his feet and pointing skyward with a thick index finger.

"What's that?" asked Colin.

"Sounds like trumpeter swans," Maggie replied, rising to her feet and scanning the skies. "But so much louder—oh, look up there! They're enormous!"

"And black," said Pop. The cacophonous calling died away long after the seven ebony giants had flown beyond the horizon limited by the tree tops. Maggie watched the sky, however, till the last note faded, then looked back to her companions. Ching was again swelled to double his normal size.

Maggie chuckled and kneeled to stroke the spikey fur of the familiar's spine. "Don't expect you'll be hunting those birds, eh, old boy?"

For an answer he sat down and began to wash the area beneath his tail.

"I suppose we had better start back for your father's place, Maggie," Colin said. "Too bad we'll lose a whole day, not to mention my favorite instruments."

27

"Wait a bit," she said, rising slowly and walking towards the trees. It was not until she reached out and stroked the unicorn's nose that Colin actually saw him. Knowing through legend and song of the magical creature's exclusive preference for virgin maidens, the minstrel prudently refrained from making any sound or gesture which might cause Maggie's new acquaintance to take flight.

After a brief exchange and one or two mutual nuzzlings, the unicorn melted back into the willows and Maggie returned to her companions. "Moonshine says he'll check a favorite watering-hole of his. If the horses aren't actually stolen, but have only wandered off, or been driven away, he says there's a good chance they'll be there. Of course, I could always go on alone on Moonshine." From her tone, Colin knew that the last was not an afterthought, but a fond wish which the theft of their horses had given her an excuse to voice. Colin had only to bow out of the quest, to return to his own concerns, and fashion new instruments, and she would be free to go with her new friend through the magic trails in the forest as far as they extended, however far that was.

Pop the Gnome was apparently dubious about the last, for he looked disapproving.

"What's the matter?" asked Maggie, for even her charmed distraction was not impervious to a gnome's disapproval.

"How many mortals do your suppose would see you when you had been forced to take Moonshine onto the open road before they decided to slay you, unicorn, cat, maiden, and all, for the sake of the magic horn?" He was struggling, it was evident, to ask the question civilly but his voice emerged harsh and stern. Maggie opened her mouth to protest, looked at him, at Colin, and Rabbit, and cat, then closed her mouth and nodded. Her eyes, when she lowered them, were oddly bright.

"Come now, witch," said Ching, rubbing at her ankles, "Don't go clouding up. You've lived here near this wood nineteen years, and never knew till today there was a unicorn in two hundred miles of the place. Or a gnome, for that matter."

Maggie made a face, but said nothing, for the horses trotted up to them then, supplies and instruments still strapped to their saddles.

Moonshine made no secret that he was as reluctant to part with Maggie as she was with him, and even allowed himself

28

to come in full view of Colin as he followed them at the edge of the wood where it bordered the highway. He exerted no other spell to keep her near, however, and as the wood and road parted to make way for a stream, parted from them with a last flourish of his tail, releasing her after an orchid-eyed good-bye to vanish into the forest.

That night, as they camped far from that section of the Northern Woods, Colin had to occupy himself with his music and Ching with his toilet, and they all had a cold supper, for there were no comments, nor questions, nor answers from the witch who had belatedly found reason for homesickness.

As she finally rolled herself in her goosedown blanket, Ching came and lay in the crook of the arm that cradled her cheek, purring, "Poor Maggie. Why can't you content yourself with a broom, like your foremothers?"

4

Colin woke to another muffled, mist-shrouded day, and to the smell of fresh-brewed herb tea and berry cakes. Maggie was sitting on a rock by the fire, a clay mug of tea warming one chapped hand while the other turned over the iron trap that had nearly ended the rabbit's life. She looked up as he rolled over, and poured him a mug of tea.

"What do you intend to do with that, anyway?" he asked, accepting the tea and indicating the trap.

"My aunt, the one we're supposed to see on the way, does a little metalwork. I thought I'd see what she makes of this. Berry cake?"

"Please." He got up and stretched, then hunkered down again to enlighten his inner workings with the hot tea and fragrant cake. He was surprised, when he woke up enough to think about it, to find the warm breakfast fire. It had been such a wet spring he wondered that she was able to locate any dry wood. "Ummmm—these are delicious. A little early for berries, isn't it?"

"Not for me. I just dry them when they're available and freshen them up when I need them. Same with the cream. Would you care for some?"

"Yes, thanks."

She poured a little white powder into his tea and it turned a soft toffee brown. He tasted it. "That's amazing."

"Glad you like it."

They passed that day and the next pleasantly enough, once more reaching a village and scattered outlying houses by the middle of the third day. Colin remembered as much as he could of unicorn lore, and entertained Maggie with all the stories and songs he could think of concerning the mystical beasts. He even made up a unicorn song, on the spot, which delighted her so much that she managed from somewhere to

30

produce an excellent meat pie for lunch and fresh peaches for dessert. Colin hadn't eaten so well since he left East Headpenney, and fitted the long discourse he was delivering, on the difficulties of keeping the proper dramatic tension present in one's lyric while doing an appropriate number of aesthetically correct doo-dahs in the music, in between appreciative slurps and gobbles of peach flesh and juice. He quite forgot to wonder where she found peaches six months before they would blossom and nine months after they should have rotted, or how she had dried them to include pits and all.

"About that song you don't like, for instance, Maggie," he said as an example. "There *is* something about it that bothers me."

Maggie, who could only stand so much jargon about someone else's specialty, shot her peach pit into a puddle of water. "There's a great deal about that song that bothers ME, minstrel," she said.

Ching was giving his full attention to his lunch of reconstituted trout heads and had not so much as a glance to spare them. Cat music tended to consist of one pleasant long hum of lyric and he saw no need at all for any other kind.

"Well, I *know*, that, of course, but what I mean is, there's no proper *ending* at all. It's anticlimactic, don't you think?"

"I certainly hope so," she replied. She would hate to think it would all end like that—with Winnie riding off for no good reason with some grubby gypsy while her bewildered husband rode home scratching his head. She began to see what Colin was talking about.

"Just so. Well, I'm actually very glad, indeed, you had me come along to protect you on this journey. Perhaps our investigations will suggest a more poetic conclusion."

"Oh, please," Maggie groaned. "Not one of those where he cuts out her true love's heart and hands it to her in a cup of gold, following which she either dies of despair or he cuts her in half and then throws himself upon his own sword in remorse. I'm ever so tired of that one. It's Gran's favorite."

"Hardly surprising," Colin mumbled, dousing the fire with a cup of water from the puddle and commencing to pack things back onto the horse. "Your grandmother is a—er—temperamental lady, isn't she?"

Maggie grinned evilly. "You think *she's* bad, you should hear her and Aunt Sybil go on about the REST of the family!

31

I believe Aunt Sybil's cottage is supposed to be an inheritance from a great-great-granddam who was fond of luring children up to the house to snack on a bit of roofing. Then there was Great Grandma Oonaugh. Now *there* was an old horror!" But she said it, Colin thought, with the same pride others might display in royal ancestors.

"You hardly ever hear of any really wicked witches anymore." Colin said. "Since under King Finbar's rule, criminal offenses are prosecuted equally, whether of magical or nonmagical nature, and are tried by a group of the offender's peers, I suppose there's not much percentage in doing anything really awful. Your ancestors may have been a bad lot, but you're really very nice, now that we're better acquainted." She gave him a sharp look, as though she were about to take offense and he hastened to explain. "I mean, even UNICORNS like you, and I guess one has to be pretty pure of heart for that . . ."

"Hearts apparently have little to do with it," she said with more objectivity regarding unicorns than she'd shown since just before Moonshine had declared himself smitten.

"And then you did catch your cat and stop him from—you know—"

"Oh, that. Well, I suppose Gran must be right. She says our bloodline has become increasingly impure in the last few generations. She likes Dad well enough, you understand, thinks he's wonderful and all that." She swung up into the saddle after settling Ching in his basket on the pack horse. "Probably because he was such a raffish sort in what the two of them refer to as his misspent youth." She smiled. "I suppose it just wasn't misspent enough, and I got tainted by his decent side."

"What sort of witch are you then, exactly, if you don't consider it impertinent to ask?"

"You hadn't noticed?" She gave him a queer sidelong look, and clucked to her horse, kicking its sides with her soft-soled boots as they clopped back out into the muddy road again.

"No." Colin followed behind her, leading the pack horse.

"I'm a hearthcrafter. Where do you suppose the warm fires and fresh fruit have been coming from?"

"I wondered," he admitted, digesting this new information as they rode off downhill again, the muddy road little more than a track through spreading marshy meadows and newly lush hillocks that gradually gave way to a few sparse slim trees flush with new green leaves. "It seems very useful then, if you can do all of that."

"Oh, aye, it's that," Maggie said, making a face. "That's what Gran says too—but I'm afraid useful doesn't really do me all that much credit in our line of work. It takes passion and power, Gran says, to be a really first-class witch, though I think at times she only says that to justify her beastly temper. No one has ever accused me of lacking that sort of passion either—but Aunt Sybil's got a lot stronger magic than I do, and she's a far more placid person than Gran or I either one—I suppose it comes of knowing what to expect. You'll probably really like her." She looked at the tortuous track ahead of them. "It's still quite a ways though, I reckon. I don't suppose you'd know that song about the silly nobleman who died of indigestion from eating eels, would you?"

Colin did know the song about the nobleman, a fellow named Lord Randall, and the song about the fiddle and the wind, which was one of his own personal favorites, and the one about the laddie-cut-down-in-his-prime. Maggie sang along in a voice low and rough for a woman, but with a lot of power and vitality, and she was even very often on key. She expressed a strong preference for murder ballads and the popular songs women sang over the loom or field hands sang while doing whatever there was to do in the field. When Colin tried to introduce an occasional romantic air, she interrupted him with a request for a work song sung by bandits as they plundered helpless villages. If he tried to ignore her long enough to finish a chorus of one of the charming love ballads he preferred, the black and white cat made it a point to rouse himself long enough to produce a terrible yowling. It seemed that any tender emotions the lady had were addressed exclusively to unicorns, and other expressions thereof were not to be tolerated.

By the time they camped that night, the minstrel had exhausted his repertoire of murder ballads and was considering applying for a teaching position at the Minstrel Academy, where he would present a course on the musical proclivities of the Northern Sorceress Personality, a subject he now felt he possessed more expertise in than he really cared to.

A technically impossible evening meal of Queenston Quiche, artichokes in almond sauce, and chocolate fudge layer cake, served with a blue wine equally correct with meat or fish, and equally delicious with either, helped to alleviate some of

Colin's artistic aggravation, not to mention his empty stomach and dry throat. As he was hoarse from singing, he limited his musical endeavors that night to a soft lament played on his fiddle while Maggie, arms clapsed about her knees, stared into the fire, rocking a little in time with his playing. Ching sprawled at her feet as comfortably as though on his favorite rug beneath his mistress's loom at Fort Iceworm.

The morning again just missed being rainy, the sky the color and texture of raw wool, with the sun invisible except as a light patch stifled by bales of clouds. Damp and subdued and tired of being threatened by the weather, neither Colin nor Maggie felt like singing or talking or doing anything but sitting half-slumped in their saddles, absorbing bumps and uneven jarrings as their horses plodded down the mushy trail. It took Colin a few minutes to notice when his horse stopped.

"Oh, no," Maggie said, drooping wearily forward on her mount's neck. Stretching out before them was a vast sea of swirling, frothing water. Debris, natural and manmade, swept along in the churning muddy flood, and trees caught up in it genuflected at its perimeters. How they could have dozed without hearing the roar and rumble of those waters was amazing.

"It wasn't like this when I came north," Colin said. "It doesn't look the same at all."

"This IS the Troutroute River, then?" Maggie asked.

Colin nodded. "According to the maps—and I remember the path this far too, but the bridge that was here is gone."

"How are we going to get across, then?"

Ching growled low in his throat and hopped down from his perch, stalking forward to crouch low on the path ahead of them. Except for his growl, his total green-eyed concentration was fixed on the flood. With a whip of his tail he stood up and turned to Maggie. "Well. If that doesn't beat all. This is the first time I EVER saw a dragon climb a tree."

"What?" she asked, a little snappish at being interrupted while she was trying to plot how they were going to cross. She personally was not overly fond of large bodies of water, and Ching was even less enamored of it than she. There were far too many trees on and just beneath the surface, and the water was far too fast to make swimming even a fleeting consideration.

34

"Maggie, look out there!" Colin pointed. "There's a dragon in that tree."

"Silly creature," sniffed Ching, cocking his ears again for a moment. "She's crying for help. Of course she's stuck. Any dragon dumb enough to go out in THAT stuff." He shuddered with revulsion. "And then climb a TREE it—well, she deserves to be stuck."

"Can't she fly out?" Maggie shielded her eyes with her hand to try to block out the sparkles of light bouncing off the water to obscure her vision.

Ching was still for a moment, listening, for he seemed to need to cock his black ears even to hear with his mind. "She's moaning something about her wings being tangled."

"Still don't see why she doesn't fly out, great beast like that . . ." Maggie said, riding a few paces up, then back, to get a better view of the dragon.

"At least we won't have to worry about a dragon as well as a flood." Colin shivered and dismounted. "Perhaps your sister would appreciate your visit more later, when she's—you know—had more chance to adapt to the nomadic life." He really didn't expect her to insist that they sit to wait for the flood to subside, which would surely take at least days, if not weeks. And they definitely could not cross it, which would be at worst a sodden death, and at best a dreadful way to treat his instruments. "We could try again later—maybe in midsummer?"

Maggie only favored him with a venomous look and dismounted, first continuing her shoreline inspection of the stranded beast on foot, then plopping down onto a fallen tree trunk. Cupping her chin in one hand, she stared moodily out at the flood, plucking angrily at the tall grasses that grew around her with the hand unoccupied with chin.

Ching joined her, settling his white stomach onto the soft, mossy covering of the log. "Well, witch, what now?"

"I don't know. I've never seen this sort of thing before. This *is* the first journey I've taken more than a day's ride from home, after all, and I can hardly be prepared for everything." She gnawed a grubby and already abused thumbnail. "Wish I had some of Gran's good strong transformation magic, instead of just hearthcraft. I could change these horses into whales or something. As it is, we're as stuck as that dragon."

"I suggest we give up." The cat closed his eyes and looked away.

"No, really, Ching, what can a hearthcrafter do in this kind of situation? I could spin a rope, but we'd never make it all the way across the river." She reached out and snapped off one of the tall reeds at the edge of the torrent.

"Don't be silly," the cat scoffed. "What would I do with a rope anyway? Walk tippy-toe across it, or hang by my tail?"

"I don't know," Maggie snapped, nettled by the cat's sarcasm, her inability to produce a solution, and the party's generally negative attitude. "But I'm sure not going to carry you." She curled her lip at the water. "I'm not all that fond of that stuff myself, you know. If my magic didn't require extensive contact with scrubwater, I'd probably be as likely to melt of it as Great-Grandma Oonaugh." She twined a second weed around the first and forced them into a rough coil in her hand.

The cat swatted at the end of the reed that protruded from her hand. "Going to make a bathing dress of these, witch?"

"Take a swim, Ching. Maybe I *will*," she stared at the reeds, replying to the concept of constructing reed bathing dresses, not to the swim. "Minstrel?" she said.

Colin hoped she had decided after all that they would turn back, now that he had patiently given her time to reflect on the impossibility of their situation. He expected she, as would any reasonable person, would reach the obvious conclusion. "Yes?"

"Help me pick some more of these rushes, please."

"Uh—why?" A qualm made him pause before he picked the first of the reeds.

"Umm—just a little idea of mine," she replied, as she energetically began to snatch up every reed in sight.

His qualm became an uneasy twinge as he dropped an armload of reeds on top of those she'd already gathered. She stopped gathering finally, but signalled him to continue, and sat down and began to weave the rushes into a large, flat coil.

"Funny time to make a rug," Colin remarked, smiling at his own humor as he dumped more rushes on the pile.

"One does the best one can with the talents allotted one," she replied with a suspicious expression of self-satisfied false humility.

His suspicion was confirmed. His twinge became absolute fear as the rush rug became a basket large enough to hold, technically speaking, either a man or a woman. Colin had the distinctly uncomfortable feeling it was intended to hold a man.

"It's a boat!" Maggie exclaimed proudly, as pleased as if she were announcing the sex of her first-born babe, as she floated the flimsy-looking thing on the edge of the flood.

"Uh-uh," the minstrel said firmly.

"Oh, *really*. It's quite strong. I'm sure it will hold you." She looked up at him with an expression of purest concern for his safety and comfort.

"Hold me while I do what?" He stood very still as he waited for her answer.

"While you rescue that poor stranded beastie, of course."

"That DRAGON!?" The stillness exploded into an orgy of pacing and wild gesticulation and he changed octaves several times as he spoke. "Look here, Maggie. I'm every bit as much an animal lover as you are, but why in the name of all that's sane would I want to rescue that dragon? I like it exactly where it is!"

"We have to rescue her because she flies, of course, is why." She used the sort of voice she might use to explain to a small child why the sky is blue. She didn't stay within earshot of his indignant sputterings, either, but went to the pack horse and began unstrapping their belongings.

"Well, see here, Maggie. Now just stop. Just because I don't agree with you doesn't mean I'm about to leave you here alone! Put those things back, won't you?" By the fury with which she was unwinding the bindings of their packs, throwing the bundles indiscriminately on the ground to fall where they may, he reckoned she was ready to remain behind if he insisted on sensibly returning to civilization. He perceived her bizarre unpacking methods to be a demonstration both of the sorcerous passion, if not power, she'd discussed earlier, and also any possible determination to remain at the river as a means to make him guilty enough that he'd stay and do as she demanded.

She ignored him, however, as he flapped around putting things back on the horse which fell right back off, of course, without the benefit of the length of braided leather rope that had bound them on. This rope Maggie was busying herself winding around her hand and elbow. After trying to replace the cat basket one more time to have it fall to his feet, spilling out the snug old piece of blanket intended to insure Ching's

37

comfort, Colin decided against trying to strap his fiddle back on and instead replaced it gently on the ground, out of reach of the chestnut's hooves should it decide to take a stomp or two.

Maggie was looking pleased as she wound the rope. Fortunately, they'd brought far more gear than they really needed and the rope was quite long. Rummaging in the pile of belongings, she removed the extra clothing she had brought from its sack, and stuffed it in with the foods. The sack she began to fill with mud from the banks of the swollen Troutroute, digging the stuff up in great gooey gobs, and depositing it in the sack with a sucking "plop."

Colin had continued to pursue her progress with alarm and not a little personal interest. Perhaps she had not been entirely frank about the scope of her magical powers, and was capable of a great deal more than she'd admitted. Perhaps she was now concocting a gigantic, magical, enormously powerful, arcane—poultice—though whether its purpose might be for rescuing tangled dragons or chastising recalcitrant troubadours he was uncertain.

She lashed the muddy sack securely to the end of the rope and hefted it. Turning to him, she inquired sweetly. "I don't suppose you're a fantastic shot with a sling or anything like that?"

"Not particularly."

"Alright then, stand back." She began to sail the muddy sack in circles above her head, bits of mud decorating her hair and spattering her face, arms, clothing and companions as well as the inanimate environment in the immediate vicinity. Colin ducked and Ching took shelter behind a tree. When it seemed to her the proper impetus was reached, she let fly with the bag. It landed, splashing an upwardly exploding fountain of water a short distance from the dragon-inhabited tree.

Hauling the sopping bag back again, she inspected the rope and then the bag itself. The rope was braided for utility in a fashion that minimized its tendency to shrink. The bag was not in a condition ever to hold clothing again. By the time she finished her inspection, Maggie's hands were so slippery with mud she had to wash them off in the river before resuming her sack-whirling stance. She let fly, and this time the bag snaked its way into the appropriate tree, and its weight wrapped it twice around a branch. Maggie leaned back on the rope, testing it with her entire weight. Satisfied, she took the end and tied it securely around the trunk of another tree.

She wiped her still far-from-immaculate hands on her skirt, and glared triumphantly at the minstrel, who had arranged himself in a nonchalant position against a tree that lent itself to lounging. Applauding slowly, he complimented her feat with mock graciousness. "Very ingenious, Mistress Brown. And nobly done. Nobly done, indeed. Now the only problem that remains, I suppose, is for person or persons unkown (unless, of course, and I can't discount the possibility, you mean for that very remarkable cat of yours to do it) to surrender his or herself to the doubtfully enormous strength of your oversized poultry basket, haul themselves across that charming laundry line you've so cleverly employed, and reach the tree, where the dragon trapped therein will meekly cooperate in having its appendages broken and its wings mangled while its benefactor frees it, after which it will follow us all over Argonia in unending and everlasting gratitude. Providing, of course, one doesn't overbalance that silly-looking boat, providing, too, that the clothesline doesn't work its way loose from its moorings, and providing the dragon doesn't immediately roast one well done before it learns of one's beneficent intentions, just in case it's interested in them."

It was Maggie's turn to applaud. "From your pretty words, minstrel, I gather you appreciate the possible difficulties of my scheme. However, I would like to point out that those things may just as well NOT go wrong, and, as they say, nothing ventured, nothing gained."

"Whereas if I should venture in this case, I might stand to gain a charring?"

"As I was saying before you gave me the benefit of your immense wisdom, I do intend to get across this river and to the other shore, and I don't intend to go the whole width by means of rope and basket. So if dragons frighten you, my faint-hearted friend, I suggest you stand back."

"I still don't see how you propose that that dragon will be of any benefit to us once you acquire it."

"Once you have helped me rescue her, she will fly us across the river, naturally."

"Oh, she's agreed to that, has she?" He raised a questioning brow to the cat, who had sauntered over from behind his

39

tree and was sniffing without interest at the spilled contents of the packs. Looking up, he met the minstrel's eye, flipped his tail, and stalked off. He had better things to do than talk to tree-climbing aquatic dragons or, for that matter, to so-called musicians who talked to cats.

"Maggie, I know you want to see your sister, but this is rather extreme, isn't it? I mean, the river *is* dangerously flooded, and the dragon and all—" He could hardly believe she meant to go on with it, and kept waiting for her to say that of course he was right and she would naturally go back to her father's hall and wait like a good witch for conditions to improve.

"Have you another suggestion?" she asked, with iciness that warned him he was likely to wait a long time for her to say what he wished. He coached her a little.

"We ought to wait a few days, perhaps, for the flood to subside, and then cross it the usual way."

"No!"

"Why not? Oh, Maggie, what difference could a few days possibly make?"

"I don't know—it all depends—it could make all sorts of difference. Abandoned lords have been known to do all sorts of awful things to wives who run off from them, and that gypsy is no gallant protector, believe me. He ran off with two of the dairy maids and then just left them to their—er—fate. What if he leaves Winnie stranded in the woods, or something? Even if Rowan doesn't murder her, there's robbers and wild animals and—"

"Dragons?" Colin suggested helpfully.

He received a glare for his trouble but she continued. "Of course, dragons. She's quite alone, actually. Maybe hungry and cold, and most certainly confused and lonely. If the gypsy should run true to type and abandon her, she would simply not understand it. People are just never unkind to her—she wouldn't know what to think. She'd be brooding about what she might have said that vexed him, and not be on the lookout for murderers or dragons at all . . ."

"If all of that's true, she'll probably be far beyond your help by the time we get there, anyway."

Maggie's eyes ate caustic holes in him. "She certainly will be, if we sit tamely by and wait for the river to go down—or I waste all my time debating the matter with craven minstrels."

He shook his head stubbornly. "Stop debating then. I'm done trying to keep you from risking your life. But I'm certainly not going to risk mine." He leaned with greater determination against the tree, looking if possible fiercely dedicated to languishing there for the duration. "I'm sorry, old girl. A lot of people have control over my life. My craftmaster has power over my music, your father and other aristocrats have power over my comings and goings, and your grandmother has power over my shape. You, however, don't have any power over me at all, and I refuse to allow you to push me into something stupid and dangerous."

"Coward."

"At your service."

With one last glare, she arranged herself in the boat, holding on to the rope for balance. Then she had to stand again, one foot on the basket and one on shore, to push the basket boat out into the water.

Her arms were almost yanked from their sockets as the tide jerked her and the boat downstream of the rope she clung to. She regained her seat and began hauling herself hand over hand down the rope, thinking stubbornly that she was certainly showing the minstrel that she was not a girl to stand around and wait for the men to do everything, as he obviously thought. Her ruminations were extremely brief, however, for the rope was slick and wet and her shoulders ached horribly with the strain of clinging to it against the current. In no way did the pain lessen as she strove to get enough purchase to pull herself and the boat against the tide, closer to the rope. Her body stretched so far between her lifeline and the boat that it arched, her belly almost grazing the water, her knees barely in the basket, head buried between wrenching shoulders and straining arms as she struggled for a better grip on the rope. A passing log swept the little rush boat out from under the precarious purchase her knees had maintained, and she dropped with a shocking icy splash into the river, the water soaking her to the waist. Inexperienced as she was at rivercraft, she did realize that her most desperate and immediate priority was to retain her grip on the rope at all costs.

She was actually only a few feet out from the shore, but even her work-hardened hands were not used to supporting her entire weight from slick, cold leather thongs against the force exerted by the river. The icy water chilled her to the top of her head, and she couldn't feel her fingers after a short time.

Abruptly she sank to her armpits in the biting cold river. A weight jerked on the rope and it slipped agonizingly in her hands. She could not be sure when one hand slipped from the rope, but suddenly her body was floating on the surface, tossing and turning with the torrent, the arm that kept her from drowning an arrow of pain that felt as though it were breaking her back.

She was hauled partially out of the water as Colin's arm caught her clothing, then her waist. "Got you!" he yelled above the river, nearly breaking his own hold on the rope with the shock of her added weight to his own. "Grab on, now!" He had slid along the rope far enough to catch hold of her. Flinging her free arm wildly in his direction as she tried to obey his order, she nearly throttled him, hooking her elbow around his neck.

He gargled at her.

They did so much thrashing around themselves that they scarcely noticed when the waves began to break over their shoulders, submerging the rope for a moment. Maggie clung to Colin's belt, twisting her head to keep the water from her mouth and nose. Colin was finally able to get them back to the shore, and they lay there, half out of the water, just as the tension that had been fighting them for the rope went slack.

As Maggie clambered out of the water and up Colin's legs and onto the bank, to lie panting and choking beside him, she heard Ching translate for the big green and turquoise dragon who was drying herself in what little sunlight there was. "Ah hah," said the cat in his pseudo-dragon voice. "Dinner is served."

5

Fortunately, the dragon was so surprised that they did not incinerate immediately when she breathed on them, that she completely forgot she outweighed them by a few hundred stone, and had sharp claws and teeth as well as fire-breathing potential.

For a witch, Maggie was very adept at being self-righteously indignant, and when she had spit out the river water, she took advantage of the dragon's confusion to display her talent for invective. "Ching," she ordered, "will you tell this foul-mouthed, fetid-breathed, carrion-eating crud that she is the most ungrateful, rude and—and not a very nice creature at all!"

"I will not." The cat sat upright, tail curled sedately around his front paws. "So far, she looks on me as not quite bite-sized. I have no desire to jeopardize our relationship by conveying such familiar irresponsible messages."

"Some familiar you are. You're supposed to protect me."

"Only from—ahem—a fate worse than death. Other peril, up to and including death, were not in my job description, particularly at the cost of my own tail."

Maggie threw up her hands. "I'm surrounded by cowards!"

"I beg your pardon!" bubbled Colin, still dripping from saving her life. "Now who's the ungrateful crud! My hands will probably take weeks to heal well enough that I can play bar chords again."

She shot him a look of simultaneous apology and annoyance. She wished he would not pick such awkward times to be sensitive. If she couldn't enlist the cat's help he wouldn't have to worry about playing his bar chords.

"Now just how was it you were planning to negotiate with this eternally grateful creature?" Colin pestered. Not having heard the remark about dinner, he remained more unalarmed than he should have been.

"Ching can talk to him, you see . . ."

Colin looked at the cat, who was yawning, and at the dragon beside him, who was concentrating on puffing up and down the scale of dragon puffs, forte to pianissimo, trying to rekindle the fizzled flame. "I'm not sure communication is the key—I can talk to a Brazorian bandit, too, but that hardly means he'll refrain from skewering me—"

"Precisely," she said, hastily returning her attention to the cat. "You ought to be ashamed, Ching. I've helped take care of you since you were a kitten."

"Yes, wasn't I cunning?" He licked a paw clean of an imaginary speck.

"You were. You were the most promising of the litter—your mother, Sacajawea, was the loveliest, loyalest, most magical of all familiars—many's the time I held you both purring in my lap and fed you dainties from the banquet table and told you . . ."

"Oh, very *well*. You've made your point. But I will *not* insult this discriminating creature. Perhaps if you prepare some food for her which will provide a nutritious alternative to yourselves as a main course, she'll accept it in your stead. She's missed her last feeding, she said. She'd have gobbled me up, bite size or no, but says she finds a cat who speaks impeccable dragonese a diverting novelty."

Maggie didn't wait for the cat to finish his long-winded speech before she rummaged into the foodbag and came out with a piece of dried venison that, with a bit of stretching, became a whole deer, considerably roasted for the flameless dragon. After four more such delicacies, the dragon daintily mopped her long, royal-blue snout with a ruby-colored forked tongue, and settled back with a gale-force sigh against a convenient grove of trees.

Colin released the breath he had been holding during the exchanges that passed from Maggie to cat to dragon. He had watched his companion address the cat, who had of course said nothing in reply, but had flicked his whiskers and twitched his tail tip occasionally. The cat had then turned to rub against the dragon in a most affectionate manner, after which performance Maggie had produced the miraculous venison, the dragon had devoured it, and the dragon had retired to leave the cat gnawing at the meat left clinging to the shards of bone overlooked in the dragon's glutting. The cat could obviously converse with Maggie, and through the cat, Maggie could converse with dragons. That was all very well and good, but it did make him feel slightly left out, but since he was also evidently to be left out of the dragon's diet, he found it fairly easy to reconcile himself.

While he and Maggie changed into dry clothing, the cat chatted casually with the dragon.

"It's quite a touching little story, really," Ching informed them as they emerged from the woods, fully prepared to run back to the cover of the trees at any sign of hostility or renewed appetite from the great beast. The cat assured them that they were safe, as the dragon had pronounced herself quite well fed for the time being. "Poor Grizel," Ching mewed his most plaintive, "has had a simply dreadful time."

Dragons are notoriously long-winded, being so full, generally, of hot air, and Ching had begun to fancy himself a raconteur, so what with the cat's speech having to be translated for Colin after it had already gone from dragon to cat to Maggie, the narrative became somewhat garbled at certain points. Nevertheless, what Grizel actually said was interpreted as the following, in as near to the dragon's own mode of expression as is possible to relate:

THE DRAGON'S STORY

"I never thought of myself as the suicidal type, not even when I found myself tumbling down the river, but I suppose I must have been, a little bit, to have sought a cave so near the river's bed, when for eons and eons that particular cave has been flooded at the same time every year.

"The heart, alas, knows no season when it's breaking, and I heeded not spring nor flood—I almost wish your violent agitation of that branch out there had not freed my wings and claws. For though I was able, having recovered my senses, to swim here, where I encountered this charming little furry friend and was given the benefit of your hospitality," (she licked her snout in remembered appreciation) "you have freed my body but not loosed the chains that bind my heart.

"Of course, I might at any time prior to my entangle-

45

ment in that tree have swum to shore. But I was asleep when the flood waters filled my cave, and before I had quite gathered my faculties, I was struck behind the ears with a portion of a nearby mountain, which must have become dislodged in the flood. At least, I suppose it had to be something as substantial as that, for I am quite well-armoured, you know.

"Oh, yes, we dragons are almost completely protected externally, but ah, the searing pain that can burn within! I see you appear puzzled, but it is true, my friends, it is indeed true that we, too, have feelings that cannot be shielded by our scales, and bear passions hotter than our own fires. Though the flood has extinguished one flame, that other within me burns like a torch I carry—for him. And I had always considered myself to be such a cool-headed sort!

"Ah, but that was all before I met—*him*. If only you could see him! A dragon is surely just a dragon, you may say. How quickly your preconceptions would melt away if only you could see my Grimley! Brilliant red-orange scales glittering in the sun! The liquid reptilian grace of him as he sails through the Southern Aurora! The sensuousness of his slither when he turned to sear me with that earthquaking smile from those hypnotic garnet eyes of his! Ah, Grimley, Grimley, my heart, my flame, my own!"

(For a moment she seemed quite overcome but was finally able to proceed in a calmer fashion.)

"We were very happy for a while—he scarcely left my side nor would he allow me to hunt for myself, but fed me from his own snout the choicest morsels. We were so blissful! How could we have quarreled and parted over such a small thing? I tell you, I am quite, quite bereft! Absolutely bereft. I simply felt, you know, that it was demeaning to my darling to let that MAN choose what he ate from our range, instead of raiding the herds and villages at the dictate of his dragonly will. He took my concern amiss, and called me a little hothead who had no concern for the security of our future offspring. And I—oh, the terrible things I said—still . . . I feel, you know, that I must resolve in my own heart this matter of dragonian dignity. On the river, as it all flashed before me in the extremity of my need, I decided that if I

46

should be freed, I would fly to the east to consult our great queen. Perhaps her wise counsel could heal those harsh words. If our queen agrees with me, then I shall return with her to my love in a blaze of glory, and how can he deny me then? If not, I shall crawl all the way back home and beg his forgiveness."

(Another flood impended, as the great dragon tears rolled off her snout and down her stomach, further saturating the sodden ground surrounding her. She sniffed a giant sniff and continued.)

"At any rate, I drifted unconscious downstream after the mountain hit me, until I became entangled in that tree, as first you beheld me. Although I possessed the strength to free myself, I was afraid of injuring my wings, which are ever so fragile. Then, when you people were playing about on that rope, you jarred the tree loose that had pinioned my wings, and set me free, and—and here I am—flameless, loveless wretch as you see me!"

Colin, his poet's sensitivity aroused, had quietly drawn his fiddle from his bag and was playing a little lament for the creature as she finished her tale.

Uncomfortable with the surfeit of sentimentality, Maggie squirmed a bit, but did feel sorry for the beast. She was actually, objectively speaking, an attractive thing. From royal blue snout to spiked and slender tail tip, her color altered many times to blend from blue to turquoise, aquamarine, and other blue-green distinctions, to sea green, and mist green, and forest green, and emerald green, to finally tip her membranous wings and frost her spikes with a chartreuse of the same beautiful shade as her big, limpid eyes, pools of misery that were, as has been mentioned, quite overflowing.

Maggie let out a long breath and rolled up her sleeves. "I can do something about the flameless part of her problem, at least, if she will promise to help us," she told Ching. "Tell her that if she will fly us across the river, I can help her by restoring her fire."

The cat relayed the message, and Grizel pronounced herself quite amenable to flying them across, all except the horses.

She would not have been able to provide such ferry service, she told them, if it were not for Maggie's generous

47

offer. She asked Ching to explain that dragons fly not only by means of their wings, which were insubstantial compared to the rest of a dragon's bulk. The fire-breathing mechanism created a cavity of hot air within, that served as a buoying agent. Maggie looked down the dragon's open mouth and concentrated on her hearth-building spell. Soon Grizel was smoking cozily away.

Colin, meanwhile, unsaddled their horses and gave them a smack on the rump to send them home, so that they might reach safety before Grizel's next feeding time. Maggie joined him in making packs of their belongings which they strapped to their backs. Ching settled himself on top of the pack Maggie wore, and Grizel knelt, allowing them to mount above her wings upon her neck and shoulders.

They felt the air rush up at them as they rose faster and faster and higher and higher. Maggie had to catch at her skirts to avoid having them singed by the backlash of the dragon's flame. Below, the river rushed heedlessly on. They sailed a dizzying height above the trees, and could make out, just beyond them, fields plowed in patchwork patterns.

Extending her feet, then gradually folding her wings as she damped her flame, the dragon brought them to a safe landing at the edge of a forest clearing.

"Farewell!" she saluted them. "I cannot go near the town in daylight for fear of my life. You have fed me when I hungered and enflamed me when I languished, and I shall ever be your friend, but I ask you grant me one final request."

The people asked the cat to tell the dragon they would be glad to grant the request, and of what did it consist?

"That if you meet my Grimley before I do, should you survive the experience, you would tell him that his Grizel burns for him still and repents her inflammatory words and—and that I shall return to him anon!"

Aunt Sybil was slogging about in a puddle of syrup, trying to reshingle her house with fresh gingerbread cookies. Maggie and Colin had smelled the cookie fragrance as soon as they'd left the highway just past the village and turned off onto the path, which a child had eagerly volunteered to show them. The child also volunteered to guide them to the aunt's house, but, as it appeared a fairly uncomplicated journey, they declined.

48

"Little chap seemed disappointed," said Colin.

"His folks wouldn't like him coming along, I think," Maggie said. "They surely must remember the previous tenant of Auntie's house. Great-great-great-Grandma Elspat liked children—but not in the conventional sense. It's a wonder the rest of the Brown line continued—I believe, you know, that it was no little woodcutter's daughter that did her in. Gran said it was her own daughter, to save herself. It will be interesting to see the place."

"But you—uh—your current aunt—she doesn't—indulge?"

"In gobbling children? Oh, no—but she keeps up the original architecture, I understand, so that they'll come out to see her, and she can treat them. With her specialty, she gets rather lonely."

"Oh?"

"Yes, she sees the present in her crystal ball."

Colin scratched his head and for a moment seemed to accept this, then said, "Huh?"

"She sees the present in her crystal ball," Maggie repeated.

"Why does she need a crystal ball for that? Most of us see the present without one."

"Well, yes, but Aunt Sybil, you see, doesn't have to be present to see the present. I mean, she can see what's happening to OTHER folk now . . . not just herself—you understand?"

"I guess so."

"That's why she has no neighbors. In the old days, I guess, she might have been actually persecuted. People like a witch who can look into their private lives far less than one who eats their children. Though of course, if she accepted all the consultations for that sort of thing that are available to her, from what Gran says I suppose she could have a house of gold, instead of gingerbread."

It was then that they rounded a turn in the path and saw the clearing containing a house, which was not charming at all, but appeared to be the victim of some natural disaster, the roof half off, the walls slanting in, and the door ajar on its jamb. An elderly woman, who at first glance looked to Colin alarmingly like Maggie's grandmother, was occupied with a bowl and spatula, and had a pile of cookies the size of dinner plates on the ground beside her. The entire woods smelled like a bakery.

49

Ching jumped down from Maggie's back and raced to where Sybil was working, where he began mewing raucously and rubbing himself against her, before sitting down to clean the syrup from his paws. Sybil turned a beaming face to them, so pretty and friendly and benevolent that the resemblence to Maggie's grandmother was all but obliterated for Colin.

"Maggie, darling, and Colin! I am so pleased you've made it with no further trouble! I nearly burnt the gingerbread when you fell in the river and the dragon got loose!" She had set down the bowl, which Colin could now see contained fudge icing, and, after wiping her hands on her ample apron, embraced them both.

"Auntie, what's happening to your house?"

"I tell you, dear, I was about to send to your Gran and see if she would like a guest till high summer. Have you ever seen such a sticky mess?" They both agreed that they had not. "You should know, Maggie dear, since I have no daughter of my own, I had intended to pass this place to you, but the practical problems of a house made of sweets far outweigh the security of owning one's own home."

Surveying the ick and goo, Maggie certainly understood what she meant. She bit her lip for a moment, then picked up a shingle and bit that instead slowly, chewing carefully as she circled the house, noting that even the foundation of peppermint stick logs was sagging and melting into the ground around the house. "May I use your oven?" she asked finally.

"Oh, of course, darling. You must be famished."

"We are, a bit. But if you'll find something for Colin and Ching, I'll undertake the repair of the cottage for you."

"Could you do *that*, dear?"

Maggie shrugged. "Well, it's a bit trickier than preparing a banquet for 1500 after a lean hunting season and a drought, but if you have the raw ingredients, I can tackle it."

It took even Maggie's magic the remainder of the light part of the afternoon to make the required candies and shore up the foundation, shingle the walls, and patch the roof with fresh sugar wafers. Fortunately for her, the power that defined her hearthcraft talent as that of hearth and housework took the term housework literally, so that it included a bit of light carpentry.

Colin and Aunt Sybil sat on stumps in front of the house,

50

drinking tea and munching the fresh roofing material, watching Maggie apply the fudge at strategic points so that it could spread itself before she applied the shingles.

"I only tuned in when you children were in the river, young man," said Sybil conversationally, "Have you known my niece long?"

Though Colin's experience was limited, it was not so limited that he had never before heard that tone of voice from fond female relatives of unmarried girls. "Er—not that long. We're traveling together on official business actually—Sir William's orders."

"I see. Maudie's message hinted that there had been some unpleasantness?"

"Message, ma'am?"

"My familiar, my budgie bird, flies messages between us sometimes—to keep in touch, you know."

"Isn't that a little awkward, considering?" He nodded to Ching, asleep in Sybil's lap, face nestled in his front paws as completely at home as though Sybil were her sister.

"Oh, Ching knows he mustn't be naughty and bother Budgie. Maudie has made that quite clear." She stroked the cat's spotted fur. "Our mother wouldn't have needed a budgie for her messages, of course."

"She wouldn't?"

"Oh, no. She could talk to you plain as day through HER visions. She talked Maudie all through birthing Bronwyn, even though she had to be in Queenston just then."

"Bronwyn?" Colin asked, sipping his tea. Maggie certainly had an extensive family. More of them just seemed to pop up in conversation all the time.

"Maggie's ma. Lovely girl she was, Bronwyn."

"It seems like Maggie has an awful lot of relatives, and they're all ladies. Tell me about Bronwyn, will you? Maggie talks about distant ancestors, but hasn't said much about her immediate family, other than that she's frightfully worried about this one sister who doesn't seem to be entirely a sister."

He felt a bit guilty for taking advantage of Maggie's doing a favor for her aunt to pry, but his horse and his musical instruments, as well as her things, had been stolen in this venture. He felt, under the circumstances, he really ought to have the whole story. Besides, it could add immeasureably to the background he needed to improve that song . . .

Aunt Sybil was a kind person and a lonely one, however,

she was not stupid. She gave him a hard look from under her brow that considerably heightened her resemblance to her sister. Maggie, having finished the foundation and the walls, and having patched the hard-candy windows with an extra shingle or two, had climbed the ladder her aunt used to climb to her bed-loft. With this she mounted the roof. She was again applying the fudge as binding material in strategic places so that it would spread itself properly to be ready for the application of the sugar-wafer roof tiles. "Well, young man, I can understand your curiosity. I suppose I can tell you something now, but the rest I'll save till Maggie's done there and we can all have a bit of supper. There's a lot she doesn't know, either, that I think she ought . . ."

"Any enlightenment you can provide would be appreciated, ma'am," Colin said. He had finished his tea and roof tile and had taken his guitar from its bag. He strummed lightly the strings as he fingered the keyboard. It kept his hands limber.

"I suppose Maggie has told you that she is a love child?"

"A—? Oh, yes, she did. I thought that was a little strange, because she and Sir William and everyone else acted as though she is a legitimate heir."

"She is, she is. But only because Sir William chose to acknowledge her, when he married her mother."

"I think you had better explain about that part."

"Well, let's see, now. How it was was that Willie Hood, Sir William that is, and my niece, Bronwyn Brown, were fond of each other from—oh, from when they were little bitty tykes. Childhood sweethearts, you might say. But Old Tom Hood, Willie's father, he had grand ideas, you know. He never did take to Willie being so sweet on the village witch's daughter. I lived there then, with Maudie, my powers not being so well developed at that time as they are now. Folk could stand to be around me then. Our mother lived here with our little brother, Fearchar, and they were both querulous, discontented folk mostly, not easy to be with. So I lived with Maudie and her little girl, and often this little lad, Willie Hood, was there to play. Stop that, kitty!" she cried, as Ching jumped off her lap and ran after a bird. He did desist, but not without an unkind glare before he sat down to wash his paw. Sybil tried to pick up the thread of her story. "Oh, my dear, now, let me see, where was I?"

She found a bit of metal wire in her pocket and began to twist it as she continued. "Oh, yes, Willie Hood. He did come to visit, but Himself, Sir Thomas, didn't like it. So he arranged a marriage with some foreign faery folk who had a daughter with a dowry so large as to buy title to all the Northern Territories for Willie." She crocheted the wire with her fingers into a double-linked ring. "If he'd been a braver boy, I suppose Willie might have taken Bron and run off—but they were only sixteen years old or so then, and he was fond of his father, for all that he was an old rogue. And Bron wasn't so sure that she wanted to run off and marry anyone, even Willie. Not that she didn't care for him, but she still hoped then to see her own talent blossom into some sort of respectable witchery, and there was only Maudie and me could teach her. She didn't mind not marrying, like some craftless village lass might, of course. Few of us have married, in the Brown line. I believe Elspat was wed to an ogre for a short time, if you could call such a union a marriage, and later there was Bron herself, but that's all I recall."

"Surely that's a little unusual?" Colin asked. He put a hand across the strings to stop their vibration. "Most ladies need a husband to protect them and provide for them."

Was there a hint of mockery in that gentle, dimpled smile? "And that's what you'll do, I'm sure, young man, when you marry. Protect and provide for your wife."

"Well, minstrels don't marry, as a rule. At least not until they've retired from the road and obtained positions as professors," he explained. "It's too difficult being on the road all the time, giving all your attention to music, to really be seriously involved with somebody—and girls take a great deal of involvement."

She laughed outright this time. "Dear, dear lad, you have just made my point for me! Boys take a lot of involvement too, that a witch may not have time for. Bronwyn was a sweet, dear girl, but she never really developed her powers before she died, because she was always spending so much of herself on Willie. Do you think Maggie's craft," she nodded at her niece, still busily shingling the roof, "takes less of her than your music does of you?"

"Er—I suppose not, but Maggie's—"

"Maggie's very like we all have been, even Bron. Which was why, as I was saying, she told Willie to never mind, she didn't care if he married Ellender. She even went to the wedding, pregnant and all. Her uncle was furious."

"I can see his point."

"Yes, I guess you could. Maudie was a bit put out too, but she'd raised Willie as much as Tom Hood had, and was delighted she was going to have a grandchild. The only time it looked as though there might be trouble was right after the wedding—Willie became genuinely attached to Ellender, the faery bride, and stayed away for a time from Bron. But faeries— and Ellender was a good quarter-blood faery, it was easy to see that—they smile and nod a lot, and are ever so lovely to look at while you're speaking to them, but you go away feeling that you've been talking to yourself. Have you ever noticed that?"

"No'm, I can't say as I've met many, at least not that close to the old blood." There *had* been a girl in East Headpenney, though, that, try as he might, he could never compose a really decent song about her, for all that she had long blond hair, big blue eyes, and all the really admirable feminine attributes.

"I see that you have."

"What?"

"I don't need my crystal ball to see what's so close to me, laddie. Why do you think I must bide alone?"

She went on. "At any rate, for whatever reason, Willie soon was coming back to the cottage, and asking after Bron, and bringing Maudie a bit of this or that from the castle gardens for her crafting. Pretty soon it was as though the wedding had never taken place."

"Didn't people talk?" Colin asked, again remembering East Headpenney.

"I suppose they might have, but they were careful not to let Sir William Hood hear, if they did. For he was now Sir William, as Sir Thomas, having wickedly succeeded at separating the children, as he thought, had taken to his bed. Folk were careful not to let Maud or Sybil Brown hear either, and I hear many things that are not meant for me to."

"Well, they certainly must be a high-minded lot of villagers to not be right in the middle of it, nevertheless. In East Headpenney there'd have been an awful scandal."

"It's amazing how fair and generous folk can be when faced with their own mortality. It's the uncertainty, I'm thinking, that adds a spice to life, keeping a body more immediately concerned with his own problems than other folks'. Even a loose-tongued person who knows that he might wake up as a crow can find his own fate a good deal more absorbing than his neighbors'."

"I never thought of it that way."

She nodded wisely. "Brewing beer and mixing healing herbs is the least of the good that Maudie does for that village." She stuck the wire back in her pocket. Maggie was now circling the house, hands waving designs in the air in front of her. She appeared to be mumbling something, but her voice was too low for Colin to hear. "What surprised everyone most, though, was when Bronwyn was birthin' Maggie—what do you suppose?"

Colin looked at Maggie. Obviously the birth had taken place. What else, then, could be the punch line? He had to admit he didn't know.

"Why, Her Ladyship, Ellender, came trippin' down from the castle to the cottage, is what! Maudie nearly threw her out at first, but I could tell she meant no harm and made Maudie let her in. Do you know, young man, I think that right there is where Maggie and Winnie got to be such great friends?"

Colin, having no idea what she meant, nodded and kept quiet, and hoped she'd elucidate so that he wouldn't have to seem ignorant.

"Ellender was pregnant at the time, poor thing, and her people, the foreign faery folk I was telling you about? They'd sent her some special elixir for labor pain. Faeries intermarrying with mortals had caused some difficulties with the birthings, but this elixir was to make it all seem like a walk in the garden. Bron'd been having a hard time of it, you could hear her hollering all about, I would imagine. Clear to the castle, probably, which must have been what brought Ellender down." Tears began to gather in her eyes. "Do you know— um—in spite of what Maudie could do, none of her medicines were of any help to Bron, and she could give her nothing more without harming the babe and—do you—" she stopped for a moment to compose herself. "Do you know that that silly faery lass gave Bronwyn her elixir? Just a bit at first, but as it only helped some, she gave her more and more, till it all was gone."

"That was certainly a very kind thing to do."

"It was kinder than that. Her own folk never got more elixir to her before little Amberwine was born, and she died

55

herself giving birth. That was when Bron moved into the castle to care for little Winnie along with Maggie, and when a decent time of mourning passed, Willie married my niece and acknowledged Maggie as well." The old lady was quiet for a time. Maggie had disappeared into the house, which caught the last pink rays of sundown on its soundly wafered roof, as tight and neat and pretty a cottage as any made of more conventional building materials.

"In East Headpenney, people would have said Bronwyn personally saw to it that the lady would die in childbirth so she could take over and be a wicked stepmother and..."

"If anybody had said such a thing, they'd have had the whole clan down on them, particularly young Winnie, for Bronwyn was the only mother she knew. Funny, you know. I myself wouldn't think being a crow would be such an awful thing, but—"

"I take your point."

"Oh, Auntie, that was so good," Maggie sighed, leaning back in her chair.

"Your voice is a bit crackly, dear," said her aunt. "Care for some honey in your tea?"

"Don't mind if I do, at that." She cleared her throat and rubbed her arms with the opposing hands. "I'm so hoarse and weary from all that spell-casting, I couldn't boil water for tea right now."

"Well, it certainly looks lovely, darling. I appreciate it so much. Under normal circumstances it's an enormous chore to keep this old place up, but with all this rain I was quite sure I'd finally be forced to move."

"Just don't let the children eat at it any more, Auntie. You'll have to keep a conventional cookie jar for that I'm afraid. I put such a strong preservative spell on it, it will be quite inedible."

"Don't worry about it, dear. It was a wicked idea to begin with, that has deteriorated into being merely frivolous. I'll be glad to have a roof over my head that won't turn to goo. When mother and Fearchar lived here the two of them could keep it up—he was rather handy as a boy."

"Tell me about Uncle Fearchar, Auntie," Maggie said. "None of the villagers seem to know much about him, and Gran never speaks of him at all."

The old lady didn't say anything for a moment as she

cleared the table and poured the tea. Ching was stretched full length in front of the emberous hearth fire, dying now that it was not needed for cooking. The evening sky had been clearing as the three people and Ching had come into the cottage for dinner, and the night was warmer than it had been at any time on their journey.

"I was going to mention Fearchar anyway, Maggie. Colin and I were having a talk while you were working and, as I told him, I wanted to tell you one or two family things that might be—painful—for Maudie. You may think that I'm an interfering old woman—" she held up her hand to ward off Maggie's protestations. "Yes, you well may. Quite a few do. But someone with my talent—to see so much denied the rest of you—it may be arrogant of me, but I feel that I have an obligation to give you some advice, to make things easier. And I'll do a sighting, as well, of course, but we can do that later."

She stared for a moment into her earthenware cup. "You see, dear, there was a quarrel, years ago, before you girls were born, and Fearchar left, and we haven't heard from or seen him since."

"Not even you?"

"Well, I did for a while, actually, but it wasn't a very good contact—a lot of static, you know, interference—till finally I could scarce see him at all."

"He was—somehow, do you think he was *blocking* you?"

Her aunt nodded sadly. "I think so. He was most upset when he left—it can't have been easy for him, the first boy in our long line of females. And then, mother died just before."

"Before what, Mistress Brown?" asked Colin, as the old lady was looking increasingly embarrassed. She looked, in fact, as though she wished she had not opened the subject and was reluctant to continue.

"Before Willie and Ellender." They nodded at her encouragingly and she went on. "I told you, Colin, that folk in the village thought little and said less of Maggie's mother being with child and her love wedding another. That was very true. Our brother was not so prudent."

"Being family, of course . . ." Colin began.

"We realized that, and that it was hard on him, particularly since he had always rather looked up to Willie—tagged along, making a regular nuisance of himself when he visited us at Fort Iceworm, he did. But he took on so long and so loud and

57

in such a temper, that it was all Bron and I could do to calm Maudie. See, Fearchar challenged Willie to a duel, of all the silly things, for the 'ruin' of his niece—and he no more than thirteen years old—when anybody could see she was not ruined, being a bit more than she was, rather than a bit less." She turned to Maggie and smiled. "Your father made some mistakes when he was young, but he's a good man, for all that. He just told Fearchar in front of the whole tavern that he wouldn't fight him and that was that. Fearchar called him a coward and slapped him publicly, and Willie just nodded and went back to his brew. The men at the tavern said Fearchar would have jumped onto him anyway and give him a thrashing, but they held him off. Finally he had to go away. Then he starts in pestering Maud to change Willie to a hare, saying he was like a hare because he was scared, y'know, to fight Fearchar. Maudie wasn't happy about the wedding, nor about Bron being so sad with missin' Willie, but she weren't daft."

"Gran would never do anything to hurt my Dad!" Maggie said stoutly. "And she told me herself Mama wouldn't elope with him so he wouldn't have to marry Ellender. What was all the fuss?"

"Just as I said, darlin'. Your uncle didn't see things that way. He kept pestering your Gran for that spell till she finally told him if he didn't be still she'd turn him into a magpie. That was when he left."

"Sounds like everybody should have been relieved, to me," said Colin.

"It was quieter," Sybil admitted. "But it was a shame too. He was a disappointed young man, not yet come to his powers, and mother only barely in the ground. He felt we'd all disgraced him and turned against him. I trust the years have shown him better." She poured a little more tea and said. "So I was thinking, dearie, that if your travels looking for Winnie take you to Queenston or thereabouts, you might ask after him. That was where my last sighting of him was."

"Of course," Maggie stretched and yawned, and in her stretch her eyes fell on her pack, hanging from a nail on the wall. "Oh, Auntie, I brought you a present." She got up and fetched the trap, setting it on the table before her aunt, who pounced on it.

"An iron trap!" her breath sucked in and she clicked her tongue, "Oh, child, where did you get such a wicked thing?"

58

"Colin took it off the foot of a rabbit. He said he thought it might have been set by the same man who shot at my dad last winter; the rabbit said so, I mean."

Gingerly, Sybil carried it to a little cabinet next to the fireplace. Inside this were metal-working tools, a small anvil, hammer, and tongs among them, along with some others Colin didn't recognize.

"I'd pity the bandit that thought to rob your life savings!" Colin said. "Who'd ever think you were a blacksmith, ma'am?"

Aunt Sybil dimpled with pleasure as she returned to the table. She carried a crystal globe with her, about the size of a small pumpkin. "Metalwork is a hobby, really. I don't get to use my craft professionally as much as I would like—a body has to be scrupulous with a gift like mine or cause a lot of damage."

Maggie laughed, a bit rudely, Colin thought. "Auntie, you must be the first one in our entire family to seriously worry about her magic causing damage!"

Aunt Sybil looked at her for a moment. "Not quite the first, child, nor the last, either." She sat down and placed the crystal before them. "I suppose it comes of being able to live other people's lives, second-hand though it is. It's a hard thing to hurt someone you understand. Troubles the sleep. So I do my metalwork when I can get metal, and peek a bit for the fun of it between serious craftwork commissions, and with that and keeping this old cottage together, I do keep busy."

"Can you show me what's happening to Winnie now?" Maggie asked, leaning forward and looking into the blank glass.

"To be sure, to be sure," replied her aunt, turning the ball over in her hands and looking deeply into it. What at first appeared to be a stray flicker from the candle stirred in the center of the ball, to gradually grow into a bright glow that began suddenly to fragment, sending motes of colored light dancing about the room.

"Ah, yes," said Aunt Sybil with satisfaction. "I believe that must be it."

All they could see was the image of a dagger, glittering nastily through the rainbow lights. Slowly, that moved away, and a throat came into view, slender and pale, and above that and around it a swath of cornsilk hair. Long, tapering fingers with broken nails dragged the hair back, and a pair of sleep-dazed, startled green eyes peered out through the parted curtain of hair.

"Out, you hussy!" hissed a voice behind the dagger. "Leave this camp at once if you want to stay alive and pretty!"

Amberwine gulped. She was not used to threats. "I beg your pardon?" she said.

"Oh, I'm sure you do that, my fine fancy lady. But begging is for honest gypsies, not faithless false trollops such as yourself! Out with you!" The voice turned into a black-haired woman, who leaned into the range of the glass, the better to menace the shrinking Amberwine. Except for the color of her hair and the green of the dress she wore, the second woman's image was indistinct.

Aunt Sybil frowned and put fingertips to her forehead. "Let me just see now if I can fine-tune this."

"Ooooh, Auntie!" Maggie's nose nearly touched the glass in her anxiety to see more. "You've got her! Poor Winnie, what an ugly customer that old bat is!"

Colin and Sybil each touched Maggie's shoulder and she scooted back so they could see.

Sybil's breath hissed out in surprise. "Well, I'll be burned. If it isn't that charlatan, Xenobia. I might have known she'd be behind this sort of thing."

"Xenobia?" Maggie asked. "Who's she?"

"She's *beautiful*," sighed Colin, evidently not referring to Xenobia, who was flashing her knife in glittering arcs at Amberwine, who finally had wakened to her danger and was reaching to pull on her boots before making an exit.

"Not so fast, my *lady*," said Xenobia. "You can just leave those behind to pay for your keep."

Amberwine complied, but said, "Quite a costly straw pile you have here, your highness. Four gold rings, a silk dress, a fine woolen cloak my sister wove for me, my moonstone necklace, and a good gray mare. Now my fine leather boots." She stood up barefoot in her shift and Sybil gasped.

"Consider it your dowry for coming away with my son, girlie!" laughed the other woman. "Pity you couldn't hold him, weren't it?"

"Pity my husband didn't kill him when he found us together on the moor," Amberwine replied over her shoulder as she hurried out into the dimness beyond the glass. "And me along with him."

60

The dagger flashed as Xenobia threw it and the glass went dark.

"Get it *back*, Aunt Sybil!" cried Maggie.

"I'm trying, child, but violence disrupts my concentration—ah, here," the rainbow colors danced briefly to show Amberwine hurrying down a path. Still vibrating in a tree she had just passed was the gypsy dagger.

"Perhaps we should start tonight," Maggie said. "She seems to be in terrible danger."

"Yes," Colin said. "Perhaps we should. For that lovely lady to be so mistreated by that AWFUL witch—oh, excuse me, I do beg your pardon!"

Aunt Sybil grinned at him. "The false part of your statement, lad, is that Xenobia is not a witch at all. Doesn't even have the second sight a lot of her people have. She's just a charlatan who calls herself Queen of the Gypsies." She turned to Maggie. "How long has your sister been missing, now?"

Maggie shook her head and looked at Colin, who replied, "From the last full moon to this, from what Giles said, but I can't be sure. Perhaps half again that time since I met him and Maggie and I started this journey."

Sybil nodded. "Good. Then it could hardly be the gypsy's child."

"Child?" Maggie asked.

"Haven't you helped your granny midwife, girl? Your sister is at least five months into her pregnancy."

"I thought they'd been feeding her well—she did look a bit stout."

"*I* didn't think so," said Colin.

"As for leaving tonight, that would be foolishness. You're weary to the bone on my behalf now, dear, and both of you on foot. Rest well this night and you'll make up your lost time the quicker for it."

"I don't think I can sleep," Maggie said. "Poor Winnie!"

"Chingachgook is having no problem on that score," said Sybil, nudging the cat, still stretched out in oblivious repose, as she returned the glass to its place above the hearth.

"Odd name for a cat," Colin remarked, fingering his guitar as he always did when distracted or confused.

"It's a family name," Sybil replied. "Handed down from one of our distant ancestors, a foreign sailor. Legend has it that he was a savage warrior from far across the seas who

61

wooed and won, or was it the other way around? one of our early ancestresses. Some of our elder kin once bore his peculiar names but as we've tried to become more—Argonian —we've passed these names on to our familiars instead. Except it's difficult to keep calling a budgie bird Osawatomie all the time, so I just call him Budgie."

Maggie had jumped up and began pacing. "How can you talk of such things at a time like this! We've simply *got* to find Winnie. Pregnant! Poor dear, I've got to get to her now and take her home. If she's so far gone as you say, Auntie, it can't possibly be that cursed gypsy's. Perhaps—no, oh, I hope we can find her before something terrible happens."

"Settle down, dear. Really, you children must be off to bed."

"Sit down, Maggie," Colin encouraged. "Here, I'll play us a lullaby."

He did so, and halfway through the lullaby, which was a long, monotonous musical recitation of King Finbar's coronation address, Maggie was climbing the ladder to the loft. Colin himself was yawning, as was Aunt Sybil, who rubbed her eyes and beamed at him. "You are a very talented young man. Are you by any chance of siren descent?"

"I don't know. I'm an orphan actually. I was raised by my Uncle Jack and Aunt Fiona in East Headpenney. Of course, Uncle Jack wasn't really my true Uncle—he was cousin to my father or somesuch thing. At any rate, he didn't like to talk about my folks much."

She got up and went to her metalworking cabinet. "East Headpenney is a charming place. I was looking at the harvest there last autumn. Very well they did." She smiled. "Play one more, dear. I'll cast a little spell of enhancement, just the standard one, and with your ability you should be able to put yourself to sleep with it. I must stay awake tonight and make a little going-away present for Maggie, but I'm sure if you sing The Minutes of The Seventh Tribunal that would do the trick for you." After casting her spell she stuck bits of cloth in her own ears.

He did as she suggested, and it worked so well that neither he nor Maggie were wakened by the firing, hammering, and polishing of metal that went on throughout the night.

6

"Remember, dear," Aunt Sybil told her as Maggie tucked the magic metal mirror into her apron pocket. "I could only give you three visions, so use them wisely to find your sister."

Maggie hugged and kissed her aunt one more time, then Sybil embraced Colin as well before the young people and the cat set off back down the path to the highway.

It was a long way yet to Lord Rowan's hall, and longer yet on foot. Determined as Maggie's heel-and-toe stomp approach to getting to their destination was, Colin had to hold back his long-legged stride to avoid leaving her behind. By suppertime the first night both of them were exhausted, and sat glumly nursing their blisters by the side of the road. They were unwilling to make even a small detour now to find a private place to camp for the night.

"Your aunt is a lovely old woman, Maggie," Colin said, painfully easing off one of his boots. "But I can't help wishing she could have loaned us something more immediately useful than a magic mirror—say, seven-league boots, for instance."

Maggie clenched her teeth and fought back the tears that lurked just under her eyelids as she removed her own boots. "*I* wish we at least had some of Moonshine's healing water, so our feet would be fit for travel tomorrow. We should have gone back to that village we passed just before Auntie's house and bought horses."

"That's what I *wanted* to do, if you'll recall, Mistress Brown," griped Colin. "But, no, you didn't want to spend the time."

"If we come to another place tomorrow, maybe we can buy a horse."

"A horse?"

"Dad didn't give me enough money to buy a *lot* of horses

on this trip, since he supplied us with some. Do you have enough for another?"

His eyes fell under her challenging stare. "No."

"Oh, don't look so put-upon. We can ride double or take turns. I didn't intend to hog it all for myself."

Colin poured a little water from his waterskin over his sore feet, then passed the water to her. "I hope your sister appreciates all this worry and pain on her behalf!"

"She—oooh, that hurts!—she will. She'd do the same for me, or have some knight or other do it for her, at any rate." She had finished bandaging one foot, and bathed the other from the waterskin before bandaging it as well. "If you knew her, you wouldn't mind this so much, really."

Remembering the green-eyed, pale haired, lithesome-though-pregnant vision, Colin nodded. "I suppose not."

"Here," Maggie said, finishing her own feet. "Put your foot up here and I'll bandage it."

"My boot won't fit tomorrow with all that under there."

"So tomorrow we'll take it off. Tonight it'll keep from rubbing your blankets." As she wrapped she continued. "The thing about Winnie isn't so much just that she's lovely, or charming, or any of that stuff."

"It helps," Colin groaned.

"I guess it might, for you. But—you remember the unicorn?" Colin said that, naturally, he did. "Well, Winnie's a bit like him. She makes you feel good—as if you're very important to her. Of course, I know *I* am—we've always been friends since we were babies. But she makes everybody feel that way." Colin appeared skeptical of such boundless grace. Maggie continued, determined that he should understand. "Many's the time when I was small I was teased by the other kids because I'm different, being a witch, and dark, and all. Gran couldn't turn every child in the village into something animalistic and similar—the little brats would have loved it! And Gran couldn't understand why I wanted to be like them anyway. She thinks we're a lot better, and, though I agree now that it would be boring to be the same as everyone else, I felt differently then.

"They all wanted to play with Winnie, of course, but she'd turn her back on them in a minute if they didn't include me. She always listened to me, even if she didn't understand all of the witching stuff. She cared about it because I do. When

64

Dad gave us a tutor and classes in how to be ladies and have manners and social style and such, Winnie didn't even need to be taught but I could never get the way of it. She'd coach me extra so I woudn't look the fool in front of Dad, then make jokes about how silly the whole thing was, anyway."

Colin withdrew his freshly-bandaged feet and Maggie looked down for a moment at her rough, dirty hands. "I've missed her a lot, Colin. I could only stand for her going away because she really seemed to swoon over Rowan, once she saw him, and would have a lovely big house and meet all those court people. I was planning to go visit her this summer, if it hadn't been for Dad's accident and Gran needing me at home."

The minstrel was not wholly convinced. "I find it hard to imagine such a virtuous person as you are saying she is doing what she did."

"I didn't say she isn't an ass sometimes," Maggie admitted. "If she had to run her own household and do all the chores without the benefit of servants, it would have been impossible for her. She's good with servants though. They all like her, and she knows how to get what she wants from them. She's just not very good at handling any sort of unpleasantness. People are never unkind to her, so I suppose unkindness isn't very real to her." She winced, remembering the vision in the crystal, and continued in a smaller voice. "She'd rather just go to sleep and forget about it than have to face doing something to make someone unhappy. That always has made ME unhappy. I could never see why she's not better at making decisions. She said she didn't have to be because I did it so well. " She frowned. "That's why it's difficult for me to credit your song. If she were to go off with someone, it might be for a little while, on the spur of the moment, while she could still see the turrets of her own home across the moors and know it was all very safe and romantic and fun. But to leave altogether? Without asking anyone or packing anything?"

"People do change," Colin said gently.

Ching came bounding out of the woods with a rabbit in his mouth.

"The gnome would throttle you, but thanks," Maggie said, accepting it.

"Excellent," Colin said. "I was getting sick of gingerbread."

They did pass through a small village the next day, and were able to purchase an aging plow horse who had not yet been killed for his meat. They rode double till Ching conveyed the message that the horse was going to lay down and not get up again if one of them didn't dismount. Maggie was restless anyway, and took the first turn walking, and in this fashion they progressed surely, if not swiftly.

The conversation had been far from lively, Maggie brooding over her sister's condition, desperate enough now to be considered a "plight," Colin humming and nodding to himself in the throes of a fit of creativity.

Finally, after many miles had passed, he asked, "Here, now, Maggie, what do you think of this?"

He sang:

> "When they came to the gypsy's camp
> The lady met his mother.
> She said 'This is no gypsy girl
> You'll have to find another.'"

Maggie shook her head. "I don't think so, Colin."

He looked offended. "Why not?"

"It sort of spoils the drama, don't you see, for him to have a mother. Evil seducers *never* have mothers, do they?"

"Artistically speaking, it's a toss-up who seduced whom, isn't it? Now, don't be angry. I'm thinking of this in terms of posterity."

Promenading along in front of them, Ching smirked a great cat smirk and said from over his shoulder. "Another crack like that and he can forget about having his own posterity, eh, witch?"

"Okay then, how about this verse, Maggie?" Colin persisted, attempting to save himself from another tirade. "It ought to work up some popular sympathy for our side:

> "A beggar lassie, dressed in rags,
> Still in her heart a lady,
> She mourns the day she heard his song,
> The song of Gypsy Davey, the song of Gypsy Dave."

"It has possibilities," Maggie admitted. "Still, I hope you won't be stuck with such a gloomy ending, even though that's the sort people like Gran prefer."

66

"Maybe I can come up with something better when we've talked to Lord Rowan," he said.

"You'll have to do most of the talking, you know."

"I will?" He was unsure whether to feel pleased at being assigned an important role or wary of assuming any responsibility in the matter beyond being General-Protector-Against-Bears and Chief Observer.

"Well, I hardly think my brother-in-law-is going to lay out a feast and spread the red carpet, as it were, for the bastard sister of his defected wife, do you?"

"I guess not."

Since leaving Sybil's cottage the days had been uniformly as sunny and clear as before they had been dreary and damp. Hills and forests and forested hills rolled gently back from the road. Wildflowers began to show themselves overnight, embellishing the carpeting of tangy new grass with clumps of blue and purple and yellow and pink and white, mixed and scattered by the roadside and upon the waving meadows. People and houses and roads branching off theirs appeared with increasing frequency, and soon they left the main highway and began having to ask the way to Lord Rowan's private estate.

The road that was pointed out to them led down the thickly populated valley, pleasant with fresh-plowed earth and neat stone houses. Maggie was continually delighting in some new aspect of the southern springtime. At Fort Iceworm it would still be as dim and dank as when they had set out on their journey.

The valley road began a gradual climb that nevertheless nearly finished off the old horse. Their feet had hardened slowly enough, spelling riding with walking, that both Maggie and Colin were now able to walk all the time, and lead the horse, who carried only their packs and the cat, when he chose to ride.

The next valley beyond those hills held the majority of Lord Rowan's vassals, those wealthy ones with good, arable land. The remainder of his holdings were the rocky hills and mountains of the Argonia-Brazoria border. Only a few scattered villages could be found in all those tortuous peaks and plunging canyons, but it had been the task of the Lords Rowan since the birth of Argonia to patrol those high hinterlands, and to this the greatest part of his time and effort was devoted.

Through the rocky foothills, then, Maggie and Colin and the tired old horse trudged, the road getting ever more steep and ever more winding as they traveled.

"I hope he doesn't live in the middle of those mountains," said Colin.

"The top of a hill, I think the people at the wedding mentioned."

"Which one? We've topped several." The minstrel kept having to wipe the sweat from his forehead to keep it from trickling into his eyes. He had already removed his vest and rolled up his shirtsleeves. His fair skin was burning a hot pink, in spite of the sun they'd gotten before. It had been several years since he'd worked in the fields of East Headpenney. He was no longer accustomed to hard work under a hot sun and was extremely uncomfortable, more so since he did not feel at liberty to give in and be miserable beside Maggie, who plodded along as steadily as the horse, her coarse wool clothing heavy but not confining, hair braided, kerchief tied around her forehead as a sweatband.

"We may as well stop here for rest and a drink," she said finally, when the path began to widen, and trees grew along the steep cliffs going abruptly up on one side and abruptly down on the other.

They sat for several minutes catching their breath, drinking from their waterskins and refilling them at the little stream of water that cascaded down the side of the cliff which formed a wall on one side of the road. Ching returned from a trot around the next bend, his fur lightly ruffled and his tail switching.

"The castle is on the next hill over," he told her. "But there are people on horses coming this way. A *lot* of people."

Maggie passed the information on to Colin, who sighed gratefully at the first part, although he hardly saw, really, how he could brave another hill, even one more, and agreed with her about the second that the best course would be to climb to the top of the hill and wait until the party passed them. "Who knows?" Colin remarked. "Maybe they'll be going back right away and won't mind giving us a lift."

Maggie said nothing, but was clearly dubious.

Ching scampered ahead and back several times. At the next bend the path reached its zenith. The descent was not by means of a rocky path such as the one up which they had come. The path sloped gently down, dividing a broad field

68

from a wood that covered the land as far as they could see, including the rounded dome rising from the floor of the valley beyond them. The wood only covered the dome to a certain point, however, for the rest was taken up in the structure of a castle, smallish as castles went, Colin thought, a circular wall enclosing a circular moat dug into the top of the mound. The circular moat surrounded a circular structure flanked by six semi-circular towers. That was it, a simple but effective, and incidentally rather beautiful, design.

"Achoo!" Maggie sneezed and scratched her nose, rubbed her eyes, then pointed. "Here comes that party Ching referred to. Best get over to the side." It took them a few moments to convince the horse, by which time the procession was upon them.

Although Maggie's actual rank as her father's acknowledged heiress and acting steward was rather ambiguous, Colin's presence and their by-now shabby mode of dress dictated that they follow the custom of standing as the obviously noble caravan paraded before them.

Accordingly, Colin took his cap in his hand and wore his best humble look as the first horse, which contained a man in a military uniform, passed.

Maggie sneezed again and watched the upcoming equestrians with bold and open curiosity. Colin's elbow jabbed her ribs. "Come on, Maggie, you'll get us whipped. Do TRY to look the modest maiden, won't you?"

"Sorry," she said, and trained her eyes on her great toe which was now protruding from her boot. Only occasionally did she sneak a peep at the procession. She could hardly help the sneezes, however, which occurred with increasing frequency.

"Imagine, receiving us with no chamber prepared, nor lamp lit, nor tea laid!" a well-fed figure who looked as though missing her tea would do her no harm at all complained to a thin and delicately handsome man. Both were well mounted and well dressed, the woman perspiring through the limp lace collar of her lavender brocade riding costume, which threatened to collapse at the seams at any moment, with the stress placed upon it by her numerous bulges and protuberances. She was red-faced, either with indignation or the effort of riding, it was difficult to tell which.

"I was talking with the serving maid . . ." the man began.

"You would talk to the serving maid," snapped the lady.

"And she said that the lord had not informed the servants of our impending arrival, nor had he given orders of any sort regarding his household since he ordered his horse and rode off after Lady Rowan."

The lady sniffed. "What would you expect of a northern woman but that? They're all half-wild up there, so I understand."

"Nevertheless, it's a great pity. Poor wretch. I understand Lady Rowan is very beautiful." Maggie sneezed again. "Bless you," the man said absently, taking no note of the origin of the sneeze. The fat woman leaned across him from her saddle to glare at Maggie, who, fortunately, was too occupied readying herself for another sneeze to glare back.

"I don't care what *she* says," snipped a plain-faced girl three horses back from the apparently noble couple. She was addressing a somewhat prettier maid who rode beside her. Both were clothed too grandly for the road, in silks and satins and laces repaired with other materials and much taken in, evidently cast-off gifts from their lady. "What's that old bag know of true love, anyhow?"

"Not a thing from him, I'll wager," the other girl agreed, chuckling behind her hand. "He's too busy trying to catch us at the bedmaking."

"No wonder, either, poor man," said the first girl, "But Ludy, one of Lady Rowan's personal maids, come from our village, you know, and *she* was actually *there* when the gypsy actually came into the actual castle!"

"No!"

"Yes! Handsome as anything, she says, though swarthy, of course, but I find dark foreign types attractive, don't you?"

"Oh, my, yes. That brooding, unknown quality!"

"Prouder than any noble, he was, she says, though not too proud to give a girl a pinch." She giggled "Ludy showed me her bruise to prove it."

"Well, they are all alike "

"Indeed."

"What happened then?"

"Oh, it was SO romantic! Ludy says first he come and asked for a meal, you know, and the lady, she was just passin' by. He offered to sing to pay for his lunch."

"Ooooh, he *sang* too?"

"My, yes, that's part of it. you know. There's a lovely song about it all." The girl went on to tell with great relish and considerable colorful embroidery how the Lady Amberwine had been so thrilled with the singing she'd invited him into the hall, and then at his slightest suggestion had ordered her horse saddled, pausing only long enough to pull on her fine leather riding boots and warm woolen cloak over her green silk morning dress before following her new love off across the moors.

"I didn't see any moors hereabouts, meself," said the other girl suspiciously.

"They're on the west side of the castle, silly, where you can't see them for the trees around the hill."

"Well, moors or no moors, she didn't let any grass grow under *her*, did she?"

"Oh, no, she was gone by that evening."

Maggie's sneezes interrupted their conversation and the plainer girl looked back over her shoulder at them. "Ugh! Scraggy-looking pair."

"He's rather dear, though, don't you think?"

By the time they had climbed down the hill, crossed the valley, climbed up the dome, crossed the drawbridge, and gained entrance to the inner courtyard, Maggie was not only crying openly, she was gasping for breath.

The closer to the castle they came, the more blurred her vision became from the itching and tearing of her eyes. Her constant sneezing kept her from drawing a decent breath. She stayed bent over with convulsions of katchooing, and Ching no longer rode on her shoulder but regarded her with wide-eyed alarm.

Colin gently guided her across the courtyard to the hall and pounded on the door. A servant on his way in by a side door noticed them at first with disapproval, then saw the state Maggie was in and sympathetically motioned to Colin to come round to that entrance which led to the kitchen.

"Your woman looks sick," observed the sturdy female who, by the ladle she brandished, Colin took to be the cook.

"Yes, ma'am, it came upon her suddenly. Though we may not appear so, my traveling companion is of noble blood, and I accompany her with a message for the Lord Rowan. Do you suppose she could be made comfortable till this illness passes?"

Ching lingered in the doorway for a moment, then, confident that the two-legged members of his party were looking out for one another, went to see if there was a barn available

71

with the possibilities of a good brawl with some of his own kind, and other feline diversion. Perhaps he would get friendly enough with the locals to acquire some gossip useful to their mission, hastening the acquisition of his mistress's step-granddaughter and his own return to his favorite rug under the loom.

"Poor dear can scarcely draw a breath!" the cook said, supporting Maggie in her meaty arms. "To bed with her, and hot herbal towels for her face and chest!" She gently lowered Maggie into a chair and left the kitchen, to return an instant later with a pretty if somewhat vapid-looking girl. "Ludy, put this lady in the North Chamber. She's too sick to be drug all over the castle."

Ludy looked askance at Maggie's disheveled state, and the cook, clearly a person of some authority, said with exaggerated patience. "The lad here claims she's noble enough for our guest chambers, and if she is or if she's not, in the state His Lordship's in he'll never know the difference anyhow."

The girl nodded and guided a streaming, sneezing, gasping Maggie from the kitchen.

Turning back to Colin, the cook said with mild severity, "Your message for His Lordship will have to wait, young man. His Lordship is—er—patrolling the borders at the present time." The minstrel's personal fragrance and grimy clothing, skin, and hair, drew a sniff from her. "Might be best you tidy up a little first anyway."

She showed him the serving men's common quarters and the well. He hauled four buckets of water to the trough for himself, and three more to wash his clothing. He wore the blue twill britches and ochre skirt, smocked for warmth, that he had worn the first day at the inn at Fort Iceworm. He hung the road-worn clothing to dry in the sun. His hands were quite shriveled and soft from all the washing, and it was some time before they dried sufficiently that he could pick up his guitar. Sitting on a servant's straw mattress, the guitar on his lap, he strummed and thought.

What on earth would he say to His Lordship? How could he breach such a tricky subject as a wife's abandonment without causing an offense which might not get him turned into cat food, but could certainly get him hung or something equally uncomfortable and debilitating? He wondered, too, what was wrong with Maggie, and wished she were there to consult. It was very inconsiderate of her to leave him in an awkward social situation that concerned, after all, her relatives, not his.

Maggie awoke from a nightmare in which she was being pressed to death. Although her breathing had been none too easy when she went to sleep, it was practically nonexistent now, and only panic forced her return to consciousness

In her dream, a lion's roar subsided into a menacing growl as the heavy paws pressed down on her shoulders and the mane bristled against her face.

Struggling to open her stone-weighted eyelids, she found they stubbornly remained closed. Body and will were made of syrup.

A growl so real that she knew she dreamt no longer rewarded her attempt at movement, and curdled in her ear as the lion's acrid breath came to her nostrils.

Odd, she thought. One would suppose a lion's breath smelled rather like old blood and such, but this one had obviously been drinking wine.

Curiosity accomplished what fear would not. Although her eyes would not open entirely, they did open enough to disclose that what pressed her to the bed was indeed a maned beast, but not one of the feline persuasion.

With hair and beard of bright red, her oppressor looked blearily into her face as she heaved herself upright enough to partially dislodge him. She noted that his eyes matched his hair. Sprawled across her in a drunken stupor, he had snored loudly enough to sound very much indeed like a snarling jungle cat.

Speaking of cats, where was that cat who was supposed to preserve her maidenly honor in such situations, she wondered. From what her granny had told her, drunken red-headed men who sprawled across a girl while she was sleeping constituted a definite threat thereto.

Ever one of the direct approach, she snarled a bit herself, her husky alto voice made even rougher by the trauma caused by all her sneezing, which, happily, seemed to have momentarily abated.

"Augh, get up, you!" she said. "You're drunk as a lord!"

He'd fallen back to sleep but now roused a bit, grumbling sleepily, and waved vaguely the bottle still clutched in one floppy fist. "S'alright, me darlin'. I *am* a lord!"

Finding she was quite decently clad in her own skirt and

73

tunic, the cook's herbal towels crumpled under her elbow, she decided to extricate herself the rest of the way out from under him. Wriggling upwards, she sent him rolling to the foot of the bed as she drew her legs out from under him and hugged them to her chest, huddling there for a moment, still not feeling quite herself after her indisposition.

He flopped over on one side and attempted to arrange his slack features into a creditable leer. "Aha!" he mumbled. "Spirited wench. Likes 'em with spirit, I do."

"If you'll pardon my saying so, your lordship, I think you've already had an overabundance of spirit."

"Oh, no, m'dear," he said, playfully swinging one shovel-sized hand in the general direction of her ankles and swigging from the bottle with the other.

She fetched him a kick that caused him to withdraw the hand for a moment. She wished she could drop one of her grandmother's powders into his bottle to convert it to something less intoxicating.

He nursed his hand tenderly. "You've hurt me," he blubbered, his bloodshot blue eyes filling with tears.

"Well, I'm very sorry, I'm sure, but you shouldn't go around lying all over people and grabbing at them like that," she said.

He looked slightly more alert, and also more dangerous, as he said belligerently, "You could have fooled me, woman. I thought that's what you were here for, because you wanted me to grab you." Seeing indignant denial oozing from her every pore, he flopped face down in the bed again. "Then do me the courtesy to get out of me bedchamber."

"This is *your* bedchamber?" Maggie looked around at the sumptuous room, with draperies masking its curved wall, rich rugs on the floor, and tapestries, and the enormous bed on which they argued. "Sorry," she got up and looked at him curiously, having recognized her brother-in-law and being at a total loss for a decent way to save the interview.

"It's one of them," he said. "Kept THIS here," he swigged from his bottle. "Dammitall, it's empty." Before she quite realized what was going on, he had hooked a brawny arm about her waist and pulled her back down beside him. He breathed a winey whisper into her face. "Cook hides it from me, if I don't hide it first. Bloody servants have the gall to say I've been drinking too much. Don't know their place. Ought to thrash the lot of 'em." He grinned conspiratorially. "I fool 'em though. Hide it in these chambers. Don't want any guests anyway, and the lazy buggers never touch these rooms otherwise."

"How clever of you," she said, drawing back from him as far as she was able. She was just about to open her mouth to scream when he gave her a hard look and shoved her away from him. She tumbled to the floor.

"Go on then, you heartless cold wench!" he sobbed with maudlin abandon into his big hands. "Bloody awful women. Always wantin' this and that from a fellow for nothin' but a how-d'ye do, then along come some other fellow and you don't even want that! Use a poor devil and throw him away!"

Maggie stopped at the door. To leave him in this state of mind would probably alienate him for good and defeat her entire purpose in coming to the castle. She looked at him for a moment, trying to see the stately nobleman at Winnie's wedding, the man they said might succeed Finbar as king, and whom her beloved sister had pronounced handsome beyond her wildest dreams. Picking up his empty jug in one hand and concealing it, just in case, in the fold of her skirt, she walked back to him and put a conciliatory hand on his massive shoulder. He did not even look up.

"Don't cry, your lordship. It's not at all how you think," she said. "You're really much too good for the likes of me, and I'm honored by your attention, really, but I've got these—um—pressing family obligations. I have this grandmother who'd turn us both into frogs, you see."

He passed a hand over his face. "Did you say—? I'm drunker than I thought."

Maggie extracted the jug from her skirts, and poured a drop of the remaining dregs onto her finger. She mumbled a brief spell over it, sprinkled a powder from her pocket over it, and wiped it on the lip of the bottle. Then she cast a general expanding spell and held the bottle out to him. "Have a bit of this, Lord. It'll clear your head."

He swigged a few draughts, gagging on it at first, but eventually both his posture and vision appeared to improve, and he regarded Maggie more soberly, "Can't think how I ever went after such a red-nosed, puffy-eyed, tangle-haired mess of a wench at that." But he grinned, if a little sadly. "Looks like you've been doing some bawling yourself."

"Sneezing, m'Lord."

"Sneezing?"

"Yes, I've had a strange reaction to something hereabouts. I was put to bed here to rest when I became ill."

He said nothing for a moment but looked sheepish. "I—um—didn't exactly advance your recovery, I suppose?"

"Well, I did wake up in a hurry."

"Sorry," he said. "Sneezing seems to be done."

"It does."

"Let's have a truce then, little lass. Come sit by me and I promise not to bite you. I'll finish this brew. Have some? No? I suppose you know, like everyone else knows why it is I'm actin' unbefittin' m'station, as cook says."

"I do—I mean—you're not . . ."

"Oh, I am. I am indeed. But how is it that you know? Not one of our girls, are you?" Able to see color again, he was curiously aware now of her darkness in a country of mostly fair-haired women.

She felt her cheeks go hot under his scrutiny where they had not with his more direct advances. "No, m'lord, I'm not from here."

"But—you *have* heard."

"I've heard."

"How? Has it gone so far abroad then?"

"Oh, no, you might say a little bird told me."

"And did he tell you why she did it?" he asked softly. "Because if he did, I wish you'd tell me. No one has. Amberwine—well, she just said she was going with him, she didn't say why." She looked away. She didn't know what to say. "What's your name?" he asked.

"Maggie."

"Pleasure to meet you, Maggie. I'm Roari Rowan and this is my place, but since we seem to be so close on such short acquaintance, you can call me Red."

Maggie nodded and he continued as though he hadn't interrupted himself. "She just sat there, Maggie, on that horse I gave her, looking bonny as ever with the wind kinda liftin' her yellow hair, and she says to me, 'I'll leave you now, Roari, and the house as well, and go with Gypsy Davey.' I was so mad I could have cut them both in half, and the horses too! How could she prefer that low-born greasy wretch to me and all I gave her—all I was going to give her? Oh, I know I was gone a lot, searchin' for the border raiders, but for the sake of all that's sacred, Maggie, how could a sane woman leave her man like that with no word at all and just GO?"

In his agitation his voice had risen to a shout, and his fists were clenched menacingly. A shudder ran through him, and for a moment his shoulders shook. Maggie awkwardly patted his back. His fists relaxed and he shrugged. "Ah, well, what good could it have done to kill them? To dirty my honorable sword with that gypsy's filthy gore? To kill the woman I hoped would be the mother of my children? No. I suppose they deserve each other." The tears were flowing freely again, and Maggie could think of nothing to say, but just kept patting him on the back. Red had a passing ignoble moment when he wondered if she might not be ready to offer more substantial comfort, when footsteps came pelting down the hall and the door crashed open.

Colin and the cook tumbled in with Ching at their heels. Rowan leaped to his feet.

"Unhand that woman, sir!" demanded Colin, boldly brandishing the fire iron. "Or you may find yourself scampering to a mousehole to escape yon cat!"

"Keep a civil tongue in your head, young man!" scolded the cook. "Oh, my poor, poor boy. At it again, are you, Red?" she asked, snatching the bottle from him. "Never you mind nasty young men and lewd women, dearie, go to your chamber, and cook will make you a nice pot of tea and fix a bag for your head."

Maggie was going to say something rude about being called a lewd woman, but Rowan was ahead of her.

"Has a man no privacy!" roared Roari Rowan to cover his embarrassment. He had found a roar a very effective measure to hide one thing and another, such as the tears that still glistened on his cheeks and in his beard. "I need no tea nor bag for my head. What I need is a drink!"

Re-entering a state of inebriation with a minstrel, Red found, was a most economical way to drink. The fellows sang more than they drank.

First drinking songs, then ballads of love lost, love spurned, love unrequited, love unconsummated, and love unconsecrated, both men singing with tears streaming down their faces in poetic abandon, until Colin was afraid his fiddle strings would go limp from the soaking.

Ching sat on Maggie's lap and purred. At first she sang along with them, but she didn't really care for their selection. The sleep which would have rested her from her illness had

77

been interrrupted by Rowan's admittedly collapsed lust. She yawned in her chair as Colin and Rowan wailed on. Eventually she leaned over Ching to fold her arms on the table and rest her head on them.

When she woke in the morning, she was in the same lavish bedchamber as the day before, quite alone this time, she noted with relief. She poured cold water from a painted pitcher into a matching bowl, washed and dressed herself, and set out to find the others. Ching hopped down from the bed and followed on her heels.

The stone floors rang hollowly beneath her feet and the place seemed deserted till she once more found the kitchen. Colin was not in sight, but Lord Rowan greeted her as she entered. "Ah, Maggie. The servants obviously must prefer you to our last guests. Squire Bumple and Lady Limely's quarters were not so grand as yours." His eyes were a bright, clear blue this morning and Maggie wondered if perhaps Cook had not after all got to him with her healing poultices and herb teas, though when she might have done it was beyond Maggie. The sky had already been lightening when she herself had succumbed to sleep. "You rested well, I hope?" His Lordship inquired.

"Very well, m'Lord," she replied primly before reverting to type and asking boldly. "Were Squire Whatsis and his lady the people we met as we came down to your castle, Lord?"

"Aye, they were." He gestured to a chair at the table, the same where she'd fallen asleep earlier. He sat with his legs straddling his chair, elbows resting on its back. "Of course, Cook didn't fancy them as she did you, lewd woman or not; they were only neighbors and not kinfolk."

"Well I must say I'm glad not to have to formally introduce myself again," she said.

"A more informal re-introduction would have scarcely been possible, eh, little sister-in-law?" He got quite a hearty laugh from the black look she gave him for his impropriety. "Family obligations, indeed, m'dear!" His laughter wheezed to a stop. "Ah, damn, that felt good. I haven't laughed in a long time. You and the minstrel are better than all of Cook's tonics."

"Where is Colin?" She touched the mirror in her pocket and remembered with a spurt of impatience her sister's image in the crystal.

"He's about. Choosing a horse for the rest of your journey,

I suppose. Gypsies have good mounts. You can't hope to overtake them on foot."

She stared at him.

"Oh, aye, Colin told me of your daft plan." He shrugged. "I did my best already. If you can talk sense to your sister, I hope you'll find her then."

"When we saw her in my aunt's crystal ball, she was leaving the gypsies," Maggie said. "And she was pregnant, my aunt said. *Very* pregnant."

"Very—?" He looked irresolute for the first time that morning. "Too—?"

Maggie nodded in answer to his garbled question "Five months at least by Aunt Sybil, who knows quite a lot about such things. Way before the gypsy came. I don't suppose you'd want to come along? Pregnant women have been known to do odd things before, and it surely must be your child."

Rowan was quiet for a long time. "What do you want me to do, Maggie? How can I take her back, if she'd come? She's shamed me before my own folk. They'd expect me to do something vengeful, and it's not in me to harm Amberwine. I need the respect of my people to lead them, Maggie."

She nodded. She wanted to tell him of her suspicion that Winnie had somehow been tricked, that, in spite of all the evidence to the contrary, including his own painful confrontation with her, his lady had been forced to leave her home. Remembering his confusion of the night before, she decided regretfully that it would be unfair to add to it, to raise her hopes when she had no real proof that her feelings were based on fact. "But you won't stand in our way? If we find her and she'll come home with us to Iceworm, you'd bear her no malice? You won't mind if she comes home to me and Dad?"

"No, little darlin'." He patted her hand and held the pat a moment too long. "I won't mind that. But I think I mind your going." They each looked in an opposite corner of the room after he said that, searching for a change of subject.

Uncomfortable, Maggie rose to her feet and went to the kitchen door, thinking she'd check on Colin's progress with the horses. As she stepped a foot into the tree-lined courtyard, she sneezed a mighty sneeze and retreated, still sneezing, into the kitchen.

The door slammed as she backed into the table and gropingly

found her chair, sinking into it as she gasped for breath between sneezes. As she held her head in her hands in the enclosure of the kitchen, the sneezing slowly subsided.

Red looked alarmed. "Poor lass. Perhaps you've simply caught your death of cold. Minstrel Colin made up a song, you know, about your tryin to save that daft drownin' dragon."

"He—gasp—he did?"

"Aye." He rose and touched her shoulder as he crossed the room in one stride. "You just let me show you how to build a roarin' fire in the hearth here. Cook wasn't expectin' us up and stirrin' so early today, y'know, after our little commiseration last night." He pulled a door in the wall beside the fireplace open and began throwing logs into the hearth's open maw. "She doesn't reckon with me constitution. M' family's descended from the owd frost giants, did you know that? Hell, I can drink like that all night and march forty leagues the next day."

Maggie was paying no attention to Roari's bragging, for as he lit the tinder to the kindling her sneezing once more erupted. "It's ahhhhh—it's—ahhh—it's CHOO! It's the logs!" Although what she said was fairly unintelligible, her frantic gestures and the commencement of her sneezing just as he lit the fire finally made sense to Lord Rowan, who was not a stupid man. He doused the fire with the pot of water in which Cook had been soaking wine cups. The fine pottery tinkled in the hiss of the dying flames. He swore as he both cut and burned his fingers pulling the embers apart, and found the rinse pail, dousing the embers again till they were completely dead. When the fire was out, he threw the sticks of kindling and logs back into the bin from which they'd come, and slammed the door.

Again Maggie's wheezing and sneezing began to abate, and she breathed normally again.

"I never saw t' like of that." His Lordship sat down again and stared at her curiously. "The good rowan logs, is't? From my own trees?" He was still shaking his head when comprehension came crashing down on top of it. "Wait a bit—that trick you did with the wine jug—and your owd granny turning folk into frogs and t' like. I heard Amberwine say she was a witch—you're witchfolk yourself, aren't you, girl?"

Maggie nodded, speech still being difficult.

"It's a wonder then, dearie, that you're sitting there to nod at me."

She looked quizzical.

"Didn't your granny or that aunt of yours tell you anything? Rowan trees are dead poison to your kind."

Maggie shrugged and said in a voice half her usual volume, "I suppose they never thought of it. That kind of tree doesn't grow at home, and I've never left there before."

"For one of your kind, it should have been a standard warning," he said, his booming voice still harsh enough to make her shrink from its noise. "Should have told you that along with telling you to wrap your cloak tight and stay indoors on rainy nights. I don't know why the reaction didn't kill you, but if it had my enemies would have said I murdered you from spite over Amberwine."

"That's ridiculous," Maggie replied with some of her old assurance.

"Wouldn't have been unheard of," said Cook, coming in from the courtyard. "'Course YOU wouldn't, m'Lord, but there's them..."

His glower persuaded her to continue at a more subdued level.

"Anyhow, just fancy poor Miss Maggie being a witch and your rowan trees making her ill!" She heaved a deep, put-upon sigh. "I suppose that means a cold breakfast and no herb tea for you, with no fire."

The positive aspects of witchcraft were displayed by Maggie who, having recovered her strength, produced ham and ginger omelettes, and two loaves of bread, one for Rowan and the other for herself and Colin, who came in while preparations were in progress. Rowan's omelette consisted of a ham and two thirds of the morning's eggs. The other third was more than enough for Maggie and Colin and the servants. Thus they breakfasted comfortably enough to please even Cook, although the older woman did voice the opinion that somehow such fare lacked the taste of food made the conventional way, with elbow grease and a fire of the usual kind. Both minstrel and host assured her that such views constituted nothing but traditionalist propaganda.

With a napkin-ruffling sigh, Lord Rowan pushed himself away from the table, wiping his mouth with the back of his hand. "Now then, minstrel, m'lad, you have the horses?"

"Yes, m'Lord." A sober Rowan, Colin felt, was entitled to formal address, although "Red" was good enough for a drunken one.

"And the provisions?"

"As much as we'll need. We can travel light on that account, m'Lord, due to Mistress Brown's—er—skills."

"Very good. Weapons?"

"Weapons, m'Lord?"

"Weapons." Rowan nodded encouragingly. Colin cast a quizzical glance at Maggie, who shrugged.

"No weapons, m'Lord. Our mission being—uh—in the nature of a family disturbance, you might say—"

"Laddy, there is NOTHING," Lord Rowan jabbed a sausagelike finger emphatically into the table top, "*Nothing* more dangerous than a family disturbance! Were I not so sweet-tempered in my cups, had you not known so many good drinking songs, and had my in-law here not been sae bonny, you might well have found out from me *how* dangerous. You won't be so lucky as to charm the gypsy camp in similar fashion, I'm thinkin'."

He leaped up and stalked into the dining hall and back before Maggie and Colin had time to do more than exchange bewildered shrugs. When he returned there was clasped in his great paw a broadsword whose enormity was minimized only by his own. He whacked and whooshed experimentally at the air around him, then ceremoniously presented the sword to Colin, who found it awkward to keep aloft.

"I don't see how he can carry that," Maggie said.

"Right!" barked Rowan, springing off again to return with the scabbard, which he plopped on the table. He sat again, drawing his chair up to the table once more, beaming like an excited child. "It's my second best family sword, y'know. Figure if you're off to find *my* wife you may as well have *my* sword to help you wade your way through her admirers. We Rowans are a warrior clan, really, descended from a rowdy bunch of fellows called frost giants from someplace past the Sea of Glass. Since we've been in Argonia there've been so bloody many heroes on both sides it's difficult to say who's bravest, but it's generally agreed that my sword, Owd Gut-Buster, belongin' formerly to that famous berserker, Rowan the Rampager, is the best. This one," he glowed with pride as he reached across the table to finger the sword as it lay in front of Colin, "is the legendary Obtruncator. Owner was not only a fella of great bravery, but possessed the most marvelous restraint and foresight of all the Rowans before him."

"What was his name?" Colin asked.

"Rowan the Reckless." He placed the sword in the scabbard. "I'm considered somethin' of a sissy by the chroniclers of my family, I would suppose, but most of the heroes, you must understand, served as one-man fronts in some king's war. I'm the first to be considered for nomination to the throne itself. Bumple came here to pledge himself to me before the fact. When you've gone I'm going to have to ride over there and make amends, I guess. Can't just go discarding peoples' allegiances if you're going to be in politics."

"You'll make a splendid king, I'm sure." Maggie said it politely, but was surprised to find she felt considerable conviction behind her statement.

"Damn right, I would," agreed Rowan. "Doesn't look too well, actually, though, Bumple says, what with her potential royal highness not exactly givin' me what you might call her vote of confidence." A few minutes passed in silence, then His Lordship banged the table as he got to his feet. "Well, lad, I'd best show you how to use this second-best family sword, eh?"

"Thank you, m'Lord, I'm sure, but really—"

"Oh, yes, and Maggie darlin', you'd best have this along." He tossed her a sheathed dagger. "All the gypsies carry at least one, and you oughtn't to be unprotected." The hilt was notably unencrusted with gems, but was made of a beautiful purple colored wood, and appeared quite sharp enough to slice anything requiring slicing. Maggie devoutly hoped she could confine its use to game meat and fresh fruit.

7

Colin groaned with pain as he half slid and half fell off his horse and onto the ground, where he lay like a freshly landed trout. A long night filled with too much wine and not enough sleep, followed by the unsoothing clang and banging of Gut-Buster and Obtruncator as Rowan attempted to teach him the rudiments and a few of the finer points of swordplay (as far as he could tell it was all rudimentary, and though he felt the point often, he didn't find it particularly fine) had gotten his day off to an inauspicious start. Maggie's insistence that they leave immediately after she had been unable to use her aunt's gift to locate Amberwine from within the castle had not been a welcome development. It had become even less agreeable when the decision was made by Maggie and Rowan that in order to keep to a minimum the effect of the rowan trees upon her, Maggie was to ride Rowan's swiftest steed at maximum speed out the west gate of the castle and across the moors. Colin was to trot behind with a packhorse and a fresh mount to replace the lathered one that would carry the heavily-veiled Maggie away from her nemesis. That was all very well for Maggie, but Colin hardly felt up to walking on tiptoe very quietly, much less trotting.

Neither had his sacrifice of his own best interests in order to preserve hers met with deep appreciation and profound gratitude. Maggie was turning the mirror over in her hands, staring at it moodily when he rode up, and she continued to be quiet and uncommunicative, nodding or shaking her head or answering in the shortest possible fashion when he addressed her, if she answered at all.

Now that he was finally allowed to rest his throbbing head and aching limbs, he was prodded out of his misery by Maggie saying, "If you don't want any of this, I'll give the rest to Ching." He looked up. Maggie was seated on her bedroll, toasting her toes before one of her fuelless campfires, eating a wing of the roast pheasant that turned on the spit above the fire. dripping juices into the flames with a sizzling pop that even sounded delicious

After feasting on the rest of the bird, two potatoes with fresh herbed butter, and half a loaf of hot bread, Colin thought he might survive after all.

With surprise. he saw that Maggie had spread his cloak across her knees and was reweaving one of the collection of rips and tears and holes that were its only adornments.

"Thank you," he said. "But you don't have to do that."

"I like sewing," she replied without lifting her eyes. "It calms me."

"Well, if it's calming you want, listen to this!" In spite of his afflictions, new verses for the song about Amberwine and the gypsy had been worming their way in and out of his aching brain all day long. He fetched his guitar down from the horse and sang:

> "Go saddle me my good gray steed
> The brown is not so speedy
> And I'll go racin' 'crost the moor
> To overtake my lady.
>
> "When he saw the man who wronged him so
> His anger it did kindle,
> But thinkin' on his lady's love
> His wrath did slowly dwindle.
>
> "How could you leave your house and land
> And all the wealth I gave ye?
> How could you leave your own true love
> To ride with Gypsy Davey?
>
> "Oh, what care I for house and land
> Or all the wealth you gave me.
> I'm goin' now, my own true love,
> To ride with Gypsy Davey."

"Then I'll put those other two verses I sang earlier towards the end. What d'ya think?" Colin asked, looking up expectantly. Maggie was staring off into space again, ignoring her needle-work. When she saw him watching her, she quickly brushed her face with the back of her hand and leaned down to bite in two the thread with which she had been sewing.

"Well?" Colin asked again.

"I beg your pardon?"

"What do you think?"

"Oh—the song. Very good, Colin. You really do have a talent." It was the longest sentence she'd said all day. He was about to ask her if she'd like to discuss what was troubling her or if perhaps he was mistaken and she was merely practicing to enter a religious order under a vow of silence, when she added another comment. He grinned with relief and with the realization that for a change he was actually glad to hear her say something. "But how do you know Winnie's side of the conversation?"

"A combination of research and poetic license. Ludy, the serving maid, was listening at the door when Rowan told Cook what happened on his ride."

"I think he showed remarkable restraint for someone with his background, don't you?" She rewove one of the few places on the cloak that had remained intact.

"Well, he came off alright in the song, I suppose . . . "

"He'd make a handsome king, don't you think?"

By returning his guitar to its sack Colin was able to conceal his frown. Rowan had been decent enough to him, but Maggie was acting, now that he thought about it, a lot the way she had after meeting the unicorn. While Rowan's horns were of another variety, they apparently troubled him enough to cause him to pay a lot of unsettling attention to ordinary brown-haired girls like his susceptible sister-in-law. It would have pleased Colin a lot better if the bereaved, deserted husband had just gone on bereaving and left his own traveling companion out of it.

"Why don't we try the magic mirror again, Maggie? We ought to find out if we're headed in the right general direction before we go much further."

"I suppose you're right. I wonder why it wouldn't work this morning. Toads! I thought if Rowan could just SEE Winnie he might—oh, I don't know what I thought."

"He did try that once to get her back," Colin reminded her, disliking Rowan even more because fairness forced him to defend the fellow.

"I know. Where shall we start?"

"Where your aunt left off."

Maggie had pulled the mirror out of her pocket and polished it. She held in her mind the image of Amberwine and of gypsies, the latter image provided by the village fairs and her imagination freshly fueled by Colin's song. As the rainbow lights flashed away in the darkness, two indistinct pictures, one superimposed on the other, appeared in the mirror.

"Hmmm, let me try to clarify that," she said, and thought hardest about her sister as she had last seen her, tousled and troubled and burdened by pregnancy. The gypsy wagons that had hung ghostlike over the mirror faded and Maggie and Colin almost wished them back to hide the ugliness of the remaining image.

Amberwine huddled by a stone wall, her hair tangled in a mat that covered her face, so that it took Maggie a while to be certain that it was indeed her elegant sister who swatted the flies away from the sores that covered her arms and thin, bare legs. Her ribs showed sharply above her swollen stomach. As the sounds of a marketplace rattled through the mirror, Winnie suddenly sat up straighter and shoved a handful of hair back from her red, swollen eyes with one sharp combing motion. A peddler's cry sang out over the other noises and Winnie got to her feet, pulling the remnants of her shift over as much of herself as they would cover. The cry was repeated, and Maggie almost lost the picture in her surprise. "That's Hugo's cart!" she said, as it came into view, immediately in front of Amberwine.

At first it appeared as though Winnie might try to round the corner of the building and escape the peddler's notice, but then she seemed to change her mind and drew herself to her full height, managing to look regal and somehow, Colin thought, ethereal and heart-breakingly beautiful, for all her dirt and mats and sores.

"Why, my Lady Amberwine," exclaimed Hugo, as though he were greeting her in her father's kitchen garden. "Whatever are you doing here in Queenston?"

Though Maggie had difficulty with them, the social graces and their attendant poise had been Amberwine's by birthright, not education alone, and had never deserted her. Now, as ever, she was cool. "Oh, hullo, Hugo. How nice to see you here. I don't suppose you'd have a frock and a bit of bread or something today I might charge to Daddy's account, do you?"

The peddler's tone was sweeter than Aunt Sybil's house.

He waved a cutely admonishing finger at her. "Now your ladyship knows I have nothing fine enough for the likes of you on MY humble cart." He gave Amberwine a chance to interpret this as a rejection of her thinly-disguised petition for help, then said, "Actually, ma'am, I've been sent to look for you. Your father is staying here with a distant relative of your stepmother's. If you wouldn't mind riding in my modest wagon, I could take you to him."

Amberwine was cool, but not that cool. Tears of relief and gratitude washed her lovely face. "At last. Oh, Hugo, I don't know how to thank you," she started babbling, "if father will only forgive me, perhaps—"

She stopped herself from talking by fairly dancing onto the cart. "Is Maggie along? Will I see her?"

"Old Hugo has all kinds of surprises for you, my Lady, if only you'll just settle yourself so we can get on now," he said it as though coaxing a child.

"Oh, certainly, to be sure, oh, my, yes," she wriggled around and signalled to him that she was ready for departure.

"That slimy bastard!" Maggie yelled, as the mirror went dark. She thrust it rudely back into her pocket. "How fast can we get to Queenston from here?"

"It's about a week's hard ride, at least. Maggie, what did he mean about your father being there?"

"I don't know. It's a lie, of course. What can that vile worm be up to, anyway?"

"Can he have passed us while we were at the castle?"

"Perhaps—or else—"

"Or else what?" he asked, hoping she wouldn't insist they ride all that night to get to Queenston the earlier.

"Or else that explains the iron trap, and why our horses were stolen. But why would Hugo be the villain Rabbit saw shoot Dad's horse? And how could he move so quickly? You yourself said a week. The man must not sleep." She sighed and bit her thumb nail before spreading her blankets. "We have to though. And the horses need a rest."

His own questions about the vision were drowned out by relief as Colin spread his own bedroll.

8

They never reached Queenston.

Colin, whose ear could pick a birdsong out of a thunderstorm during an earthquake (if a bird should be so unwise as to be present and singing under such circumstances), heard the music hours before they reached the gypsy camp.

By the time Maggie heard it as well, they had spotted the gaudily painted wagons competing with the wildflowers for sheer colorfulness in the wood-bordered meadow.

At the top of the meadow they stopped their horses and watched the late afternoon activity of the gypsies. Townspeople from the village which lay nearby were scattered among the gypsies, having their fortunes told, Maggie supposed, or perhaps naively imagining they could get the best end of a trade for the gypsy horses which were tethered close by one of the wagons. Babies squalled and children ran naked among people, livestock, and wagons. The flash of bright, cheap cloth and the glitter of a golden earring or a gold coin necklace occasionally danced across their field of vision before being blotted out as the wearer disappeared behind a wagon or hunkered down to barter.

The predatory gleam in Maggie's eye, and the determined compression of her lips as she surveyed the scene boded no good to Colin. Gypsies were scarcely known for their tractable dispositions either, and he and Maggie could not count on strange townspeople to extricate them from any difficulty Maggie's temper brought upon them.

Ching sat up on his pallet and viewed the camp with precisely the same attitude he displayed towards birds. Maggie smiled suddenly, a lazy, preoccupied smile, and nodded, leaning over to scratch the cat's ears.

Hoping that the smile meant her mood was improving, Colin said, "Maggie," in his best tone of gentle but firm reasonableness. "That is no place for you. You are far too emotional about this situation, and will undoubtedly cause those people to do us some injury if you let your temper get the better of you. You can't do your sister any good then, can you?" He ended on a note slightly more confident than the one he'd started on, and stole a glance from his alert, eyes-forward posture, to see how she was receiving his speech.

To his utter astonishment, the predatory stance and the probably even more troublemaking smile had both disappeared, and it was a mild Maggie who sat on the horse beside him, her head lowered, eyes downcast, hands meekly folded atop the pommel of her saddle. Ching had rolled over on his back and was watching them, upside down, purring sincerely.

"I—uh—I feel," he finished lamely, somewhat deflated by the lack of anticipated opposition, "that an objective party such as myself is the proper one to do the reconnaisance. Besides, gypsies are pretty musical. They're not so apt to mind a minstrel."

"Of course not, Colin," she readily agreed. "A minstrel's pocket's as easy to pick as anyone's." The momentary sharp look that accompanied that statement was quickly veiled by lowered lashes. Colin wasn't really fooled by her pose of maidenly acquiescence, but was grateful she wasn't making a scene. "I really think you're probably quite right. As you say, I do get upset. So perhaps Ching and I will stay here in this part of the meadow."

"What will you do?" he asked suspiciously.

"Oh, pick a few wildflowers, gather a few herbs Gran was wanting at home. So you just run along and find that awful gypsy—but watch out for his nasty mother."

"Right," he said, still puzzled, but getting ready to take advantage of her uncharacteristic fit of good nature to click to his horse and be off.

"Good-bye!" she waved gaily to him, though he still sat beside her. In order not to feel ridiculous, he rode into the camp.

A small, grubby boy ran up to him as he stopped beside one of the wagons on the fringe of the camp. "Honorable Lord!" the youngster yelled loudly as he bowed low and grinned, "I will keep your splendid animal and treasured possessions from all harm while you enjoy the hospitality of my home and converse with my elders, you know what I mean?"

90

Colin knew. "How could I possibly repay you for such thoughtful service, young squire?" he replied with insincerity to match the urchin's own. He knew exactly how.

"By crossing my palm with a small coin or two, or a large one if you prefer, oh, not for me, but for my aged mother and fourteen younger brothers and sisters," he replied. It must have been a remarkable family for him to have fourteen younger brothers and sisters, Colin thought, as the boy himself was scarcely more than seven or eight years old.

"Of course," he said, flipping the coins to the child. Two wagons away, a woman with the raven gypsy hair and skin darker than Maggie's switched her scarlet flounced skirt back and forth the same way Ching would switch his tail as she watched the transaction with an interest not wholly economic. Her lava-black eyes infected Colin's pores with a humid pre-perspiration warmth.

Very conscious of those eyes, Colin cradled his fiddle under one arm as he sought the source of the music, a task made more difficult, as there was a lull in the performance, whether or not occasioned by his arrival he had no way of knowing.

Children clung to his britches and shirt tail as he walked from wagon to wagon, seeking the musicians, who were not occupying the bare meadow grass within the ring of wagons, as Colin had half expected. There were women poking in a cooking pot over a central campfire, and some others tending a spitted animal roasting over a pit, but they were old and unattractive, and in no way musical-looking, though he admitted he could have been fooled. Actually, the children weren't the only ones enjoying the novelty of being with peculiar-looking strangers. Colin had sung a lot of songs about and by gypsies, but like many of the other things he had sung of at the academy, gypsies were not something of which he had any first-hand knowledge. He'd sung of rowan trees too, but how good had he been at recognizing them? They'd practically had to kill a friend of his before he even knew what they were. The same ignorance held true of court life (except for a brief field trip to the minstrel hall at the capitol), the seas beyond the Gulf of Gremlins, war, bandits, True Love, ogres, flying carpets, and princesses. And of course, any number of other things, though he had been able, in the course of this journey, to withdraw dragons, unicorns, gnomes, and knights from the list. Even in East Headpenney they had had a witch, though she was of little real use that Colin could see, her main talent being the ability to communicate with dead people. Because of that talent of hers, he had met a lot of ghosts, but on the whole, he thought with satisfaction, gypsies were far more colorful and exciting. He sort of hoped this might be the wrong gypsy camp, or that if Gypsy Davey were here, Amberwine would, in spite of the evidence of the magic mirror, be with him. While Amberwine and Maggie were being reunited, Colin could befriend the people of the caravan, who would recognize him as a good and honest man and a great artist, and trot out all their best folk stories and songs to tell him, which he would take back to the academy and for which he would be given all sorts of praise and respect and a professorship with tenure (which he would humbly decline, of course, preferring the true troubadour's life on the open road).

Just as he was accepting the Minstrel's Medal of Merit from Master Minstrel Peter, he tripped and fell sprawling, face first, catching himself hard on his left side to avoid damage to his fiddle.

"Sorry," mumbled the person over whom he had tripped, languidly drawing her feet closer to her and covering them with a full blue skirt. Her mood appeared to match her attire. Ignoring him as completely as though *he* were a ghost, she sat with her head resting against the splintery rough wood of the wagon, the pretty head drooping as though her neck were inadequate to support it. Though the neck was long and graceful, it appeared to Colin to be in no way insubstantial, however. It was draped with beads and coins that jangled distractingly as the girl heaved a desolate sigh. Her chin pointed up but her mouth pointed most emphatically down, and he watched a tear balance, glistening, on the end of her nose before skipping over her lips to slide down her chin and trail off behind her ear.

"It was my fault. I ought to look where I'm going," he said, feeling embarrassed to be relatively tragedy-free in the face of such evident misery. "Beg your pardon, but could you tell me where the musicians are? I play the fiddle," he held it up, his credentials, "I thought, you know, they might let another fiddler sit in."

She jerked her head to the left. The children who had been following him had joined a group of people, liberally sprinkled with dogs, who leaned, sat, or lay in a loose cluster around five men, and around one man in particular.

Having had more than what he felt was his just portion of moody women lately, Colin stifled his sympathy, and in three strides joined an ale keg of a man who was seated on the ground. The man in the middle was telling a story, and telling it very well. His tone was ringing and true and carried so well Colin wondered that he had not heard him earlier. The fellow's whole attitude was a parody of the love, grief, hate, sorrow, and anger that motivated his audience. His was the voice of life taken lightly, and it was a soft voice, sibilant, caressing the ears of his listeners. He had a gift for timing, drama, and imitation that made him the best natural storyteller Colin had ever heard, aside from Master Minstrel Peter.

Though certainly dark, the gypsy was neither tall nor particularly handsome, having a beakish nose not uncommon on other faces in the crowd. But his black eyes sparkled with wit, his mouth was always ready to laugh, and his hands were in constant motion, making a play of his words.

They were large, thin-fingered hands and they drew, as Colin watched diagrams of battles, became firing cannon, or horses so fast as to elude all pursuit. They described with gestures to match his voice his conquests of the most beautiful women in more countries than he cared to count. Colin believed every word.

Watching the gypsy, Colin wished that he had as large a nose so that he could flare it dramatically, as though at the scent of blood or perfume—it was, on the gypsy, an excellent tool of expression. Colin also thought that his nature slighted him when it came to flashing a dashing smile. Even with brown edges, white teeth flashed so much more effectively in a dark face. The gypsy drew answering grins from the men and sighs from the prepubescent girls and the few crones.

The only physical resemblence between himself and the gypsy was that they both had dirt under their fingernails— but Colin wondered if he could move his hands so flexibly describing the curve of a lover's breast, waist, and hip that his audience would fail to notice his poor grooming habits. Probably not.

For all his talent and training, he began to despair of ever having such a manipulative narrative skill as the gypsy. Perhaps if he questioned the gypsy, who seemed to have accomplished the thing the older fellows had hinted was part of the trade of the minstrel, that of having the audience in the palm of his hand and, not incidentally, of having female persons unplatonically impressed with him, Colin would find out how it was done. It could be, of course, that practice made perfect, as it did with getting a consistently perfect high drone from his fiddle or clear barred chords on the guitar. Probably not, but he could hope so.

When the gypsies began to play once more, this tune a non-gypsy song, a bawdy ballad, in fact, that Colin knew, he put his fiddle to his shoulder and unlimbered his bow. The other fiddler in the group, a one-eyed man whose big nose had such large pores in its skin it looked like a bit of aged cheese, stopped playing. Colin played for a moment or two longer before he realized he was carrying the tune alone.

The man who spat in his general direction was as skinny as one of the camp dogs, but lacked their teeth or any of his own. "We do business with you people, but who asked you to play, eh?"

"I am the violinist in this camp," said cheese-nose.

The air had a lot the same mouth-drying heaviness it had had in Sir William's tavern just before Colin had flown off into it. He hoped the witchy gypsy woman, Xenobia, was not within earshot, as he remembered his training in dissembling class. Dissembling class had been excellent training for him. Basically much too forthright for his own good, Colin realized that every competent entertainer must be at least in part a liar. "What do you mean 'you people'?" he asked in the best imitation of their speech pattern he could muster.

"Outsiders get entertained tonight, when they pay," said the skinny man. "Isn't that right, Davey? Only gypsies now."

Colin huffed himself up indignantly. "Not a gypsy? I? Not a gypsy? What sort of people are you not to have heard of the fair gypsies of Kallanderry?" He warmed to his part. "You wound me. My violin weeps with pain—to be so ignominiously cast out by my own people—" seeing a glint of amusement in Davey's eye and fearing he was laying it on a bit too thick, he left off talking and began playing again, which suited him much better. The fiddle did indeed cry a violin's lament, a morbid throbbing tune, if to say tune was not to make it sound too lively. Before long the majority of the observers and participants looked a lot like the gypsy girl he had tripped over. It was too mournful for Colin to sustain without becoming seriously depressed, so he blended it into a sprightlier tune, one full of enough spirit and fire to convince them he had to be a gypsy.

Nonetheless, up till the moment when Davey began to first clap time and then to improvise on his own guitar, Colin had expected to have his fiddle shoved down his throat at any second. Taking Davey's lead, the others also chimed in and the hostility was forgotten. Behind his concentration on his music, Colin was finally able to exhale.

As one good drink begat another, so did one lively tune lead to the whole group joining in on a second song. Soon everyone was laughing, crying, singing, shouting, and generally carousing in an altogether friendly fashion. All except Davey, Colin was surprised to notice. Among the unabashed tears and laughter, the storyteller had stopped participating, now that he was no longer the center of attention. He looked bored. A jug had been making the rounds of the group, and when Colin next passed it to Davey, the gypsy rose to his feet. "Come on, Cousin. I'll show you around." He picked up his bolero, on which he'd been seated, and flung it casually over one shoulder. His guitar dangled from the other hand. As they left the group, he said, "My people are preparing to entertain the townsmen with a little show tonight, while the children go into the town for supplies. Now, of course, that we know you're one of us," and a twitch of his eyebrow gave Colin to understand that he knew no such thing, "we hope to enlist you in our performance. We'd be honored, you understand."

"I understand, and I'll be happy to do that, Cousin," Colin replied. "Nothing I like better than a good show. Nothing like it for—er—gathering provisions either. Are you sure the town will be empty enough to make the shopping profitable?"

"Oh, yes." His smile was wolfish. "A group of our little black-eyed beauties, chaperoned by my mother, have gone to the town to do what you might call the advance publicity. A few of them," he indicated the nongypsies still engaged in trying to trade horses, "came out this afternoon when a friend of ours who's a peddler passed the word we were here. They hope to trade horses and buy and sell orphans." He grinned broadly, apparently considering this last very humorous. Colin, orphaned since babyhood, was less amused, but nevertheless smiled his best shrewd ersatz-gypsy smile.

"I saw one pretty girl who apparently didn't go. I tripped

95

over her when I joined your group—very nice-looking, but she seemed unhappy."

"You can only mean Zorah," Davey snorted. "She thinks she owns me. She's always hanging around me, crying. I think she believes if she cries hard enough I'll drown in her tears. If you like her, take her with you, please. She's nothing but trouble. One time when I was young and stupid I gave her a little thrill, and ever since she dogs my footsteps. Her father used to be a powerful man here, could train anything, trained our first bear, in fact, but then he was killed. If Zorah weren't such a good trick rider my mother would get rid of her."

Colin felt ill at ease. This was not what he wanted to know about female admiration, its care and feeding. Infatuated girls undoubtedly must cause trouble to someone like Davey, he imagined. He knew he'd have to go right on imagining too, since few were infatuated with him, and it hardly seemed fair. Still, the gypsy seemed to have a history of such disappointed infatuations; he must be used to it by now. He seemed to make a habit of them. Hadn't he ever been smitten himself? Even with the reportedly irresistible Amberwine?

"I can't take any girls with me," Colin said aloud. "Maggie wouldn't like that at all, I'm afraid."

"Who is this Maggie?" asked the gypsy, his irritation gone and his voice regaining its former silkiness.

"Uh—one of our girls."

"Pretty?" Interest flickered in Davey's dark eyes, replacing the sullenness he'd displayed discussing the unfortunate Zorah. Colin was reminded of the hunting hound with a scent, or songs about hunting hounds getting scents, anyway. No one hunted with dogs in East Headpenney.

"Umm—so-so." He remembered belatedly that his imaginary Kallanderry gypsy tribe were supposed to fair, and Maggie was nearly as dark as any of these people. "Actually, she's the regular kind of gypsy—we—uh—adopted her."

"Oh, and you say she's traveling with you?"

Colin waggled his head deprecatingly. "She's a really shy girl. She wanted to camp up farther in the meadow—doesn't like crowds."

"What? And miss our legendary hospitality?" Davey clapped him on the back and speared a chunk of meat from the roasting lamb as they passed. "No, my friend, *cousin*, we must insist you bring her down to our camp. Never must it be said that some of our own camped alone while we had a fire and music and plenty of food to share! It would be a deadly insult!"

"It would?" Colin certainly didn't want to offend local custom. He suspected Davey knew that and was counting on it "That's very gypsy of you, I must say," Colin replied finally, feeling trapped.

Davey waved expansively. "Of course it is."

Colin was shoved suddenly forward as a small black-haired missile slammed into his back. "Davey! Queen Xenobia wants to see you *now*." A buxom gypsy lass disentangled herself from Colin and tugged at the hand of Davey, who was already following her back toward the campfire.

"Your pardon, Cousin. My mother has returned."

"Perfectly alright, old man. I'll just go along and—uh—command Maggie to pull up stakes and come back here with me to your camp and—er—no nonsense."

"Good!" hollered the gypsy, flashing one more dazzling grin as he was dragged off. Colin sighed to notice that the gypsy didn't allow himself to be dragged for long, but neatly turned the situation by catching up with the girl in two strides and encircling her waist with his arm. Colin shook his head slowly, and walked back toward where he had left his horse.

"Psst! You, Blondie!" He thought at first from the language that Ching had followed, finally deciding to talk to him.

"What?" he asked, looking around.

"Over here! Yes, you!" From behind a wagon wheel the girl who had been crying, the one Davey had called Zorah and had said such uncomplimentary things about, beckoned him. He wondered what she could possibly be doing under the wagon. Feeling a little foolish, he looked over his shoulder to make sure no one was looking before he hunkered down to talk to her. No one watched, and he imagined if they did they'd assume he was relieving himself.

Her expression was perhaps a little nervous, but no longer so soggy. "Yes, ma'am?" he asked.

"You make friends fast, eh, Blondie?"

"If you mean Davey, we just met of course but . . ."

"But you like him. Fine fellow, yes?"

"Well—"

"Sure, you do. Everybody likes him. Me, especially," a rueful shrug punctuated that remark, "but it's you who's got to help him."

97

"*Me?* Help *him?* He looks as though he's doing just fine without my help, actually."

"You don't understand."

"Can't say as I do, in fact. Say, tell me, what's a nice girl like you doing lurking about behind wagon wheels anyway?"

"Come down here and sit by me, and I'll explain it all to you, little fiddler."

"Thank you, but you see, I'd actually promised Davey that I'd . . ."

"Come."

He went.

9

As he had never seen Maggie do much more than produce something tasty for mealtimes, Colin would have been a trifle shocked if he had beheld the goings-on in the meadow above the gypsy camp since he had been absent.

The longest chore was the gathering of lichens for dyes, but even that took only a few minutes with the aid of Rowan's knife and Maggie's magic, for the gathering of plants was a legitimate household pastime at Fort Iceworm. Tree lichens next had to be separated from rock lichens. These were then divided into their respective varieties, which would produce divers colors according to their properties. Rock lichens were the best, but the most tedious to gather.

Then there was the dyepot to be fashioned. This was made of clay from the banks of the little stream that kept the meadow green and provided the gypsy camp with a water supply.

Setting the magically fired pot on another magic fire to boil with some of the dye plants and a bit of salt, Maggie repaired to the woods. There she removed her white shift from under her brown woolen skirt and tunic. One of these days she would have to conjure an anti-scratchy spell for wool, she promised herself, as she returned to her horse and dyepot, and took her extra shift from her pack. She wove a spell and the shifts unwove themselves and rolled themselves into neat balls of cotton. It was simple then, with the use of a rapid production spell and an extra-fine enchantment placed on the hand spindle she also carried in her pack, to spin out the thread from her underwear to something finer and softer and much, much longer than it had been before.

Back to the woods she went with this thread, and from the boughs of two trees that grew close together she made a loom. Powered by her magic, the crude loom warped itself and wove the ex-lingerie into a gossamer white cloth.

Maggie draped the cloth over her arms and carried it back to the dyepot. Cutting some of it off, she dipped the shorter piece in. It came out a saffron and she held it up to herself. "What do you think, cat?" she asked Ching, who had had time for a short nap during all this activity. "Do I look nice in yellow or maybe a little sallow?"

Ching growled at the herby smell of boiled lichen on the cloth, but it was a token growl only. He had smelled far more obnoxious smells than stewed vegetation in his life as Granny Brown's familiar. "What in the name of the Mother are you doing with THAT?" he asked.

Snipping at his tail with her fingers, Maggie laughed mysteriously and cut off another piece of cloth, added something from her medicine pouch to the dyepot, and withdrew a bright emerald piece of cloth. "Making a party dress, kitty dear. The gypsies are obviously planning a do of some sort, and I won't want to look shabby, will I?"

"Kitty dear?" Ching flipped his tail with a gesture of profound disgust and trotted off towards the woods. "On that note I think I'll go have a bit of a scratch in the dirt."

When the cat returned, Maggie had put the last stitch into the dress and had emptied the dyepots. With only a little water and a bit of soap root her grandmother had smuggled into the country at considerable cost to Sir William's purse, she managed to bathe her skin and hair.

"Ugh. Putting THAT stuff on your pelt can lead to a fever, witch. Don't you know anything? Why didn't you use your dry-cleaning charm?" Ching sounded casual, but if he hadn't been fairly used to the vagaries of his own mistress he would have been seriously concerned for her granddaughter's mental health.

"Believe it or not, cat, once in a while it actually feels nice to be wet all over. Particularly on a warm day." She shrugged. "And I haven't melted yet. I'm going to the woods again. Stay here and watch the horse, will you, and be prepared for a surprise!"

"Nothing you do any more surprises me," grumbled the cat, settling down to clean his immaculate white belly.

Without the thin hair necklace mostly concealed by the billows of her hair, the cat would never have recognized Maggie. Even at Amberwine's wedding she had been too

100

busy flitting hither and yon supervising preparations and yelling at people to bother much with her own appearance. Freed of the dirt and set off by the soft, colorful cloth of her new dress, her skin gleamed in the waning sunlight like freshly-minted copper coins.

The emerald bodice of the gown was trimmed with saffron embroidery, and was cut so low Maggie nearly lost her courage and stuck in a couple more stitches, just to be safe. It was a flattering style, though, as much of it as she could see in the magic mirror, and it made her neck look longer, her bosom fuller, and her cheekbones higher. Her brown hair showed glints of garnet as it flowed across her back and her eyes looked large, melting and mysterious. She fastened wildflowers above her ear for a finishing touch, but was not quite finished at that. At the nape of her neck she tied a special braided knot, and into this put two small phials from her medicine pouch.

The pouch itself, her kerchief, woolen clothes, and boots, as well as her money, she wrapped in her cloak and hid in a hole beside the stream bed. If she concealed her pack as well, it would be too obvious to possible thieves she was hiding something, and would invite search, so, reluctantly, she left it beside the horse.

"I must admit," said the cat, who had been watching these preparations in silence. "This time you surprised me. What are you going to do in that get-up?" Ching hated to appear not to know everything, but his feline curiosity was definitely activated, as he could never remember having seen Maggie in anything but the brown skirt and tunic or some variation on the same theme. He had always taken it for granted that it was part of her, as his own fur coat was part of him.

"I have a plan. We are going, old cat, to fight fire with fire because, as people are always telling me, you can catch more flies with honey than with vinegar."

"You look like you've got more use for that stitch in time that saves nine, if you ask me," yawned the cat, licking a paw and applying it to his whiskers to acquire his own party polish. "Are you sure your gran wouldn't want you to put a couple more stitches in the top of that dress?"

"Look, cat, who feeds you on this trip, anyway? Gran or me?"

"Have I mentioned how nice you look?" Ching asked. "You smell good, too..."

"Thank you," said Maggie, as pleased as if she had not coerced the compliment from him. "It's a little of the perfume Gran made for some of those ladies at Winnie's wedding—just enough behind the ears to do the trick."

"That stuff really works," the cat conceded. "I'm surprised it didn't sell any better than it did. Maybe if she'd called it something besides Gramma Brown's Balm for the Blues—I suggested "Heat," myself, but she said I was being a feline chauvinist.""

"Well, in case anyone gets wind of it that shouldn't, I have the antidote tucked in my hair, and a little more of the love philtre for when the perfume wears off."

"But what are you going to dooo?" mewed Ching in his sweetest wheedling tone. Something told him that his position as moral guardian was about to be challenged.

"You'll see," she said, starting down the meadow, her feet brushed by the soft, cool grasses, and her bright skirts swaying.

Ching jumped to his feet and stretched, then padded after her. "And I thought I was the enigmatic one in this outfit."

"THAT is why you must help him," Zorah concluded urgently, brushing the last of the tears with which she had been freely dampening Colin's best handkerchief for the last half hour.

"Why *me?*" he asked. "I hardly know the man." Or have good reason to like what I do know, he added to himself.

"Because you are a kind man, I can tell, and you do not come under the influence of Xenobia."

"But I explained that I am a gypsy really, you see—"

"Kallanderry? Phooey!"

"I see. Well, I shall discuss this with my friend—" He lost his train of thought momentarily as a flock of birds flew overhead. Where had he heard that peculiar cry before? Oh, yes, the swans... When the birds had passed over, he could hear the first chords of a guitar melody drifting across the circle from the campfire. Zorah hastily gathered her skirts in her hand and crawled out from under the wagon. "I must go now. The show starts soon, and I got to prepare my horse. Help us, mister, please. You're my last hope."

"I'll give it some thought," he said cautiously, crawling out from under the wagon less cautiously, bumping his head, and

102

then having to dust off his britches, which retained some horsey artifact that had been under the wagon.

A sound less pleasant than the guitars attracted his attention. Many more non-gypsies, distinguishable by both their coloring and their clothing, were milling around the encampment now, and a good number of them were clustered on the far side of the campfire.

From within this cluster came a roaring, growling, and derisive shouts and jeers. Investigating, Colin found a bear-baiting in progress. He could have been wrong, of course, and had it backwards, but it seemed to him that the growls and roars came from the bear, and the shouts and jeers from the mixture of gypsies and non-gypsies that taunted the beast. The bear was supposed to be one of the entertainments and was trained to "dance." Now he was merely being irritated. Colin wondered that the bear's trainer allowed it to be so mistreated. An irritated bear was the last dancing partner he himself would prefer, and gypsies, according to the stories he had always heard, were supposed to be good with animals.

Under the circumstances, he felt he could hardly blame the animal if it chose to take a bite out of someone at some time during the evening. Just so it wasn't him.

He wandered around, looking for Davey. He had to make some excuse for not bringing Maggie after all. After Zorah's disclosures, it seemed more dangerous than helpful to be there himself.

The best thing for them to do that he could think of would be to extricate themselves as gracefully as possible from the vicinity of the camp, and get to Queenston. There, perhaps, they could find where Amberwine had been taken by the peddler, collect her from him, and return to Fort Iceworm.

"Tell your fortune, mister?" The scarlet-dressed woman who had watched the child take his horse stepped out from the shadow of a wagon, causing the preoccupied Colin to jump in his tracks. Without waiting for an answer the woman sidled forward and grasped the wrist of the hand not employed in carrying the fiddle. "You got no common hand there, mister—" she began.

"Uh—I just visited another practitioner of your art a short time ago—" Colin said, withdrawing his hand.

"Oh?" the woman asked, left staring at the hennaed palm

103

of her own hand. He could see now she also sported a little tattoo beneath her right eye. "Did that fortune teller warn you your horse is about to become the main course for tonight's feast?"

Colin looked around frantically, trying to see his horse, or rather, the horse he'd borrowed from Rowan It was not tied among the others belonging to the gypsies guests "No, ma'am—where is he?"

"Really, mister, I can't just GIVE my professional services away, no matter how handsome you are." She switched the red skirt a little more and smoldered at him

He fumbled in his purse and crossed her palm with too many coins, which disappeared down her dress. And that boy looked so reliable too," he mourned.

The woman flashed such a show of great white teeth he almost thought she meant to bite him. "He *is* reliable—but I'm not. See, by having me tell your fortune, you have changed it! Now your horse is alright—he's tied up right behind my wagon, where Mateo put him."

"Oh."

"You are angry?" she asked with no abatement of the toothy grin.

"Not especially, if the horse really is alright. Relieved actually. He doesn't belong to me, you see, and I'd hate to have to answer for him."

"Xenobia thought you would be angry."

"I beg your pardon? This is really an extraordinary conversation, don't you think?"

The woman ignored his last remark and went back to switching her skirt, which seemed to be a favorite gesture of hers. "Xenobia says the outsiders are always angry when we outsmart them."

Colin chuckled. "Yes, I can see where that would probably be true." He backed away, this time occasionally glancing behind him to make sure he didn't back into anything or anybody to upset his balance. He darted down for one quick glance under the wagon before leaving the area entirely. Sure enough, there were his horse's white-stockinged feet and grazing nose placidly chomping the meadow grass.

"Hmph," said the woman, purposely shoving rudely into him as she passed to the campfire to solicit more business Colin found it difficult to understand her attitude. She seemed to feel that his money was poor compensation for the absence of the properly stimulating row she had been expecting.

He followed her stiff back and flouncing red skirt through the now flickering shadows cast by the fire. Night had come quickly, and with it a full moon. Taking the place Davey indicated with a wave that he should occupy, Colin hoped the full moon wouldn't be up to its usual tricks to making people behave bizarrely and complicating things. Even good luck charms frequently failed when the moon was in this bloated phase.

The entertainers were shabby by minstrel standards, or even by good-sized city standards, but the presence of the townspeople, who had turned out in large numbers, testified that entertainment in their own town was even shabbier. Probably almost nonexistent. As a preliminary to the flashier numbers, the woman who had accosted Colin, introduced by Davey as "Runya the All-Seeing," made the rounds of the farmers, servants, tradesmen, and craftpeople, mumbling such stock phrases as "Ah, there's luck in that handsome face of yours, mister," and "You're gonna remember for a long time what the gypsy woman tells you today, my friend." For her finale, she publicly read the palms of the mayor and the local castle's head butler. What she claimed to read in their pudgy palms was so preposterously flattering and so filled with riches, love, power, and fame as to make the recipients of her attentions fairly blush with pleasure, and the rest of the audience collapse with mirth.

The bear-baiting continued, but this time it was called dancing. Colin concentrated, during this phase of the performance, on a chord progression he thought would go well with gypsy music.

Zorah's trick riding brought the level of entertainment up somewhat. Gasps flew through the audience. "Where had a girl learned to do that, whose was that magnificent horse, and from whom do you suppose she stole it, and wasn't that a crummy trick she should be wearing britches so that when her skirt flew over her head when she somersaulted across the horse's back—" Nevertheless, this exhibition of equestrienne derring-do brought the most applause of any act yet presented.

The musicians played a couple of numbers, one gypsy, one a non-gypsy reel, and the tempo changed to a startling upbeat one, the scurrying of fiddles and the syncopated toc-a-tocing of the hand drums heralding flashing limbs and heaving bosoms as the dancing girls swirled around the campfire. Not all the gypsy girls, or even most, were really beauties, but whatever shortcomings they possessed went unacknowledged by the men, who showered them with coins. Actually, Colin thought, they were not really even very good dancers.

From what he remembered of his instruction in gypsy culture, designed to give him background for the music he was learning, the constant traveling kept them hard at work maintaining a semblance of order to their home life, and left little time for the eternal dancing popularly believed to be their main occupation in life, besides stealing. Consequently, the only time they really danced much was at their entertainments, at festivals and fairs, and whenever they were allowed near enough to a village to interact with its people.

Whatever these dancers lacked in beauty or skill they made up for in sultry appeal and enthusiasm, and in spite of himself Colin found his hands getting quite sore from clapping time to the complex rhythms of their music. He started to dig out his purse to throw a few coins himself, but found someone had been there before him. He hoped Maggie's resources would be adequate for the rest of the journey. It was, after all, her sister.

As the final dance tune began, the girls grabbed some of the townsmen and pulled them up to dance with them in crude imitation of the folk steps the gypsies had displayed. As the last notes died away, the girls sat down next to their erstwhile partners, in order to relieve them, Colin felt sure, of whatever coins they had not extracted by their performance.

Again the musicians began playing popular songs, and once or twice Colin found himself playing a solo part. It was Davey, apparently flattered, who introduced the song about himself and Lady Rowan.

They were into the second verse when a drunk hollered, "Hey, Gypsy. How about that? What happened to her highfalutin' ladyship, anyway?"

Davey stilled his strings with one hand and the other musicians stopped playing, as well. He paused, caressing his chin with his fingers, appearing to weigh the question carefully. "Now, you know, I really couldn't say, boys. That was a nice girl, a beautiful girl, but hardly up to one of our little gypsy temptresses, eh?" He hugged the girl beside him, the same

106

one who had earlier brought him the message from his mother. "No. Really, friends, she was as charming as could be, but we couldn't keep her here forever. Mum had to run her off, finally. Stole things, if you know what I mean." He led the crowd in an uproarious laugh. Colin felt nauseated. A tap on his shoulder and a hiss in his ear prevented him from an indelicacy.

"Can you get them to play for me?" It was Maggie who hunched down, unnoticed, in the darkness behind him.

"Sure," he said, too glad to create a diversion from the present line of discussion to question her more closely.

"Something fast, slow, then fast again, in their type of music," she said.

Colin raised his bow, tucked his fiddle under his chin, and hesitated only a moment before sweeping into the lead-in of one of the more classical pieces of gypsy dance music. The other musicians seemed as happy to play, and stop discussing Davey's love life, as he was, and joined in quickly. The hand drum beat rhythmic counterpoint to the whining, interwoven harmonies of the two fiddles and Davey's guitar.

The opening chords were fast, as Maggie had requested, and she used them to come whirling out before the fire, an emerald and golden dervish casting her own dancing shadows under a pale yellow moon.

Colin was suitably impressed. For the first time since he'd met her, he realized she certainly was very much a witch indeed. As surely as Granny Brown had transformed him into a bird, Maggie had transformed her prosaic assistant scullery-maid self into a seductress to be reckoned with.

For only a moment she paced the measured beat with saucy thrusts of her hip, her fingers snapping in time. The lack of the silver finger cymbals worn by the gypsies didn't trouble her, it seemed, and she made an instrument of her own hands and body. Colin decided she was manifesting musical talent after all. Flowers appeared and disappeared in the tossing dark waves of her hair as she whirled. Her skin was less like the satin which was the popular conception of ladies' skin, and more like burnished metal, as it sheened with her perspiration. Her bosom rose and dropped sharply in time with the drum, while her mid-section did something serpentine and her shapely legs, apparently unhampered by the bright skirts molding against them, pranced and twirled and wove their own patterns in the circle beyond the campfire.

As the music slowed, becoming almost sinister in its insinuation, her arms joined her torso in the undulations and Colin was reminded of the cat having a nice stretch. or so he told himself. He was trying to believe her dancing was a musical interpretation of the cat or a snake or a variation of the folk steps the women had done earlier. Following the sequence she had requested, using his instrument to guide the others, he found it difficult to keep his mind on anything but his friend's disturbing behaviour.

What bothered him most was not the antics she was performing with her body, but the way her eyes first locked on Davey's to hold his as she executed a turn. Her head and upper body strained backward to maintain the contact as she danced, then, emerging from her turn, she let her eyes slip slyly away. A phantom smile played on her lips, which seemed somehow fuller and redder than Colin remembered. but that might have been a trick of the full moon.

Davey was apparently as enchanted by all of this as anyone, and watched her with a sort of predatory possessiveness while he continued to fondle the girl at his side..

The tempo picked up, and her steps again became more prancing, hips keeping time, fingers clicking, ribcage bobbing to the music. The eye contact changed too, and she gave the gypsy only an occasional smile, then slipped away to bestow a full-blown silent laugh on another member of the audience. It was difficult to tell who was mesmerizing whom, but a glimmer of understanding began to dawn when Colin noticed Davey's hawklike attentiveness become irritation on the occasions when her attention was elsewhere

With a drum roll, the music ended, and Maggie sank from a graceful turn to her knees, arms extended, palms up. She was pelted with the coins not already gleaned by the pickpockets, as the townsmen and gypsies both applauded.

Colin was working at fighting off a sense of betrayal. While this was certainly an interesting side to her personality, he trusted better the one he thought he already knew. If his suspicions were correct, this scheme of hers was more harebrained than the one that nearly got them drowned in the Troutroute. He had better catch up to her quickly, and let her know why what he suspected she planned was futile.

His opportunity dissolved as Davey, dumping the girl who had leaned heavily against him during the dance, rose to his feet with a feline flourish and offered his hands to Maggie.

She smiled and accepted the courtesy, rising to her feet with his help.

Colin fumbled into action and dashed over to the pair, who seemed in immediate danger of disappearing into the shrubbery. "Ah, Magdalene, my dear, you did join us," he said. He considered clapping her on the back but decided against it. "Davey, this is my friend Maggie. I was telling you about her earlier."

Davey didn't break eye contact with her as he replied. "Ah, yes. The shy one."

Colin's laugh was shaky as he sought to keep the conversation from degenerating into nonverbal communication.

"Oh, she is, aren't you Mag! But—er—a real trouper."

"She certainly appears to be," said a woman, emerging from the bustle of the departing crowd. It was Xenobia, the woman in the crystal. Now her hair was smoothly tied into a crimson kerchief, which was trimmed with the same coins that adorned her ears and neck. The coins represented so many different countries and denominations that Colin felt sure she could have easily been some kingdom's national treasury.

He saw Maggie's face as she recognized her sister's green silk gown bulging to encase the gypsy woman's pudgy body. The green silk didn't quite manage to be a decent covering, so the woman had piled a purple and orange flounced skirt on top of it.

Although it was well-known that a person's wickedness was reflected in the face as age advanced, Xenobia had few wrinkles, and her nose, while straight and proud, was not prominent. In fact, she still bore the vestiges of beauty, an effect spoiled only by her garish clothing and harsh expression.

"Mother," Davey said jovially. "This is my good friend, Colin. I told you of him earlier and this—"

"Yes," Xenobia said succinctly. "My son, I would talk to you. Come to my wagon. I have this problem I want you to help me with."

"Of course." Davey replied, piqued at the interruption. "In a moment."

"Now." said Xenobia.

Davey shrugged and smiled at Maggie. "Now." He repeated it with an air of resignation, and ran a finger down Maggie's arm. "You don't leave, eh?" He strode away after his mother.

"Whew," said Colin. "That was close."

"Yes, I almost had him," she snapped. "Colin, why did you have to interrupt?"

"You should have seen yourself!" he said more vehemently than he had planned to. It occurred to him that he sounded priggish. "I mean, alright, so you were beautiful, but *where* did you learn to dance like that? not from your grandmother, I'll wager."

"As a matter of fact, I did," she replied hotly. "It is part of the ceremony of welcoming young witches to adulthood, and we do it every year at our Sorcerous Ceremonials, so there!"

"I guess that *would* get them into adulthood fast, alright, if they do it the way you did."

"It is a beautiful and meaningful ceremony, I'll have you know—" the witch began her retort but was interrupted by Ching sliding between her ankles.

"It seems to me that that silly minstrel is more concerned with your virtue than I am, and I'm the chaperone! You'd better come out with it, witchy, and tell us what you're up to."

"Alright, then," she said to the cat and turned to Colin with exaggerated patience. "I thought I would make him fall in love with me, then I could reject him and give a little of the anti-love potion to his other conquests and leave them to their mercy. That's little enough revenge for what he's done to Winnie."

"That ought to do it, for sure," he admitted.

"So you think he is?"

"Is what?"

"Is in love with me, of course."

"No. Heat, maybe."

She looked mortally offended. "Well, how would you know anyway? Is it so impossible?"

"Oh, don't pout, Maggie. Ordinarily, of course, it wouldn't be impossible. If we had that whole silly village following you like puppy dogs I wouldn't be the least surprised. But in his case it is impossible. That fellow can't give you his heart, because he hasn't any."

"Excuse me? Would you repeat that?"

"I said he hasn't any heart. One of his childhood sweethearts has become disenchanted enough with the present Davey to try to persuade me to help her do something about

110

it so she can return him to what she insists was his former perfect self. She told me the whole story."

"Which is?"

"His mother had the heart removed when he reached puberty." He was about to explain further when Xenobia and Davey reappeared

Xenobia smiled. "Here we are again. It didn't take long at all, now did it? I trust you will stay with us tonight?" Maggie noted that the hissing element in Xenobia's voice that had so impressed her through the crystal was actually a lisp. It was somehow more unpleasant than the hiss

"As a matter of fact," Colin said, not caring at all for the gypsy woman's manner, "as a matter of fact, we must be getting on. There's a fair at Queenston market in a day or two where we're supposed to perform."

"Odd," said Xenobia, still smiling. "I heard of no fair. We naturally couldn't allow you to travel so far at night, could we, son?"

"No, indeed." He circled Maggie's waist with an embrace that appeared affectionate, but which she found painful. "I choreograph the dance numbers for our entertainments, you know? I intend to persuade you to share a few of those beautiful dance movements with me, my dear, you know what I mean?"

There was no need for all of this horrible cat-and-mousing, Colin thought indignantly. A ring of shadowed faces and the occasional glint of moonlight off metal, barely visible behind Xenobia and Davey, undoubtedly accounted for the prickles running up his spine.

"Oh, I'll gladly show you those steps, Great Gypsy Prince." replied Maggie. Colin groaned inwardly. "Great Gypsy Prince." Now really! "But in privacy, please. You know already how shy I am."

He laughed what to Colin was a very nasty laugh, and led her off to the woods.

"Here." his mother cried after him, apparently unable to bear the pretense that theirs was just a friendly little seduction. She tossed him a length of leather rope, which she had concealed in the folds of the garish skirt. "Tie her up when you're done with her, or you won't get your rest."

"Who said I plan to rest?" grinned the gypsy with a moonlit flash of white teeth, his jewelry jingling against his bare chest

111

as he leaped to catch the rope with one hand while retaining a firm grip on Maggie with the other. The rope apparently dispelled any illusions Maggie might have had about making matters go according to her plan, for she yelped indignantly as the gypsy began once more to propel her toward the woods. Colin urgently wished for Lord Rowan's second best family sword. He might have at least looked sufficiently frightening to wipe the smile off that ogre's face, even if he couldn't wield the thing properly.

"As for you, my merry minstrel," Xenobia said sweetly, "You could prove less easy to handle than the girl."

"A lot you know," he mumbled under his breath, but replied more clearly. "Why are you treating us this way? Your son was bragging about your famous hospitality. Is this how you treat your distant kin?"

"MY kin?" She really did hiss now. "You're MY kin? Say something to me, then, in our own secret tongue, relative." She chucked him under the chin with her fingers so hard it made his eyes water. "Sing me a sweet gypsy lament in the old tongue. No? I thought not." She turned to the shadows behind her. "Mateo, my boy, show this false gypsy what you found on his horse."

Triumphantly, the boy dragged forth the second best family sword, House of Rowan crest and all.

"This sword, I am told, is the property of the enemy of a great sorcerer who is friend to my people. If you're such a fine gypsy, how come you have it, eh?"

"I stole it."

She shook her head. "No. And there are no gypsies in the world who look like you, as my son well knows. He only liked your singing and playing and thought, 'ah well, he's harmless enough.' Then we found this. Too many of your kind mixing with my people is what I say." She spat the last and turned from him to give a command to her guard. When her back was turned, Colin amazed himself with his own ruthless cunning as he snaked an arm around her throat, catching her neck in the crook of his elbow. "Nobody move," he ordered. "Or I strangle the old witch." He was snarling in the voice he used when singing the villain's part in a murder ballad, and was gratified to see how effective it was. Xenobia clawed at his arm and he tightened his grip.

"Mateo, if you are fond of your present form of government, it would behoove you to replace that sword in its scabbard and put it back where you found it. Then you will bring my horse right here."

How was he going to elude them long enough to free Maggie from the gypsy's lustful clutches and ride away through the thick wood beyond danger of capture was quite beyond him. It was better than listening to Xenobia's melodramatic threats, though.

The boy hastened to do his bidding, the sword thumping on the ground behind him as he scurried away.

Although he didn't actually see them move, the other gypsies seemed to melt back into the shadows. He heard his heart in his ears and felt as though he had a chill. He couldn't have held onto Xenobia much longer when the boy led the horse into the clearing.

He was just breathing a sigh of relief when a blow from behind knocked him down. The witch fell on top of him, wriggled away from his grip, and emerged to stand above him like a knight who had just vanquished a dragon. His focus swam as he concentrated on trying to stop the ringing in his ears.

"No, you fools. Not with daggers." She halted the threatening jabs at him with a gesture, then scratched her chin. "For this offense to my person, something messier, I think. Let's see if our friend the bear can improve this one's singing voice, eh? Throw him in the cage!"

Colin's only good fortune at this turn of events was that he was a minstrel, not a hero, and so felt free to kick and scream with no appreciable loss of self-respect as they dragged him to the bear's wagon-cage, and shoved him at the opening. The smell alone nearly killed him before he was rudely kicked inside.

"Too bad it's all closed up, like. I'd enjoy watching," he heard someone say as he landed.

"We'll hear, right enough," said someone else.

A deafening roar was the first indication of their veracity.

10

The gypsy had his love nest all arranged. Since he shared his mother's wagon, he found it convenient to prepare such trysting places wherever their band went. It made an interesting game, to find a suitable spot to woo, and, naturally, to win, his loves. The locations were varied enough to titillate his sense of adventure: a hay mow, an outbuilding, an open field, a deserted woodcutter's hut, or, as it was tonight, a comfortable bed of fragrant spruce boughs and soft moss, all ready for him to lay the lady down beneath the rustling willows.

Leaves and laying down, however, appeared to be far from the lady's mind. He was finally forced to give her a shove. Awkward, true, but effective.

"You louse-ridden, horse-dewed son-of-a-" she began before he caught her in his arms and hushed her with a hard kiss. The harshness of it became satisfyingly soft and melting and mutually nibbly and she surrendered sufficiently to allow him to go on to the next phase and locate a limb to caress. The nearest was a velvety thigh.

He murmured softly, as usual, "Your skin—oh, darling, it is so very soft."

She broke his hold and looked at him with astonishment, then burst into a fit of laughter totally inappropriate for the mood of the moment and offensive to his sense of fitness.

"What is so funny?"

"Me—me and my soft skin. What did you expect, anyway?" she was so amused by her own joke she collapsed once more before she could continue. "I mean to say, did you imagine I would have scales, or what?"

For such a ravishing girl she clearly didn't understand the first thing about being ravished. She was drearily unaware of the protocol of such matters. That was a classic compliment! Offended, Davey decided that perhaps she preferred a more basic approach, which also happened to suit him at the moment.

He grabbed the front of her bodice and pulled. It ripped apart long enough for him to catch a moonglow swell of copper skin, then it wove itself primly back together again.

"Ching was right," the girl muttered to herself, "a stitch in time would have indeed saved nine this time."

Though her perfume was driving him mad, he thought it prudent to employ more circumspect tactics with young women who caused their clothing to automatically mend. "However you did that," he grumbled, "you're certainly a lot more modest than you were a while ago." He had relinquished his embrace, but retained her wrists.

She glared at him.

"Of course," he added quickly. "On you, my lovely, modesty or immodesty are equally becoming."

Seeing that he was making no headway, he reverted to persuasion. "Come, now, my sweetheart. I won't force you to do anything you don't want to do. Not until you're ready. I'm sorry I tore your dress—I am too impatient to taste your charms. I can't help myself, you know. Passionate gypsy blood, and all that." He pulled her back into his arms, where she lay for a moment against him while he kissed her neck and munched her earlobes. He had found ninety-nine percent of the subjects tested responded favorably to such embraces.

She sighed deeply and almost snuggled against him for a moment. "You don't intend to harm us, then?"

He looked down at her with annoyance. The little wench was trying to take advantage of the situation! "Well, I didn't say THAT. You are spies, after all. But I wouldn't want to have to force you, dear girl. Think how bad that would sound!" He considered that for a moment, while defining the contours of her bosom and experimenting with a couple of squeezes.

A lupine grin replaced his unaccustomed meditative air. "On the other hand, who would you tell? Not many more get-togethers with the girls for you, sweet."

The breath was knocked out of him as he was flung backwards by the unexpected force of an enchanted shove. By the expedient of informing her magic that she wished to push the cow aside for milking, Maggie had employed it in her

115

personal defense. "I cannot believe Amberwine's incredible lack of taste." She enunciated each word with finicky precision, and shook herself as though infested with spiders.

Davey, after inspecting himself for damage, was preparing to leap upon her and crush her into submission, in the course of which he was certain she would come around to her senses and enjoy it all tremendously. Her words, however, had given him pause.

"Amberwine? You mean Lady Rowan?"

"Yes. I mean Lady Rowan, you cad." Her formerly voluptuous mouth was now set in a thin line, and her fiery eye reminded him uncomfortably of his mother.

"Must you bring up ancient history?" Sighing dramatically, he let his fingers crawl toward the leather rope at his left while he raised himself casually to his right elbow, as near to her as he dared.

"I certainly must," she said.

"You haven't got much sensitivity, have you, wench?" he asked critically.

"More than you have. I say, is it true you haven't a heart?"

"You really are an insensitive little witch."

"Precisely."

"As a matter of fact, I don't. Part of my puberty rite as a gypsy prince required its removal."

"What a quaint folk custom! Oh, Mother!" she swore, catching sight of the rope in his hand. "You aren't going to use that thing, are you?" She tried to scramble away, but he caught her by the foot and slammed her against the trunk of a tree before she was able to contemplate cows.

"I don't see why not." He yanked the knot tight. "You are a spy."

"I am *not* a spy, and you *are* awful."

"Not entirely. If you'd only have given me a chance I can be quite amusing, really." His protestations were limp, however, and he had lost a good deal of his inspiration for the moment.

"Oh, to be sure. I think you're funnier than a hanging, myself," she said acidly. "Really, how do you keep walking around without a heart?"

"It was magically removed, silly girl. Not surgically."

"I see. You have a blood-pumping apparatus, just no feelings."

116

"You might put it that way. Scientific turn of mind you've got, for a spy."

"I told you I'm *not* a spy. I only wanted to find out how you managed to make off with my sister, and why you allowed your mother to drive her away later. As a matter of fact, now that we're better acquainted, I'm amazed Winnie didn't leave without being asked."

"You don't like me, do you?"

"No. You do have a certain superficial charm—" He cocked an eyebrow. "Alright then, a deep superficial charm. But though Winnie might occasionally do something batty, she's very discerning about people generally, and men in particular."

"Perhaps you're not being discerning enough, my dear," he suggested. "She, perhaps, saw some of my excellent qualities you insist on overlooking."

She snorted in a most unladylike manner. "I'm very sure one of them is that you're unbeatable in a horse trade."

"True. But other things, as well." He looked at her as longingly as though she were a jam tart and he suffering from both appetite and indigestion.

"Be a good fellow, prince. You really don't fancy my berry-brown body any more, do you?"

"The night is young. A gag, perhaps . . ."

"Don't be a toad. Let me go. I'm not really a spy. My sister didn't do anything to you, and you know it."

"She did."

"She didn't. She couldn't—wouldn't."

"She did."

"How? You can't be hurt without a heart, can you?"

"I have my pride," he said stiffly, then snarled so nastily at her that in her helpless condition she was quite alarmed. "There is something very wrong with the women of your family. I should have known you two were related by the way you act."

"What do you mean?"

"I mean your father will have no grandchildren, the way you and that lily-white sister of yours behave."

"Nonsense. Winnie is pregnant already."

"So I noticed, once mother confiscated her gown. It has to be a changeling."

"Be reasonable. The baby has to be born for faeries to

117

substitute a changeling, and Winnie's part faerie herself. Nothing like that could possibly happen." It occurred to her then to stop arguing long enough to understand what he had been telling her. "You don't mean you—um—she—you mean there's no disgrace to Rowan then?" That was as delicately as she could put it.

"Well, she did tell him to go mind his towers and battlements when he came riding after us, right enough!" He laughed. "You should have seen his face. Red as his hair!"

"I don't think it's funny," she said severely. "But why would she go away with you and then not—you know..."

"Good question. Unless like you she's nothing but a tease. The sorcerer personally told me she fancied me when she saw me perform at Fort Iceworm two years ago, before she married. He even taught me a special song he swore was her particular favorite. It had the same tune, in fact, as that ballad they sing about me now."

He shrugged. "It worked very well at first. She fairly fell into my arms and couldn't get her boots and cloak on fast enough. A damn sight faster than I was able to get her out of them. When she told her husband off I thought to myself, I thought 'Davey, lad, you have by your side a lady good for hours of fine entertainment!' Then—nothing. No sooner had we reached my camp than she turned cold. Wouldn't let me touch her." He glared at Maggie accusingly. "Never in my life has such a humiliating thing happened to me. What a lot of trouble for nothing! Oh, the sorcerer was pleased, I suppose, but what of me? She wouldn't return to her husband—of course, we wouldn't have allowed her to before the story was circulated enough to make it awkward for him, but she didn't want to go when I gave her the chance. She wouldn't eat, wouldn't work, wouldn't make love. She just slept."

Maggie nodded sadly. Winnie had napped through a great deal of unpleasantness in their childhood. When Maggie's mother had died, the only mother Winnie had known, her sister had slept steadily for almost two weeks.

"Finally, mother drove her out. Who needs another obstacle to walk over?"

"But why did you want her in the first place? Aside from your low-born lust, I mean. I'd think that all that would be a great deal of trouble for *just* that."

"I *beg* your pardon. As a matter of fact, it *was* a practical arrangement. A friend of our people—the sorcerer I mentioned—has political ambitions. He wished to discredit Lord Rowan in some subtle way, as he cannot do him direct damage. The rowan trees that surround Rowan's castle protect him from sorcerers. They are murderous to witches."

"Yes, I know."

"I was naturally happy to be of help in my modest way," he shrugged his most charming humble shrug. "We are loyal friends, we gypsies."

"Provided there's enough gold and silver to sweeten the deal," Maggie amended.

"You insult!" He made a jack-knife leap to his feet. "I try to act nicely to you, to make love to you, and you insult me. I shall leave you here, tied to this tree, to die." He started to stalk off.

"Oh, Davey, don't go being offended!" Maggie talked so fast she almost stumbled over her words. It would cost her a lot of valuable time to figure out which household spell to apply to loosen a leather rope. She could have simply unspun a hemp one, but the leather was difficult. "I didn't mean to insult you, truly. I didn't think I could, you being heartless and all."

"I may not have a heart, but I'm a very sensitive man." He fairly spat at her.

"I can see that now, and I was wrong, and I'm very sorry. You're absolutely right, of course. You really are irresistible. It's just that odd things are expected of us younger witches by our elders and there's this unicorn at home and—well, you see, I can't afford to get involved with *any* man right now."

"That is your affair entirely, madam." He turned once more to go.

"I can help you, you know."

He stopped. "What did you say?"

"I said I can help you with your problem."

"What problem is that? The one you caused or your concern for my lack of useless sentiment?"

"No, no, no—not that. Those are just small difficulties. Come on, prince. I can't shout your worst problem all over the woods, can I? Do be patient with me a bit longer, and come back here and sit down."

"Well," he said, looking back through the trees to the camp where the embers of the evening's fire still glowed in the darkness. "It *is* early yet. I think it would not look g—I think, so, I would not like to go back so early." He sank to the ground near her. "Now, woman, tell me what it is that you have to help me."

"That girl you were with tonight—"

"Lahara? What about her?"

"You're—um—lovers?"

"Yes, of course."

"Well, what if you get tired of her?"

"Then I find another one."

"What about her? Doesn't she make trouble?"

"*That* one? No!" He laughed. "She wouldn't dare. What trouble could she make?"

"How about the others?"

"How about them? Zorah, she just cries all the time. Dalia's husband is afraid of me. And Runya..." he broke off thoughtfully.

"Runya the all-seeing?"

"Runya, yes. All-seeing, fortunately no. I admit, at times she has worried me. She is very capable with her knife, and she is my cousin, on my mother's side." He winced.

"You see, you do have a problem."

"Mostly they do as I tell them, though."

"Mostly. But as you say, you folks have all this passionate gypsy blood, and once in a while a little of it is bound to be spilled. What if some night you're all snuggled down in the shrubbery with a new friend, and Runya decides to take up whittling?"

He shuddered.

"It can't be much fun for you, either," she pointed out. "It must be depressing having all those women crying over you all the time."

"No. One can only do so much for them. It's the price of manhood, I suppose."

"Runya could take care of that too."

He gulped. "What did you have to say, witch?"

"Just this. What if I were to give you a potion that just sort of de-ignites the passion of the ladies no longer in favor? A kind of anti-love serum?"

"You could give me such a thing?" He sounded tempted, then a troubled look crossed his handsome face. "But they would forget me then. What if I wanted to try again with one I had given this potion to?"

"Oh, Davey," she smiled from beneath coyly lowered lashes.

120

"Do you really think you'd have any trouble if you chose to overpower a little potion?"

"No, that is true."

"And it could be so useful. Just a drop in food or drink."

"You want only that I release you?"

"That, and get my friend loose, and tell me how to get to this sorcerer who's plotting against my sister."

"You ask a lot, witch. What's to keep me from taking your potion and whatever else I wish?"

"I can change the potion into extract of skunk gland without batting an eyelash."

He began to untie her.

11

Colin's horrible screams and the bear's ferocious growls made it difficult for even the most hard-hearted of the gypsies to get to sleep. Xenobia had thought the minstrel's execution would be noisy, but was beginning to wish the bear would eat more daintily. Zorah cowered beneath her blanket and whimpered herself to sleep, all of her own hopes dying in agony with Colin. And in the woods, Maggie cut short Davey's explanation of how to reach the sorcerer's castle. Her heart sank as she shoved the potion at him and began to run through the edge of the wood to the point of the encampment closest to the commotion.

In the bear cage, Colin shook with genuine fright, and followed his first, authentic scream with a repertoire both blood-curdling and heart-rending. Ching, the cat, sat switching his tail, clearly promising to give him another taste of his claws if his performance was substandard. The bear, likewise under the influence of the cat, snuffed and whuffled, bellowed and bawled, growled and grumbled his most challenging, while finishing the remains of the meal his keeper had left in the cage before the bear-baiting began.

With a particularly satisfying chilling gurgle, Colin reached his finale. The bear ate more quietly as the cat sank down onto the floor of the cage to lick his front paws and wash his ears. Colin wiped the perspiration from his brow with the side of his arm. "That was close," he whispered to the cat. "I don't know how you talked him out of eating me, but thanks a lot, cat. I swear to you that none of your kind shall be mistreated or hungry as long as I'm about."

Ching's eyes gazed greenly up at him in the darkness, his purr almost as loud as the bear's growls. Colin scratched the cat's ears and considered. "Still, I don't imagine you're magical enough to open this cage, are you? No, of course not. At least you've given me time to think." Ching presented the side of his face for a whisker scratch. Colin regarded him thoughtfully.

"Yet you can understand me, can't you? I mean, I know I can't tell if you're saying 'meow' or reciting poetry when you and Maggie chat, but you're a clever fellow. You can understand everybody, right?" Ching said "mrrp" in a pleased sort of way, and continued to encourage caresses by rolling onto his back for his black-and-white belly to be rubbed.

"There's one girl here who might help me. I don't know if she's actually a friend or not but she does dislike Xenobia. Maybe if you could get Zorah to come and get me out?" He was starting to think and talk faster, hoping there might be some way to escape in time to save Maggie.

Ching sat up, flicked his whiskers, looked about, and switched his tail so emphatically he fairly thumped it on the floor.

"No, I don't suppose you'd know her, would you? She's got on a blue dress, and she's rather smallish—a bit shorter than Maggie. She looks sad. Actually, I don't suppose she looks that sad while she's sleeping but that's the general idea." The cat regarded him quizzically. "Um—I think perhaps she lives in that red wagon with the hideous purple stripes on—" He found himself talking to the end of a tail and cat back feet as Ching leaped down. "I want you to know," Colin said to the tailtip before the cat was completely lost in the darkness. "This quite makes up for you trying to eat me."

The cat tried two other wagons before he found the right one. Even for humans, colors looked different in the moonlight (as in Ching's favorite words of wisdom from Granny Brown regarding feline camouflage—"all cats look gray in the dark."). Ching's magic operated efficiently enough, but his visual apparatus was such that Colin's red and purple had no meaning for him.

So he tried a green wagon with orange stripes, and a blue wagon with gilt stripes, where he narrowly missed being skewered by the dagger of a fat gypsy man attempting to make love. The man apparently felt that Ching's questioning mew added little to his efforts; only the cat's agility kept him from becoming fish bait.

Finally, though, he found a striped wagon containing a woman who looked worn out even while she was sleeping, a

123

girl of about Maggie's age and size, and a boy child and a girl child of tail-pulling years. Colin was wrong, though, about the girl. She did look sad, even in her sleep.

Being careful not to wake the others, who might not be so sympathetic to Colin's and Maggie's respective plights as the young woman he was sent to fetch, he hopped softly onto the girl's chest and sang into her ear. She stirred. He sang a bit louder, but she mumbled, and her arms made brushing motions to rid herself of him.

He patted her half-open lips with a paw, his nose almost brushing her teeth. Her breath smelled pleasantly of home-brewed ale and spice-root. He patted again, then leaped side-ways as she sat up, her elbow nearly striking him as she raised her hand to rub her eyes.

"What?" she asked.

Ching purred reassuringly, fixing her with a calm composed gaze. He hoped she wasn't one of those silly hysterical people who couldn't abide the presence of a cat.

Zorah liked cats, however, and found stroking Ching a soothing balm for her sadness, even though she was barely awake and afraid of waking her family. She had no idea how he'd come to her wagon, but welcomed his company anyway. When Ching was sure he had her attention, he backed off, chirruping for her to follow, advanced again to rub against her, then once more retreated when she tried to pet him. Soon she got the idea that she was being instructed to follow him when he hopped down from her wagon.

He led her to the bear's cage, but when she saw the direction he was taking she turned again to go, protesting tearfully, "Oh, puss, I can't go there. That poor man!" Ching sat thumping his tail on the ground, staring up at her until she began to realize he was not behaving in a naturally feline fashion. Most cats, if there was a great deal of blood around, would have been savagely excited. Such a description in no way fit Ching. Zorah's curiosity led her on.

More to bolster her own courage than because she actually thought she would be understood, she said, taking a deep breath and pulling her frayed and muddied cloak close about her, "Very well. I will look, then. I am a gypsy woman, and not squeamish."

A disembodied voice followed this outspoken proclamation of bravery, almost making lie of it by sending her screaming back to her wagon.

124

"Please, Zorah, do be quiet and get us out of this cage. The bear is sleeping now, and might wake up hungry."

Making the sign against the evil eye, which also included ghosts and witches, she finally managed to peer into the wagon and through the bars. There sat the minstrel, appearing more bored and anxious than mauled. He was in one corner of the cage and the bear was piled like a used fur rug in the other corner. "Will you please get me out of here?"

"If you promise to do what I asked you earlier." Not for nothing did she come from a long line of horse traders.

Colin reluctantly promised he would help her locate Gypsy Davey's heart as she had asked, and she took the key ring from under the wagon seat and fit the great wooden key into the lock.

"Now hurry," she said nervously as he jumped down beside her. "Some of my people will still be awake. We got to break camp soon and be out of here before dawn. Those town people are apt to get a little mad when they learn what our little shows really cost."

"I have to find my horse and get Maggie. If only we could delay pursuit somehow . . ."

"I'll drive away our horses. That should give you plenty of time. It may be a close thing with the townspeople while we gather them up, but it won't take that long."

"Good girl!"

The horse had to be saddled, but the saddle and bridle had fortunately been left on the ground near the animal. In the confusion, no one had taken the sword and scabbard from the ground where they'd tossed it while subduing Colin. But he missed his instruments immediately.

He followed the soft nickerings of the other horses to find Zorah again. She was busy loosening hobbles and smacking rumps to encourage them to wander off into the richer grasses of the upper meadow.

"Do you know what's become of my fiddle and guitar?" he asked.

She looked up from beneath a horse's belly, trying to avoid getting stepped on. "I don't know. Xenobia probably saved them for Davey. She's always taking other people's things and giving them to him, as though that would make him stay with his mama more!"

Ignoring the last part of her answer, Colin stormed. "Well, he can't have them!" He dismounted, tying the reins to a wagon wheel. He was so angry that he started to stride straight towards Xenobia's wagon, mindless of the few gypsies who still lingered by the dying campfire.

Zorah's skirts rustled like wings in the darkness as she overtook him, restraining him with a hand on his arm. "Hey, blondie."

He turned impatiently to her. "What is it?"

"Don't go charging in there like the bear." She hauled Obtruncator from its scabbard and handed it to him. "Listen, take some advice from a gypsy girl, and use a little stealth. If you use that and *this*," she tapped the sword, "Maybe you'll get to leave this camp alive."

"Oh. Right," he replied, dropping back behind the wagons in a suitably stealthy crouch, Obtruncator protruding menacingly in front of him. "Thanks."

But even sneaking wasn't as helpful as he might have hoped, for Xenobia had taken his instruments inside her wagon, and she was still awake. He could hear her humming tunelessly to herself. Obviously, Davey had not inherited his musical ability from his side of the family. Peeking around the corner of the door in the back of the painted wagon, he could see that she was sitting facing his instruments, counting the booty collected earlier in the evening.

He grimaced. Chance was evidently not going to help him much tonight. Resuming his sneaking tactics, he crept up into the doorway and hoped her own croaking would cover some of the noise he made as he mounted the step leading inside. In case it had not, once inside he leapt immediately for her neck again, very nearly seriously injuring himself on the second best family sword as he did so.

The gold and silver tumbled from a tower to a heap. "Xenobia," Colin said, "this is getting monotonous. Really, I don't like bullying women." He cast about for something with which to gag her. Her eyes rolled back and her mouth worked furiously as the movement he made in his search increased the pressure on her windpipe. He lay the sword down long enough to grab first his guitar, then his fiddle, and pull them back to him. He seemed to lack sufficient appendages to do everything. Finally, he snatched her own blanket up from under her, almost upsetting them both, and wrapped this encumbrance around her, all the while maintaining his stranglehold with the other arm.

126

In desperation, he finally picked up the sword and braced it, point against her back, and released her neck, saying, "One word and you're spitted. Now then, take off your stockings and hand them back here."

"Stupid! I'm a gypsy. I don't wear stockings. I go barefoot."

"Well, um, I'll wager the Lady Amberwine had stockings. Give me hers, then." He felt absolutely brilliant for thinking of that. He was complimenting himself on his quick wit as she handed the stockings to him after pulling them from a remote corner of the wagon.

Unfortunately, the sword had plopped down against her blankets when she moved forward to get the stockings. Colin rebraced it.

"Before I gag you, ma'am, you can also tell me where you've got your son's heart hidden. You can just hand it to me if it's close by."

"Now, how did you hear about that?" she asked, sounding discouragingly uncowed by his fierceness.

"Never mind that," he growled.

"Have pity on a poor woman, young man. My baby's heart was stolen from me."

"A likely story. Who has it then, if not you?"

"The sorcerer took it. He holds it to insure my cooperation in helping him with his plans."

"Now that's smart," Colin said. "Where does he live?"

"At Dragon Bay. But you'll never get that far!" she shrieked the last as she jumped forward, ridding herself of the sword. Colin had carelessly shown that both of his hands were occupied with stocking as he leaned forward to gag her. Taking advantage of her freedom, she yelled for help in a voice piercing enough to be heard in Queenston.

Colin, fiddle, guitar, and sword were out the back of the wagon and clattering toward the horse before help reached Xenobia at the front of the wagon. He ran headlong into Zorah, who was bent over, unhobbling the last of the horses.

As she picked herself up from the ground, Colin thrust his instruments into her arms. She clutched them to her and ran toward his horse just before her kinsmen came howling around the wagon yelling and screaming what Colin assumed to be uncomplimentary and disparaging remarks in their gypsy language. They were brandishing knives, clubs, and a mace left over surely from the Second Rebellion, as well as several other miscellaneous implements designed for incising and slicing, and quite a few blunt objects. Backing slowly away, Obtruncator hoisted before him, Colin faced the invading horde at first with a tentative thrust here and there. As they collectively perceived that he was no master with the weapon, they jostled each other to strike the first telling blow, crowding him back against a wagon. Colin did the only thing he was capable of doing at that point, and started whacking and banging the sword around himself as furiously as he was able to wield the cumbersome object. He hoped to create a wall of such unpredictable destruction between himself and his attackers that perhaps sheer indecision as to where they should attack would delay his opponents in dispensing with him.

The gypsies did back off in the face of his assault. The first brave soul who attempted to storm his bastions got a fearful clout on the head, which would have surely scalped him had it been from the blade rather than the flat of the sword. As it was, he fell to the ground, insensible. Another belligerent fellow, the possessor of a staff, brought the staff up to block the Obtruncator, which obtruncated it on the spot.

Whirling a sword which was taller than he was and at least a tenth part as heavy did begin to tell on Colin's strength after a time. His arms, tireless at playing fiddle or guitar, quickly wearied with the labor of bashing the sword about. He wondered, as he wearied, who exactly had originated the term "swordplay." Undoubtedly one of Rowan's frost giant ancestors. Someone sidled in then to take advantage of his waning strength, and Colin was saddened to see his fellow-fiddler, Cheese-nose, flashing his dagger in confusing convolutions.

He was also extremely worried, as Cheese-nose evidently knew his way around daggers as well as he did around fiddles. While trying to determine what the other man would do next, he saw a glint of metal from his other side. One of the worst things about this night fighting was that, in spite of the full moon, it was difficult to see in all the confusion and darkness who was doing what.

Colin switched his attention from Cheese-nose to the sneak-attacker, whipping Obtruncator to where he had seen the metallic flash, nearly beheading three people in the sword's path.

He didn't hear the barking and yapping until Ching dashed between his legs and a blur of dog knocked Cheese-nose aside. Colin regained his balance, and thrust to drive off the attacker on his right side, while he avoided the recovering Cheese-nose on his left. The right-hand attacker tripped over the dog and stepped heavily backward, grinding his heel into Ching's tail. Swords were forgotten as the dog growled and snarled at all and sundry, trying to get at Ching, who now made of himself a hairpiece and muffler for the right-hand attacker, who was no longer attacking but screaming in agony. The new hairpiece was anchored firmly to his head by four sets of claws.

Although the animals created a diversion which provided Colin with a moment's respite, he would have been cut down as soon as the first gypsy returned his attention to the battle. But it was then that the bear came lumbering into the fray.

Colin didn't stick around to see his enemies scatter, as he was too busy scattering himself. He bolted for his horse, leaping into the saddle as though he'd sprouted wings. Ching made a corresponding leap from the head of the gypsy he'd been riding, and transferred to Colin's shoulder instead. Then somehow they were on the horse and off through the open meadow. Colin was shaking so hard he nearly dropped the sword before he could return it to its scabbard.

As he galloped across the space between the circle of wagons and the wood, he saw Davey, muscles rippling magnificently in the moonlight as he sprinted at full speed toward the camp. Colin resisted an impulse to run him down, but held him at bay with the horse's nervous pawing hooves. "Where's Maggie?" he demanded.

The gypsy looked genuinely confused. "She's not with you?"

"No."

"Then she must have thought you were killed in all that noise, and run away. I let her go a long time ago." He appeared unconcerned by Colin's threatening air and shrugged impatiently, starting to walk in a wide circle around the frenzied horse. "Look after your own women. I've enough problem keeping up with mine."

Watching the gypsy walk blithely away from him and back

129

to the camp, Colin saw one more thing before he fled into the woods. Zorah, visible to him but not from the camp, popped out from under one of the wagons and waved wildly for a moment before disappearing again.

12

Colin's terrible screams had come to a shuddering climax long before Maggie reached the portion of the woods that would enable her to reach the bear's wagon undetected. For a long time after that she stood staring dry-eyed at the circle of wagons, unable to believe the evidence of her own ears. She wandered further into the woods, to the upstream end of the camp, her stomach heaving and body trembling with shock and fury.

She had to control an almost unbearable urge to fly into the gypsy camp and dismantle it and everybody in it with her bare hands. She didn't have even her dagger now, though, and if she met the same end as Colin, who would there be to help Amberwine? She was comforting herself with visions of plagues both magical and mundane which she would cause to infest the gypsies if it took the rest of her life, when her attention was redirected to the camp by the clanging of swords, the screams of combatants, and the neighings of horses.

By the time she found a vantage point from which to observe the melee, the other sounds were joined by Ching's yowl of pain and indignation, a dog's frantic yapping, the coarse shouts of the gypsies, more fearful roaring from the bear, and the thunderous thudding of unshod hooves galloping over the grass.

All she was really able to see were confusing shapes flitting about in the diffuse light of the moon, but she did finally see a streak of pale hair as Colin, on the opposite side of the camp from where she now stood, rode away across the meadow, stopping only long enough to threaten Gypsy Davey. The gypsy appeared to talk his way out of the situation, and, before Maggie could cross the meadow to join Colin, he had ridden off into the woods. Her own cry for him to wait was drowned out by the bellowings of the gypsies pursuing their horses, who were for some reason scattered all across the meadow.

She fled back into the woods and ran until she reached the part of the meadow where she had left her horse and package of belongings. Now it seemed almost a game to elude the gypsies. She was giddy with relief that Colin had escaped, and fairly skipped through the damp, clinging meadow grass as she ran to the stream. As she had anticipated, her horse and pack were gone, undoubtedly the current property of some enterprising used horse dealer. There was, of course, a good possibility that her horse was one of those trotting over the meadow just ahead of a cajoling gypsy, but she was not about to take the time to look for him, or to try to catch any of the horses and persuade one to allow her to mount.

Snatching her hidden cache of clothing from beside the stream, she heard the callings and neighings come rapidly closer to where she knelt, until the noise and thundering shadows were all around her. She had to dodge several rocketing horses to reach the safety of the willows at the edge of the wood.

When she felt she was safely concealed, she changed out of the bright clothing she'd made from her underwear and into her brown skirt and tunic. She pocketed her medicine pouch and took the remaining phial of love potion from her hair, dropping that into her pocket as well. She wadded the bright gypsy dress so that only the green showed and wouldn't betray her by its color.

Of the wildflowers which had graced her hair that night, only one remained after her tussle with Davey, and that had wilted. She could detect no vestiges of the love-philtre perfume on her skin. Taking the flower from her hair, she tied her kerchief around her head instead. It was then that she heard a horse breaking through the underbrush nearby, the voice of its pursuer close behind. With her dark skin and clothing she melted into the forest as though she were an animated tree trunk.

By the time she could no longer hear voices, neither could she find a path underfoot. The sun had risen, and as she searched it came from oblivion to reach mid-point in the warm spring sky. The leaves overhead glimmered feverishly, their tops glazed with a citrusy hue, and all around her were mosses, tall grass, fallen leaves, and the trunks of dead trees

132

underfoot. The path had completely disappeared. She had blended into the forest a little too successfully, and realized that she was lost.

Wandering, she came at last to the bank of another stream. Although willows and other taller bushes grew close by the bank in many places, at one point they did recede into a clearing, and in this spot the stream was lined with a field of berries.

She picked great handfuls, and ate them that way, having nothing to make a more fanciful concoction, and not possessing the strength or inclination for cooking, magical or otherwise, just then, anyway. They were very good just as they were, if a bit tart at times. She continued gathering after she'd eaten her fill, and tied them into her kerchief, leaving her hair to string down, hot and sticky, against her neck.

Her exhilaration over Colin's escape and her own began to fade, and she sat down on a log to think. She was tired, having been up the whole night, and now that she knew he was safe she was annoyed that Colin was not there to keep her company and help her continue their journey. Presumably Ching was with him now, and she missed the cat too.

She would have liked to discuss with Colin what Davey had told her, and plan how to get her sister away from Hugo, who she now felt sure was taking her sister to the sorcerer, if he hadn't already killed her. Although she badly wished to see Colin again, she just as fervently hoped he would continue on his way when he found she was not in the section of the wood for which he had been headed.

Still, Ching might have cheered her with his sarcasm, and not incidentally with the game he could catch and share with her. It would be nice to stroke his fur while she thought, too, instead of watching her hands turn blue from the berries. A tear of self-pity slid down one of her brown cheeks.

She was about to brush it aside when she heard the rustling in the bushes and heard a peculiar snuffling, whuffing sound and saw the leaves of the willows shake. A brown, furry nose poked out of the shrubbery.

She froze. A bear, perhaps the one from the gypsy camp. Now she really did miss Ching, and even the minstrel, who might have at least tried to do as her father had suggested and sing the bear a lullaby. She could always TRY to turn the creature into a rug. It was better than being eaten.

The bear emerged fully from the bushes and stood on his

hind legs, blinking his small eyes and looking around. Maggie sat back so abruptly when he stood up that she almost fell into the stream. Before it had occured to her that that would have been a safer course of action than to attract the bear's attention, she had caused considerable commotion flailing around trying to save herself a soaking.

The bear growled.

Maggie righted herself abruptly, sitting up so quickly that the kerchief-tied bundle of berries rolled out of her lap and onto the ground beside ner foot. She nudged the berries toward the bear with her toes.

To her surprise, he picked them up and carefully unknotted the kerchief before devouring the berries in two pawfuls.

"Thanks, m'dear. These are excellent."

She shook her head sharply and pounded above her ear with the heel of her hand. "Excuse me. Did you say something?"

"Yes—the berries—very good indeed. I say, you wouldn't have a little honey about, would you? Since I've been in this form I've had such a great craving for it, but of course, Xenobia would never let anyone give me any."

"No, I'm sorry. Perhaps I can go find some—" Seeing a chance to escape, she tensed herself for flight, then hesitated. He seemed completely uninterested in eating her, at least so long as berries were available. "Excuse me, bear. How is it you—or rather, I—I mean, how can we understand each other?"

"You young folks broke part of the spell. Didn't you know?"

"Spell?"

"Yes, indeed. Xenobia's spell specifically stated that if I were released by—say—a magic cat—and my son's own true love, that I should once more be able to talk and act as a man. Of course, I can't *look* like myself again unless I'm able to recover young David's ticker." His little bear eyes looked at her shrewdly. "I trust I'm not incorrect in assuming you're part of that group—with the charming animal and the clumsy young chap who screams so beautifully? I know Xenobia's folk, of course, and you have a different look than the townspeople."

"Oh, yes, those are my friends, Colin the minstrel and Chingachgook, my grandmother's familiar. But if you're not really a bear, then who are you?"

"I am Prince H. David Worthyman, formerly known at

home and abroad as Prince Worthyman the Worthy, heir to the throne of Ablemarle. I suppose now my brother, known in my day as Prince Worthyman the Worthless, has been kind enough to fill the vacancy left in the crown princedom since my bearship."

Maggie nodded. "We don't get much political news up where I live, but Dad did say that since the death of your late father, King Worthyman the Worthy, things have really deteriorated over there." She was silent for a moment while His Highness, having finished the berries in her kerchief, shoveled them off the bushes into his muzzle with both front paws.

"Excuse me, though, Prince Worthyman. How did you come to be enchanted, if that's not too personal a question? My aunt says Xenobia's a charlatan, not a proper witch at all . . ."

"Your aunt is absolutely correct, m'dear. She's not a witch, of course. She custom-ordered the spell from her patron sorcerer."

Maggie snorted. "That fellow has caused a great deal of trouble!"

"Aye, he has indeed." He turned a berry-stained snout to her, then dropped down onto all four paws and settled himself beside the stream for a drink. "I'll tell you, gurrrl," he said, shaking the water from his snout when he had finished, "If you'll be kind enough to scratch behind my ears and along the top of my nose—ahhhh, yes, that's good—I'll tell you all about it."

THE ACCOUNT OF HIS ROYAL HIGHNESS
PRINCE H. DAVID WORTHYMAN,
ALSO CALLED THE ENCHANTED BEAR

"I suppose you can't really be too hard on Xenobia for a lot of the things she's done. I didn't realize at the time what a sensitive girl she was or I shouldn't have—er—loved her and left her, as they say.

"But I was just a young sprout then, and if the girls didn't like me quite as well as they like young Davey, well, they liked me well enough so that soon I grew bored with them and their fickle fan-fluttering flatteries and I preferred to go huntin' instead.

"We were sheltered up to the castle, you know, and I'd

135

never seen a gypsy wench before. But I saw a great deal of Xenobia that first time, for she was bathin' in the river. She was so pretty then, with that golden skin and those snappin' black eyes—oh, yes, I was considerably smitten. To give m'self credit, she didn't take much persuading. I visited her several times while her caravan was in the area and then, being gypsies, they left.

"I nearly forgot about her as time went by. Being crown prince is fairly heavy work, y'know. One thing father insisted on was that I choose and marry one of the local princesses. Princesses in general seemed a sorry, simpering lot compared to Xenobia, I thought then, but finally I chose Jane of Brazoria as the least objectionable of them, and we were married, and I resumed learning my duties as king-to-be while Janie and I tried to produce an heir.

"Probably because we weren't so lucky on that account, I was ready, when I got Xenobia's message, to believe her when she said little Davey was my son. By the time I heard, you see, the lad was well along to being eight years old. I didn't question that he was mine for a moment, either, once I saw him. He looks like me, don't you think? No? Oh, yes, not so shaggy—heh, heh—keep forgetting. Not used to being both man *and* bear. S'awkward.

"Anyway, little Davey was my son, and a charming, laughing child he was too. I wish Xenobia hadn't hidden herself so well when your friends released me. I'd have shown her a bear! 'Twas a terrible thing she did to our boy."

"Hmph," said Maggie. "He seemed to be doing alright for himself, if you ask me."

"Well, of course you've no idea, not having been around long. But I can tell you, gurrl, that my son is not the warm, gay child he was. He is not even a nice person now. Many fear him, and many envy him, but no one except his mother and that girl who opened my cage truly love him—and even Xenobia and the girl only love what he used to be."

"I see."

"Back to my story—I say, I hope I'm not boring you?"

"Oh, no."

"Well, then. Davey was a beautiful child, and we loved each other at once. For a week I bided with the gypsies and taught him the things I knew—a bit about hunting, a bit about affairs of state, a few songs I'd learned off the circuit minstrels. But when time came for me to go, Xenobia cornered me, wantin' to know couldn't I stay with her and the lad. I explained about learning to run kingdoms, and Jane, and all, and I s'pect she must have figured I'd gone snooty on her. With Jane and all that, I couldn't take her back to court even if they could have adjusted to the life. It wouldn't have done at all.

"I thought she understood that in spite of the fearsome frown on her face as I left them. Five years later I received another message, this one askin' me to come to young Davey's manhood ceremony. I see now that that frown, when I first told her there was no room in my life for her and our son, was when she decided to change and all three of us became monsters.

"She met me on the road before I reached their camp, and was all smiles and giggles. Even eight years ago, Xenobia was still quite a good-looking woman, and I flattered myself that my charm certainly wore well. I'd no idea it was a different charm altogether that she had in mind then, for we never went through the main camp at all, but straight to her wagon. She gave me meat and drink.

"I asked to see my son, but she told me he was 'being prepared.' After I drained my wine glass, I felt a little drowsy, y'know, so I thought I'd just have a bit of a nap.

"When I woke up I was in the bear's cage, couldn't move a muscle or say a thing. My body was changin' into a bear's then, you see, and it seems to affect you like that. It was dark, and Xenobia came up carrying a torch, hard yella light on her hard, wicked face. I wondered then what I saw in her. Behind her was this fella all muffled in cloakery, like some sort of pilgrim.

"'This here's the sorcerer, Davey,' she says to me. 'Come all the way from Dragon Bay to be at our boy's ceremony.' Then she went on, mocking me. 'As your highness may have noticed, I don't write to you overmuch, not bein' an educated woman like your wife and the noble kind. But our tribe has lately suffered the loss

137

of our beloved bear—got a bit rough in the bear-baiting, and the poor thing got killed.' Well, I thought she was daft, you know, goin' on about some bear and me not bein' able to talk.

"Then she says, all sweet and reasonable, 'So I thought we could help each other out. You want to be near the boy, and I need a new bear. The sorcerer here is obligin' us by arranging for you to *be* the bear. If it should by any chance happen, I have to tell you, that you ever get help getting loose from the cage by another magic animal— and where will you find one of them among us?—or what the sorcerer is about to make really impossible, and you'll see for yourself what I mean, soon enough—if this magical animal that helps you is aided by our boy's true love, you'll get to think and talk like a man again. Of course, anybody else tries to help you, you'll probably eat them, because in a lot of ways, mighty prince of mine, you're getting to be all bear.' She laughed then and it was spine-tinglin' to hear.

" 'After this ceremony, our sweet little boy will never have to worry about findin' a true love to desert the way his Papa did. His heart will belong to his mother and only to her!'

"I didn't know, of course, what she meant by that, but I was soon to find out, for she left the cage facing the gypsy's campfire.

"This ceremony they were having was all lit by torches carried by the friends of all the boys getting passed to manhood, and I could see well enough. Young Davey, he was all eager and excited, and they smeared paint on him and on the others and waved symbols in the air supposed to be magical, had some dances, give him a speech about how he's a prince now. Ha! If only he knew, he could be a real prince with none of that hokum about it.

"But on with what I was saying. Anyway, pretty soon it's all over for the other boys and they go back to their parents. But Xenobia tells the boy that since he's a prince and so on, he has one more bit of special rigamarole to go through.

"She takes this crystal thing from the sorcerer—what d'ya call them, gurrl? A prism. And she holds it in front of the child and tells him to watch it, to watch the fire

138

inside it, to watch the colors of it, and pretty soon he gets real stupid looking. A trance, I s'pose it was.

"The sorcerer comes forward then and takes this prism from Xenobia, places it against the boy's breast. He chants and sing-songs and makes more magical patterns in the air. Wasn't much of that went on before the prism gets brighter and brighter, and then very bright, indeed. Xenobia held out her hand for it then, but the sorcerer didn't give it to her. She put up no fuss, either, afraid of undoing the magic, I suppose.

Davey woke up then, and a great feastin' party was held. I felt hungry myself, you see, for I was this way by then, and the meal I'd had as a man was hardly enough for a bear. I was also beginning to feel stupid and dull and ornery, and I tried to lift my arms to rattle the side of the cage. I saw my paws and forelegs then, and I knew she was telling the truth, that I was turning into a bear. I tried hard to understand what they were saying as they came to the cage, hoping they'd give me a clue as to how to free myself.

"Xenobia had figured by then that the sorcerer had tricked her and was hollering at him. 'You promised me I'd have the heart,' I heard her say.

"The sorcerer was sweet as honey. 'I only promised to relieve him of it, dear lady, Come now,' he says, 'why should a traveler like yourself be needing extra possessions to cart around? I'll just keep it safe for you as a memento of this lovely party and this charmin' native ritual of yours. Someday, maybe, when I'm sure of your friendship and all, I may let you have it back.'

"Xenobia didn't say anything to that, and he raps on my cage, and I knew I was more bear than man already, for he smelled delicious. 'By the way, Highness, the lady was not exactly playing fair with you. She neglected to tell you the rest of the antidote, as I'm bound by the spell to do. If, having been freed by those other conditions she mentioned, you manage to recover this little trinket,' he flashed the prism again, dazzling my eyes and taunting Xenobia, 'so your son can be as dreary as most young men, you will regain your human shape. If you don't die of old age in that bear body first!'

"Then I'll be if he didn't mount on a great black swan and fly away before Xenobia could be at him again."

139

"I must say," Maggie admitted through her yawn, "that was an amazing story." Her eyelids had been getting ever heavier as the bear's deep voice growled on. The bear prince raised his great shaggy head from her lap, and if a bear's tiny eyes could look solicitous, his did.

"Ah, gurrrl, and you listening to all that after being up all night and none of the sleep you natural folk need. You're in sore need of hibernation." He rose to his hind paws again and looked around, then dropped once more to all fours. "You nap a bit and I'll keep watch. I doubt any of Xenobia's tribe have lingered in the area, but we'll wait for nightfall to move along all the same."

"You're the prince," Maggie agreed, snuggling down into a nice grassy place and immediately sleeping.

14

Due To The Magical Nature of This Tale
Chapter 13 Has Been Omitted

Awakening in his comfortable room at the Queenston Inn,
the homey weight of Ching's purring body stretched across
his legs, Colin felt like crying. His body ached all over from
wielding the great sword, and from riding in one day the
day-and-a-half distance from the gypsy camp to Queenston.
He had actually allowed himself to be so panicked by pursuit
as to take Davey's word for it that Maggie was safe and likely
on the road ahead of him. He had half-killed his horse galloping down that forest path in hopes of collecting her.

For the first league or two that flew beneath his horse's
hooves, he had expected to rein in at any moment to hoist a
brightly clad figure up behind him. Instead, the path had
been empty, the town at the hour of his passage had been
empty, and the highway beyond the town leading to Queenston,
while not empty, had not led to Maggie either.

He hadn't really supposed she'd get so far ahead as to reach
the highway on foot before him, but nonetheless her absence
upon it caused *him* to feel empty. It was by then too late to
turn back, or to slow down, for the gypsies would have
recaptured their mounts and been after him if that was their
intention. He could not take the chance that it wasn't.

So today he was less weary, but sore of mind and body, and
a day behind from sleeping through it if he could judge from
the ruddy sunset pinking the lace curtains that hung at the
window.

He was hungry too, and had no assets except a sword that
didn't fit him, his musical instruments, the clothes on his
back, and a borrowed cat. He also had a lack of bright notions

141

how to proceed with keeping his promises to Maggie and to Zorah.

Ching raised his black-masked face from his kneading front paws, green eyes slitted with good cheer.

Colin idly scratched behind the cat's whiskers. "At least you're in a good mood. We'd best get to work," however, before they throw us in prison." The cat didn't look particularly worried. Having no purse, he could hardly be held responsible for bills. Colin walked to the window to get his bearings. The capitol swept down to the brilliant water of Queenston Harbor, whose garden of masts and spars was outlined in sharp detail against the mountains. The sunset frosted the upper peaks, hovering protectively around the harbor, with strawberry ice. "Ah, well," sighed Colin as he pulled his boots on, "at least if we don't come up with something here they'll only jail us—if they catch us. This is a nice place. Some inns, I understand, they'd simply slit our throats and be done with it."

Fortunately, temporary impoverishment was one contingency the academy had trained him to contend with. Guitar strung across his back, and fiddle under his arm, he held open the door of the room for Ching to stroll through. "Now, cat, I promised you you'd never go hungry, didn't I? How does some nice fish sound?" Ching gazed raptly up at him for a reply.

Hoping not to meet the landlord, Colin slipped softly down the stairs, and for a change luck was with him. He breathed more deeply when they had put several streets between themselves and the inn. The salty, fishy smell of the harbor tanged at their noses, and Ching padded along in a positively frisky fashion.

Colin soon thought it prudent to lift the cat to his shoulders so he could ride between the guitar and Colin's neck. The capitol of Argonia was much busier than it had been when the third-class apprentices from the Minstrel Academy had visited their hall there years before.

Even now, in early evening, merchants and sailors and servants and nobles streamed around him. bartering and buying right in the middle of the street. Heavily-laden wagons pulled by horses or oxen parted the stream of passers-by as a boulder parts a stream of water. Carriages, gilded and probably belonging to noble court officials and administrative personnel, clattered by, heedless of the traffic, and Colin shied, nervous of so much activity after the relative peace of the highway.

He ought to have expected it would be busier, though, with the tribunal convening in only three months. Servants would be renovating their masters' and mistresses' townhouses, merchants would be heavily stocking their inventories, and, naturally, more ships would be required to bring the goods.

Country folk would be coming to town looking for work more lucrative than farming to see them through the coming winter. And curiosity-seekers would be trying to find a good place to stay before everyone else got moved in. For everybody wanted to know what would happen when the elder statesmen of Argonia met to nominate Finbar the Fireproof's successor to the crown of Argonia.

Finbar had been one of the best kings ever to rule, and one of the most colorful. The Minstrel Academy was one of the King's many educational advances, and had been founded some fifty years ago, shortly after Finbar had accepted the crown. Tax reforms, improved farming methods instituted by wise men sent abroad specifically to study advanced foreign techniques, the abolition of differences in the criminal code between magical and non-magical folk, and a general attitude of reason and tolerance I had been the result of his rule.

But Finbar, once the most stoic and courageous of princes, was finally growing old. Some said old before his time, as an unfortunate consequence of his family history. He came from a family of performing magicians, whose talents included not only Finbar's own penchant for swallowing flaming swords (which made him virtually dragon-proof) but also being sawn in half, lying on beds of nails, sticking swords into boxes containing themselves, and other uncomfortable occupations. Even those who did not agree that the king's premature infirmity at the age of eighty-six resulted from his magic had to admit that his perilous ancestral talent had cost him his heir to the throne:

For his descendants, in the same way lamented by Granny and Aunt Sybil Brown, were less powerful than he, as he was less powerful than his ancestor who could climb invisible ropes into the stratosphere. The two young princes, in trying to live up to their father's prowess, perished rather messily while attempting to master one of the more advanced skills practiced by him. The princess did happen to have a little talent for eating fire, but after the demise of her brothers she decided to retire from public life and become an illuminator of manuscripts.

Some folk were uncharitable enough to intimate that a monarch with somewhat less magic and somewhat more mortal strength and horse sense might be a wise choice at this time.

At any rate, the economy of Queenston was flourishing if the reigning monarch was not, and it was not easy for a man with a cat on his shoulders and a fiddle under his arm to elbow his way through the throngs that crowded the streets and waterfront, where if there were fewer nobles and rich merchants, there were more longshoremen, sailors, and the ladies who profited by their company.

He was about to ask one of these people where he could locate his dinner when his nose located it for him. Rancid grease, frying fish, sailors whose bodies touched water only when a wave washed across the deck of their ships, and the mingled stench of first- and second-hand ale and foreign tobacco told him he had found a place to earn his meal and rent money even before he heard the clamor of voices and the rattle of cutlery from within.

He could see very little as he entered the inn, for two reasons. The first was that a friendly pre-dinner brawl was in progress and people were flying in and out the door on their knees and by the seats of their pants in confusing profusion. The second reason was that the smoke from both pipes and unattended oil lamps clouded the entire establishment with a haze of blue-gray fumes. Colin thought perhaps the patrons were so glad to see the place after months at sea, they probably considered the fumes atmospheric.

Ducking the airborne diners, he made his way to a chair in the corner of the room where he could have his back against the wall and avoid being jostled from behind. Ching jumped down from his shoulder and went to investigate the fish smells emerging from behind the bar, and Colin unlimbered his bow.

For a time he played to himself, building his courage, and no one could hear him over the brawl. But the first of the brawlers to decide to sit and nurse his wounds over another flagon sat near him, listened to what he played, applauded loud enough even to be heard over the din, and bellowed a request. This innovative pastime quickly became fashionable

144

among his fellows, likewise seeking less painful diversion which would allow them more drinking time.

Requests were loud and competitive, and almost led to another brawl, until someone decided to influence Colin's choice with a copper coin. Someone else decided that what one copper coin could do, two copper coins would do better, and so on. By the time he had enough to buy his dinner, Colin was thoroughly enjoying himself.

All of the sailors had voices, a few of them good, all of them lusty, and they brought the same enthusiasm to the singing that they had to the brawling. Their favorite songs were bawdy and very long, since on shipboard it was a common pastime to sing and to add new verses, appropriate to the current situation, to old songs. Colin was on the sixteenth verse or the eighteenth, he wasn't sure which, of the one about the selkie who outwitted the sea serpent and seduced the siren, when the first of his listeners called the innkeeper for a pint for the fiddler.

As the evening wore on and the smoky room changed from an overall illuminated gray to an overall illuminated black, frequent calls of "Innkeeper, t'lad's dry! Ale!" reverberated through the room along with the clanking of flagons and the singing. Then Colin was good for another forty verses, and after the first few times was amazed at how harmonious the chorusing of the sailors had become.

When the second gallon had poured down his throat, a man with a striped cap and an eyepatch produced a concertina and another man produced a hornpipe, and then it didn't matter if Colin sang or not, as everyone else was making music, even if they weren't all singing or playing the same song.

As the night wore on and day approached, Colin was still singing and yarning at the table occupied by his most fervent and most intoxicated supporters. The minstrel listened to their stories and thought he'd never heard anything so wonderful, or met such fine, brave, intelligent, altogether splendid fellows in his life.

There was a lull in the conversation then as all of them took a pull at their flagons and he told them about his own adventures. When he'd finished, several pints later, his face was wet with tears. "... and so I lost dear, dear li'l Maggie..." and a couple of the tears slid over the lip of his flask.

145

"There there, lad, you'll dilute the ale," said the concertina player, thoughtfully mopping Colin's face with his striped hat, and then blowing his nose on it before replacing it on his own head.

"Ah, you loved the lassie, didn't you, lad?" asked a tender-hearted old soul, the bosun of the ship they all crewed on, and a former pirate.

"Well, she made excellent stew..." Colin said wistfully, the tears still flowing freely. "But I left her in the wood. Couldn't find her. Nothin' left of her a'tall but her pussy cat."

The originator of the ribald remark that followed that statement was awarded a scathing look by Ching, who was filled with fish given him by the friendly cook in the kitchen and perched once more on Colin's neck.

When the laughter died away, someone else said, "Sign on with us, then, lad."

"Can't. I've all this unfinished business. Got to find 'er ladyship for Maggie, and get the gypsy's heart from t' sorcerer for Zorah, like I told you." He started bawling again at the impossibility of it all, then brightened. "I say, you lads wouldn't know where I could find any bad sor—sor—men witches, would you?"

The old pirate with the romantic streak spoke up again. "Now there's a good reason for you to join on with us, laddie. The wiliest rogue of the sorcerous lot lives on an island in Dragon Bay, so I hear tell. If it's evil sorcerers you want, he's your man."

Colin, who didn't see how he could be running into two evil sorcerers on the same journey, felt sure that the sorcerer the pirate mentioned must be the one he sought. He agreed to sign on as far as Dragon Bay, and asked when they were leaving.

"First light 'o morning, which is to say as soon as I can boot these rogues out of here," said the second officer. "We wants to get into the Bay and docked before Dragon Days starts if we can, which we can't if you lads sits here all day."

"What's Dragon Days?" asked Colin.

"Aw, it's nothing. Just every month for a week or so Dragon Bay is plagued by this great beastie what it feeds before it eats everything in sight."

"How can people live there, then?"

"It's this sorcerer fella, you see," said the concertina player, warming especially to the narration now that work was in

146

sight. "He sets up this Dragon Days arrangement with the Dragon. Persuasive sort of chap, they say he is, the sorcerer—not the dragon—thought dragons do their own persuadin'—anyhow, the way of t is everybody has to give up so many of their beasts every month to feed the dragon. There's some say an occasional rival of Himself the Sorcerer gets unlucky enough to wander in among the poor beasts and be eaten, but none will swear to it. The folk drive their beasts down to the bay, and the animals are driven onto a barge and hauled out to one of them rocky patches that surrounds Evil Island."

"Evil Island?"

The man leaned forward, whispering, "That's where the sorcerer dwells, of course. Some say it's beautiful and others say it's terrible, but all say it's a bloody good thing t' sorcerer has made this arrangement so they can tithe a cow t' the dragon instead of being eaten out o' house and home in a more personal kinda way. Ah, laddie, a dragon is a terrible plague!"

"I don't know 'bout that," Colin said, trying to be fair, "I met a dragon once, and she wasn't such a bad sort once you got t' know 'er."

This remark was met with laughter that all but gusted away the atmosphere, the guffaws being so lusty as to blow the smoke clouds out the door. "Not so bad oncet you gets to know 'er! Now there's a good 'un!"

The old pirate clapped him on the back. "You surely must come with us now, laddie. It's a fine sailor we can make of you."

"But I've never been to sea."

"No matter. We can teach you the sailin' part, but the serious requirements is drinkin', singin', and lyin', and you surely do excel at that."

15

His Highness the bear, Maggie found, made the perfect traveling companion. While strong enough and bearlike enough to barge through the woods with no fear of interference from griffins or lions or much of anything else, he was nevertheless cultured, erudite, witty, and considerate. Ever courteous, he was mindful of her comfort and courtly in his manners, yet not too dignified to use his claws to dig for edible roots she could cook for supper.

The first night they had spent getting out of the wood, and had in the morning camped on the banks of a river which neither of them could name, Maggie never having been so far from home before and the bear being a foreigner. Of course, he told her, he had been all over a great many countries with the gypsy band, he was sure, but his own mind then was dominated by the bear's, and he had only a bear's perceptions of where he had been.

The worst part of the spell Xenobia had caused to be cast upon him was that he was not only a bear in appearance, but a bear in thought and deed as well. His own mind was imprisoned by the bear's, and he had only the control a bear normally had over his actions and treatment. There had been other times, he admitted remorsefully, when enemies of Xenobia not so well-connected with magical cats had been put in the cage with him. Maggie shuddered, but so did the enchanted prince.

It had been a terrible thing to watch the body he occupied murder helpless people. It was somehow not at all the same as leading troops in a border skirmish, bashing heads and laying into one another in good clean soldierly fun. That was after all a prince's duty.

Well into the afternoon they had a dinner of berries and bird's eggs. The bear had them raw as he found them, but

148

Maggie made an omelette of her share, after she had first prudently expanded both foods to satisfy their appetites and have a few days' supply in reserve. There were enough eggs left over to return to the bird's nest, if the bird would have them after they'd been juggled about by bears and magical spells.

As His Highness regally licked in the last of the blue stain from his muzzle, Maggie reached into her pocket and produced the silver mirror. "I suppose," she said, "we ought to find out where we're going."

"Good idea, gurrrl. How?"

Maggie showed him Aunt Sybil's mirror and explained its powers and restrictions. "Only trouble is, this type of gift magic limits itself to three visions only. Then it's useless unless it's recharged."

"What's the problem?"

"I think we've used two already, if the one that misfired at the castle counts. Colin and I saw Winnie in Queenston the second time we tried it. And I was thinking. If we're up against such a powerful sorcerer, maybe we should try to enlist the help of my uncle."

The bear waited courteously for her to continue. "My aunt said her brother lives in these parts somewhere, and by now he may be very powerful himself. Aunt Sybil and Gran are. Unfortunately, I'm not. Making a superb soufflé hardly qualifies me for rescuing people from the clutches of mighty sorcerers. There's also that little matter of your son's heart he might advise us on. No," she concluded, having convinced herself, "we need first-class help."

"So you're thinkin' to find your uncle in the glass instead of Lady Rowan?"

"It's an idea. Probably Uncle Fearchar knows this sorcerer, what with both of them living on the coast and all. Possibly they even play chess together once in a while—though neither of us have any reason to be fond of him, to another sorcerer like Uncle Fearchar he might not be such a bad fellow."

His Highness grumbled deep in his throat, but only said, "If your sister is with the peddler and you think he's dangerous, shouldn't we fetch her with all speed? If we delay, she and her babe may come to harm that no powerful help can remedy."

Maggie automatically started to open her mouth to argue her point of view further, then considered. Without knowing

Hugo's plans, she had no way of knowing how much danger Winnie could be in. Had she hit on the idea of locating her uncle to be of the most possible help to her sister, or merely to bolster her own confidence, which had taken a sharp drop once they were dealing with sorcerers rather than a few gypsies and a gossipy peddler?

"You're right, of course," she finally agreed. She tried to concentrate on Amberwine then, as they peered expectantly into the rainbow lights that began gathering in the silver, and she hoped the vision would be of Amberwine in better straits than before.

Again she got a double image. "I'm sorry," she told the bear. "I'm not nearly so good at this as Aunt Sybil. I keep bunching them together." The bear stared over her shoulder as the blurry vision of Amberwine's face gradually faded. "At least her hair seemed to be combed this time," Maggie remarked hopefully.

"Maybe this is where she is," said the bear, indicating the second picture, which was sharpening now that Amberwine's face had disappeared. In the mirror was the interior of an inn, as seen in front of, around, and behind a man whom both Maggie and the bear both thought they recognized but were equally sure they had never met. His appearance was strikingly unusual, not that of a person one would easily forget, Maggie thought.

He had coppery skin, lined deeply around his intensely dark brown eyes, and grooved on either side of his hawkish nose down to a thin-lipped mouth which held a faint suggestion of a smile. His cheekbones were high, and his brown hair, distinctively striped with gray at the temples, waved handsomely back from his forehead. In his hand was a wine glass and at his elbow the innkeeper's wife, pouring him a refill.

"It's such an honor to have you stay with us here at Bayshore Inn, Master Brown," the woman simpered, setting down the wine crock. "Will you be staying with us long?"

"Only till the second loading is done, Goodwife," the man replied.

"It's Uncle Fearchar!" said Maggie, now that the reason for his familiar appearance was clear.

"Of course, that's why I thought I'd seen him," the bear said, "the fellow's the spittin' image of you, gurrrl."

Maggie blushed guiltily. "I'm afraid the magic mirror must show what I want to see, not what I think I ought to see. But

I wish we could get Winnie back—maybe—" she returned her eyes to the mirror but the image was already gone. She shook her head. "Too bad. That was the last one, too."

The bear sat back down by the fire, and Maggie put the mirror away. "I propose that we use the nonmagical clues we have. All roads seem to lead to Dragon Bay. Let's get over there so I can get the boy's heart and tear out of that smiling sorcerer what he's done with your sister."

It was easier to talk of getting to Dragon Bay than to do it, for the way led into the foothills and over a high passage that crossed the Mountains of Mourn. The mountains had been named, said the bear, who had studied wars foreign and domestic as Crown Prince of Ablemarle, after a battle involving giant soldiers who landed on the shores of Argonia, wreaking destruction in the coastal villages. They were repulsed finally, at the cost of many lives, from crossing into interior Argonia when the loyal home guard defended their home from the towering slopes. It was reported to have been a terrible battle, with even the Argonian dragons aiding in the defense. Maggie said she'd heard of it too, except she had heard that the dragons only helped the Argonians because the enemy tasted better and were larger. The dragons had been concerning themselves more with their plates than their patriotism.

Although there was a footpath, perhaps left from the days of old before the Argonian Navy became strong enough that the mountains did not need to be foot-patrolled, the going was by no means easy. Road-hardened as Maggie's feet had become, her lungs were entirely unconvinced they were able to breathe the rarified mountain air, and the bear often had to wait while she caught her breath.

It was cold up there, too, and the snow was deeper than her riding boots, which were growing thinner and thinner with each magical patching. She shivered even in her woolen cloak, which was not, unfortunately, her winter-weight cloak. If she had only brought her hand spindle from the pack she might have woven some of the bear's fur into a coat, but it was too late for that now.

When they finally came down out of the mountains it had been a full seven days since they'd left the river. By noon of that day they stood on a hill overlooking Dragon Bay and the little town that lay along its shore.

From where they stood, the Bay was silver and white,

151

smooth as glass in long flat curves offset by choppy glittering expanses of water. Beyond the Bay was the open sea, but behind it was another mountain range, craggier and even more forbidding than the one they had just crossed.

Studding the waters were a number of small islands, some no more than rocks for the waves to break against, and others fairly large and green and covered with vegetation. The largest of the islands was crowned by a castle. Even from their vantage point it appeared crude and ancient, two enormous stone houses, one taller than the other, with towers stuck at each corner and surrounded by a high wall.

The town was situated on what was the only possible site for it, having been built on a beach that was backed by the hill on which they stood. Fierce rocky cliffs brooded over the water on either side of the town, their grimness somewhat softened by the sparkling falls of spring water cascading down their faces and by the wildflowers growing in the deep cracks that scored them.

"I'll wager," said the bear, "that that's where the dragons of Dragon Bay lurk." Maggie shaded her eyes, straining to see. "In those caves in yon cliffs, gurrl. Just the thing for dragons. Bears too, matter of fact."

"I was getting ready to speak to you about that, your Highness," she said, turning back to him. "I'm really afraid that the sight of you will cause undue panic in the town. Perhaps I'd better go find out if I can where the sorcerer dwells."

"No, gurrl," he replied. "You're a good gurrrl to offer to take my chances for me. But sorcerers are tricky, and you might be trapped with no way to send for me. I think if you enlarge that cloak of yours to fit me, and put a hood on it, I can pass for a foreign pilgrim, and none'll be the wiser."

Maggie had been almost afraid he wouldn't object to her suggestion, for she felt safe in his company, if not from dangers sorcerous and arcane, at least from those physical ones like ogres and goblins which were well within the competence of a bear's strength.

When the clock had been altered as he requested and he stood before her on his hind legs, paws concealed in the folds of the garment, she smiled with satisfaction at her handiwork and pulled the hood a little lower over his snout. "There. If you just keep your voice down and your claws hidden, your Highness, this might do the trick."

"You'd better make out that I'm fasting, as well, then," replied His Highness, "I'm not much for knives or forks these days."

It was odd coming into a town again after being in the woods and mountains for so long. There seemed to be too many buildings and too many people moving too quickly. The self-preoccupied looks on the faces of the townspeople as they brushed past the travelers forced Maggie to keep reminding herself that their own business was just as important and they needn't keep giving way before people. Though Dragon Bay was small, it was still much larger than a gypsy camp, where the bear had spent his last few years, or Maggie's home at Fort Iceworm. Many of the hurrying people were driving geese, ducks, cows, and pigs through the streets, so that the noises of those animals were mixed with the cries of their drivers and the general conversation of day-to-day commerce.

Careful to keep the bear as far as possible from the larger animals, Maggie looked around for a point of reference. "I'm not sure how to do this, now that we're here," she told the bear. "I feel so silly just walking up to someone and saying Excuse me, sir or madam, would you be so kind as to point the way to the nearest evil sorcerer?' I mean, how could they admit knowing someone like that? It would show they kept bad company." The bear nodded, but had no suggestions to offer.

Most of the structures along the shore street were fishermen's huts with boats docked at the front doors and nets set out to dry and mend. Several landings down from Maggie and the bear, some of the animals were being loaded onto a barge While they stood staring at the activity, a cow being driven down the street behind them came too close to His Highness's wild-smelling person and bolted, causing several other animals to engage in a miniature stampede.

The Prince pulled Maggie away before she could be run down by a flock of frantically bleating sheep, and the two of them fled up a narrow side street to avoid being trampled. When they had put another street between themselves and the bustling dock, Maggie collapsed against a building to catch her breath.

Regaining her composure, she slowly opened her eyes again and found herself staring into the open door of the

153

establishment on the opposite side of the street. Her hand went to the bear's shoulder. "Your Highness, isn't that the inn from the vision?"

"Hmph?" asked His Highness, allowing his snout to protrude slightly as he stood more erect. "I can't tell for sure. Haven't seen many inns lately, and, to tell the truth, we bears are a trifle near-sighted, but I'd say it is."

Maggie took a deep breath and held up crossed fingers to the bear before they entered the common room of the inn.

"Good day, good folk," said the same woman who had been so polite to Uncle Fearchar, sounding as though neither they nor the day actually met her specifications. She cast a critical eye over the scruffy girl and the great, hairy pilgrim, sniffed, and continued in a businesslike manner to set the table for her lodgers' evening meal. When she had finished and they still stood there, she said, "If you're looking for a place to stay, I'd think the Lorelei would be more to your liking. It's cheaper, and anyway, we're full up."

That was a fine way to talk to an enchanted prince and a semi-powerful witch, Maggie thought. She certainly hoped the woman would display more courtesy to other peculiar-looking travelers, or in this country she might find out how difficult it was for a toad to polish cutlery. At least she had been polite to Uncle Fearchar, which reminded Maggie of why they were there. "Thank you for your counsel, ma'am," she said with all the mildness she could muster, "but actually we were looking for a relative of mine."

"Oh?" said the woman. "We have few strangers here. Who is this relative?" She set down the rag and pitcher she had been using to clean the table and placed a fist on each ample hip, devoting her full steely-eyed attention to the bothersome intruders.

"My uncle, Fearchar Brown. I—er—was told he had been stopping here."

"Master Brown is a relative of *yours?*" The woman's lower jaw dropped as recognition of the common familial characteristics between niece and uncle began to redden her face. "Oh, do pardon me, Miss. As I say, we get so few strangers!" She hurried around the table to pull out a bench. "Pray, seat yourself and rest. I'll bring you a mug of tea and a bit of bread I baked this morning and send my boy around for Master Brown."

She called to the boy, who came running with much show of adolescent knees and elbows, and sent him on the errand, then turned anxiously back to Maggie and the bear, saying, "I'm sorry there's no butter today. Like all else in this town it goes bad very quickly. It's a pity the food we have to waste! There was a good catch this year, too, but how we'll get through the winter I don't know, I'm sure . . ."

"Doesn't salting and drying keep it well enough?" Maggie asked, more to stop the woman's babbling than because she was really interested.

"Salt!" snorted the wife, whose stare regained its former piercing severity. "I wouldn't poison my family and customers with that! It wrecks one's health, didn't you know that? And it has that horrid aftertaste, besides."

"It does?" Maggie's opinion that the woman was extremely peculiar and changeable and generally not much worth bothering about was confirmed. Even the bread she baked was absolutely tasteless, no doubt due to the woman's prejudice against salt, and with no butter to put on it Maggie thought she might have as well eaten a piece of the table instead. "You wouldn't happen to have a place where my companion and I could wash, would you?"

The woman's grimace of distaste said that no number of celebrated kinfolk could make up for the mess they would leave her washing all the grime from themselves. Of herself Maggie thought that that was probably correct, but it was unfair in the bear's case, since none of him was visible outside his cloak. "I'd have to charge you, Mistress," the woman said finally, "as that would require the use of one of my rooms."

"I'll trade you a preservative spell for it then," Maggie offered with exaggerated patience, "to keep your dismal fish fresh."

Making sure that Maggie kept her end of the bargain first, the woman supplied her with a bowl, pitcher, towel, and a scrap of homemade soap. She did not offer to heat a kettle of water, so Maggie had a wash no warmer than those she'd had since Castle Rowan.

She realized she had given the innkeeper's wife far more than fair value for her facilities, but she felt better when she came down the steps and saw the boy escorting a man into the room. The bear joined her silently at the foot of the steps and together they stepped forward to meet Fearchar Brown.

155

Like Granny Brown and Sybil and Maggie herself, Fearchar was clothed in brown, but with a difference.

His britches and jacket were of the finest cocoa-colored velvet, lavishly trimmed with gold embroideries of intertwined and elongated animals and intricately interwoven knots and lacings. His shirt was a shining cinnamon silk. Maggie and the innkeeper's wife curtsied. The bear pulled at the hood of his garment as though he were tipping a cap.

"The boy said a lady was inquiring for me, claiming to be some relation of mine," began Uncle Fearchar, speaking to the innkeeper's wife. She nodded at Maggie. Fearchar crossed to meet her, a smile lighting his face as he took her hands in his own well-kept and lavishly jeweled ones. "She is most certainly kin of mine! You must be the baby Bronwyn was about to have before I left!" he cried. Maggie thought she saw pleasure in his preliminary survey of her.

"Yes, Uncle. Maggie, sir."

"I gave them my best bread and tea," chirped the proprietress, "and they're all washed and rested and comfy."

Fearchar turned to her coldly. "You may leave us now, madam. But a bottle of wine to celebrate our reunion would not be amiss."

They sat sipping the wine while they talked. His Highness drank nothing, but did join them at the table, slumping somewhat, as his bear's anatomy was not well-suited to formal dining. As Fearchar began to talk, Maggie had been surprised to hear the beginnings of a growl rumble within the cloaked figure.

"Now then, dear girl, what brings you so far from Fort Iceworm? Your—ah—your mother and father are well, I trust."

"My mother is dead, Uncle."

"I'm so sorry to hear it. Your Grandmother? How is dear Maudie?"

"She's fine, Uncle. Actually, what we came for I mean— I—" she was distracted and forgot what she was going to say as the growl from the bear built to the point that Uncle Fearchar tried to peer into the cowl.

"Excuse me, good pilgrim. I didn't quite catch that?" he said.

The prince threw back his hood and jumped up on the bench, grabbing Fearchar by the jacket with his great front paws, "Prepare to die, varlet, or hand over my boy's heart!

For eight long years your hateful voice has been ringing in my ears."

Maggie tried to drag the bear off her uncle by pulling on the cloak the bear wore, but it came off as she pulled, and she fell backwards.

Uncle Fearchar seemed to have regained control of the situation, though the bear still had him in hand, or paw. "I beg your pardon, my dear bear," he said into his Highness's snarling maw. "Would you perhaps be the Prince of Ablemarle come after the remedy for your enchantment?"

Maggie thought that even His Highness felt the strong, compassionate sincerity in her uncle's voice, for he was lowering him to his seat even as he growled, "Come to you for one last drink of the marrow of men's bones if you're not quick enough about doing as I say, sorcerous scum."

Unruffled, other than his clothing, Uncle Fearchar smoothed his lapels and clucked over a winestain where his coattails had dragged in his cup when he was hoisted aloft. He returned his attention to the bear. His expression was one of mingled martyrdom and pity.

"My dear bear, it is true that I cast a spell upon you and procured for Xenobia the spell to remove young David's heart, but let's be gentlemen about this, shall we? You must realize that even a sorcerer of my stature has a living to earn." The bear's growl had died down to a grumble again but he didn't appear particularly impressed. The sorcerer continued. "It was for your own character development that you had to be transformed; surely you can see that now? In abusing the faith of poor Xenobia, you transgressed, betraying not only a woman who loved you, but your own principles. In your feckless fickle state you would hardly have made a good ruler for your country or a decent father to your son. I simply aided the lady in providing you with an object lesson. The removal of Davey's heart was part of the plan. Through the whole procedure we were only thinking of the ultimate personal growth you would achieve by the time you got to this point. We felt that in observing Davey relating to others with no regard for their emotional safety, you would come to understand how irresponsible and unworthy such behavior is. Obviously we were correct, or you would not be here now, waiting for me to institute the last of my remedial conditions to the spell."

To Maggie's surprise, the bear had by now ceased growling, and after listening quietly for a moment or two had begun nodding happily. "Yes, yes, I see it all now. How stupid of me to think that there was anything wicked in such a valuable lesson. Are you sure I'm quite worthy now to regain my human form?"

Fearchar nodded gravely. "You can be helped, yes. If you and my lovely niece will be so kind as to accompany me..."

The bear brushed his snout with a front paw. Maggie recognized the gesture as one of embarrassment. "Of course. Whatever you say. Hope I didn't hurt you there, sir," he added sheepishly, for a bear.

"Wait a moment," Maggie said, bewildered at all the revelations and sudden attitude changes taking place. "Maybe both of you understand all of this, but..." Her uncle turned a look of deep concern and interest on her, mingled with avuncular pride, and she stumbled through the rest of her phrase. "If you're the sorcerer who has caused all of his problems, then you must be the one who's caused mine too, and you must know where Winnie is, and..."

He patted her hand and looked deeply into her eyes, smiling reassuringly. "Of course I know where she is, dear child. She is at my home, an honored guest. She will be so thrilled to know you're coming to see her. When my trusted servant, known to you as Hugo the Peddler, found the poor girl in her sad state, he naturally brought her to me.

"Although Lord Rowan and I are, as you may or may not know, both contenders for the throne, Lady Amberwine is, after all, related to my family. I wished to spare her further pain and humiliation, and let her have her baby far from those who would chastise her for her girlish folly. Hugo feared if she knew he represented me, she would not come with him, so he instead allowed her to believe he came from your father. I hope we were in time. Hers is a delicate nature, and I fear her bitter recent experiences may have caused her lasting harm." He tapped his head with a forefinger.

Maggie found herself nodding agreement and promising to do whatever she could to help. She could see now that Fearchar had only been trying to save her sister, and a lucky thing it was, too. "That was so kind of you, Uncle. When is she to return to Lord Rowan?"

"To Rowan? Oh, Maggie, surely you must realize by now that while I bear him no malice, I do feel that Rowan is a dangerous and unpredictable man. I had hoped you would

158

help me persuade your sister to accept the hospitality of my castle until her babe is born and they are in condition to travel with you to your father's home again. Perhaps you, too, would grace my castle for awhile? To keep His Highness company?" His Highness bowed, and Maggie nodded her head.

Uncle Fearchar had told them the trip from Dragon Bay to his castle on Evil Island would be novel, as it was. His boat was not propelled by means of the wind, but was elegantly pulled by three giant swans, black as the pupil of an eye, the same that Maggie had seen flying over the Northern Woods.

Hugo had met them at the dock and helped them aboard and made them comfortable, but in spite of what she now knew, that the peddler was her Uncle's major-domo and confidante, she still disliked him. There was the mysterious matter of the rabbit and the arrow he saw being fired at her father that hadn't yet been explained to her satisfaction... perhaps she'd have an opportunity to talk to Uncle Fearchar about it privately. Twice the peddler touched her, once in helping her to climb into the boat and another time in settling a soft velvet robe over her shoulders to keep off the chill from the bay. Both times she failed to suppress an involuntary shudder.

As the swans pulled them noiselessly through the water, Uncle Fearchar pointed out the bargeload of animals making its way across the Bay in a course that was at an oblique angle to their own. "Ah," said Fearchar. "There's a colorful local sight for you. Our beast barge on its way to the feeding grounds."

"Why's that?" the bear asked. "Do you take it upon yourself to feed the beasts the stockmen have no food for?"

"Hardly that," he laughed. "The animals are part of my Dragon Days program." He waited modestly for them to ask about it, but when they didn't, continued. "Dragon Days is a little project of mine, you see, to rid the area of the maraudings of the monster. All it took was having a heart-to-heart chat with him."

"It seems to me, heart-to-heart chats with dragons could be a little risky," commented His Highness.

"I am fortunate enough to be exceedingly brave," admitted Fearchar, "and just happened to have along at the time a powerful sleeping powder, in case he proved nasty."

"So how does this Dragon Days business work?" Maggie asked.

"It's a simple arrangement. I persuaded the dragon that it would be less trouble all around if we, the citizens of Dragon Bay, supplied him with a diet filling and nutritious enough to meet a dragon's requirements, to be delivered to a certain place every month in time for his feedings. That way, he ceases snatching children and prize livestock, and we are no longer subject to his depredations. He also doesn't have to risk getting skewered by some knight errant abnormally strong and abysmally stupid enough to try to beard him in his den, as it were."

"Brilliant," agreed Maggie and the bear in unison, watching both Fearchar and the disappearing barge with such avid new interest that they failed to notice when the boat landed.

"You must get a lot of exercise climbing up and down this path just to get to your own front door," observed Maggie. Although she was used to the rigors of travel, or so she told herself before undertaking new ones, she found the almost perpendicular trail from landing to castle gate severely taxing.

"As I recall," said the bear, who had shed the pilgrim's robe and dropped to all fours for more comfortable climbing, "that's the way of castles. You must keep in mind, gurrl, one usually wants to keep one's own folk in, while discouraging the rowdy element without. Wouldn't do to make it easy, would it?"

"I seldom use this route, actually," said Fearchar. "Generally one of my familiars," he indicated the swans, now unharnessed from the boat and gracing the Bay, "flies me wherever I wish to go. Since Dragon Days takes place so close to home, however, I feel that when I go to the village to act on its behalf as the event's sponsor, it is incumbent on me to travel more or less in the mode of the local people."

The bear nodded gravely. "The common touch. Very wise of you. My father used to tell me that was a very important asset to a king."

Maggie murmured between labored breaths that it must be lovely to fly through the air like that, though she recalled the similar flight she and Colin had taken on Grizel's back with something less than relish.

160

The path went up even more steeply at that point and their breath was required for climbing.

The front gate was surrounded by carved stone, and its wood was embellished with carvings as well. Fearsome creatures scowled down at them, goblin guardians frozen in stone, permanently, Maggie hoped. She was considerably taken aback by its ugliness, but the bear sniffed appreciatively the work on the door, a pictorial panel dramatizing the exploits of several of the horrific creatures.

"Hmm, interesting. I say, Brown, this is quite old, isn't it?"

"I'm afraid so," said Uncle Fearchar with a put-upon sigh. Hugo opened the door and they started up a flight of stone steps which lead through myriad carved archways. The shadows in these arched passages seemed to harbor chill and gloom. "It was built before Argonia was properly settled, I believe, as an outpost for the ancient Drumclog civilization. That's all I can get out of it."

"All you can get out of it?" Maggie asked, continually astounded by the sheer breadth and miscellany of what proved to be her uncle's magic. "You mean you can talk to the walls?"

He led them through a dank gray hallway and to another carved door. "No," he said, "but there are these runes, as you see here." He indicated the characters on the carving. "Shortly after I took up residence here I noticed them and, as soon as I was able, secured wax impressions. The princess was able to —er—enlighten me regarding their meaning." Their steps made hardly a patter on the bare stone floor of the great, high-ceilinged entrance hall.

Maggie looked up, turning on her heel to catch the last rays of sunlight shining on the walls high above them. The windows were set high and narrow, a wonderful source of light for the dust motes and any possible bats, not much use for people. At least she couldn't see any bats in the plaster-work.

"You know the princess?" she asked, belatedly tagging after them.

"My goodness, yes, child." He ushered them ceremoniously through a hall, a sharp left turn, and at last they found themselves in a room the size of Maggie's village.

"My study," said Fearchar. "Drafty at times, but it has enough space for my projects." His projects, the ones they

161

could see displayed, included a complete dragon's skeleton, maps of every imaginable place made into tapestries and hung from the walls, a model of the capitol city and the palace, complete with pullaway walls to display the rooms' interiors ("I've been planning how to decorate—just in case"), and another entire wall of pigeonholes containing scrolls and parchments, presents from the princess, "all beautifully illuminated, of course." High above the scholarly materials, metal cases shaped like men caught the bear's attention and Fearchar explained. "Those were given to me by the wizard who originated the spell for turning you into a bear, Highness. Met him at the World-Wide Wizard's conference right after I moved south. We've corresponded since, and I've visited him swanback once or twice. Those cases are used to protect the bodies of the soldiers in his country from their enemies."

"Ingenious," exclaimed the bear. "What won't they think of next?"

Maggie was running from one table to another, picking up things and putting them down again, turning them over and examining them. It was the most exciting room she'd ever been in.

"We'll spend lots of time here together, you and I, my dear," said Fearchar indulgently. "Right now, come along and see the rest of my diggings, and greet your sister."

A second door led them to a dining hall, which was cozier than the study, but still enormous. "This was formerly a foyer leading from the great hall to the kitchen and the tower," Fearchar explained, "but I needed the space in the great hall for my study, and the food arrives here much warmer without having to travel the extra distance." For a foyer, it was an elegant dining hall, Maggie thought. The table was made of a massive slab of mirror-like wood, red as wine, and the legs were great beams of the same wood intricately carved and polished. Tapestries covered the walls and upholstered the matching chairs, which looked more like thrones with their high backs and arm rests. A heating stove, lavishly decorated with black and gold tiles, wrapped around one corner of the room and provided extra seating space beside itself, comfortably tiled to bring the warmth of the stove to the lounger on chilly days.

"The stove is my own addition. A suggestion of the wizard I was telling you of. Now then, Your Highness, Hugo will have a nice den prepared for you in the room next to my own, upstairs, where it's warmer." He indicated a flight of steps which led to a long, narrow landing forming a balcony high above them. "Maggie, dear, I presumed you would wish to share Lady Amberwine's tower chamber. We live simply," his sweeping arm took in the lavish room carpeted not with reeds but with the pelts of many different varieties of fur-bearing animals, "but I trust you'll be comfortable here."

"Thank you, Uncle," she said, turning toward the staircase.

A clatter from the room beyond and Hugo came bustling out, carrying a tray full of candles. "I hadn't time to put these in the rooms, master. Perhaps the prince and Miss Maggie would be so kind as to carry them up with them?"

Climbing the staircase, Maggie looked back down once to see her uncle waving her to go on up and Hugo lighting the first of the serpent-oil lamps in the huge fixture that hung from the lofty arched ceiling above the dining table. She set the bear's candle in his chamber for him, as it was awkward for him to carry it in his front paws, and walked back down the landing to the doorway set into the rounded stonework, the tower entrance at the top of the staircase. There was another stairwell within the tower, and as Maggie climbed she lit the lamps that studded the wall to light the way.

She looked forward eagerly to seeing Winnie, and found her lying fully-dressed on top of the uncurtained bed, her hands clasped above the hillock of her abdomen.

Calling to her as she crossed the room, and eliciting no response, Maggie sat on the edge of the bed and shook her. "Winnie, do wake up. It's Maggie. I'm here. I've come all this way to find you, the least you can do is postpone your nap."

Lady Amberwine opened the startling long-lashed green eyes that matched the deep emerald of her gown. Her confusion changed to fright and she shrank from her sister's touch. "Oh, Maggie. please don't slay me! I know I've disgraced you all, and you've no reason to spare me or this gypsy child I bear, but for the sake of . . ."

"For the sake of sanity, what are you talking about?" asked Maggie, sitting sharply back. "Slay you? Box your ears, maybe, for talking such nonsense but—oh, no, now, stop that. Please stop being a goose and come back here. Of course I won't box your ears, or slay you either. Why should I do that?"

"I—I don't know, but I know that's why you're here." Winnie's hands twisted and pulled at the bedcovering as she clawed her way as far from Maggie as possible.

"Winnie, it's me, your sister. I've ridden and walked a very long way, and risked great danger and more inconvenience to bring you home to Fort Iceworm, if you'll come. If I wanted to be rid of you I'd hardly have gone to all that trouble, would I?"

Winnie looked at her skeptically, but edged a bit closer. "I suppose not. Still . . ."

Maggie reached forward to touch her again and Amberwine sprang back, whimpering "no" as though she'd slapped her.

Maggie sat back up, folding her hands deliberately in her lap as she searched her sister's face for some clue to explain the meaning of her strange behavior. Had her difficulties, as Uncle Fearchar suggested, succeeded in unhinging her reason? Could faery people even go insane? Maggie looked at herself in the mirror opposite the foot of the bed. No, she had not changed into some ogress or ravening beast. What, then, could make the sister for whom she had forsaken unicorns and braved dragons, floods, ravishment, and starvation treat her like the proverbial wicked stepsister? A tear trickled down each cheek. Maggie continued to stare at the cowering Amberwine, brushing the tears away impatiently until they soon were too many for a casual wipe and she had to give in to clutching her face in her hands to try to stem the flow.

For all that she feared her sister for what she believed was good reason, Winnie loved her, too, and seeing her cry wrenched loose tears of Amberwine's own. Now—long after she believed she had cried her life's supply of them, the salty-liquid flooded her eyes, nose, and mouth, and she gathered Maggie to her, both of them rocking and weeping copiously until at last Winnie dragged forth her handkerchief. She always had been the one who had the clean handkerchief and she applied one corner to Maggie's face and one corner to her own, saying, "Do stop crying now. Come on, everything is alright and we're together. Stop now. I really can't bear it. If you don't cease this minute I shall go right back to sleep."

"It—it's just," Maggie began, her own teary purge slowly subsiding, "it's just that I can't stand it if you hate me. You've always been my best friend. How c—can you have changed so?"

164

"Hate you? Changed? Rubbish! Whatever are you going on about?" She recalled being startled on waking to see Maggie for some reason, the nerves of pregnancy probably. But she could hardly recall saying anything like that. "Of course I don't hate you, Magpie. You're my very own dear brave big sister and I love you, of course. I'm ever so glad you've come to fetch me away from here."

"You are?"

Winnie nodded and jumped from the bed to a beautifully embroidered screen close to the door, thrust the screen aside and pulled out a dress. "We really must be changing for dinner now." Maggie could see what Winnie, who never liked tears, was up to, but refused to be distracted.

"Winnie, if you're so glad to see me, then whatever was all that stuff about slaying you?"

"Slay me? What stuff? I must have had a nightmare or something. I haven't slept at all well since I left the castle, you know. I've been feeling so awful about what I said to Roari. I don't know why I said that. Roari must be very put out with me for being so pert when he asked me not to ride off with that gypsy. He was right, of course, as usual. Davey was a dreadful person, and that mother of his! I can't think why I went with him—something about that song—oh, well, I'm sure Roari won't stay upset with me after the baby's born, do you think?" She dragged from behind the screen a flame-colored dress. "Now this would look lovely on you. Try it on. We have to do our own toilette here. Hugo's the only servant, and I'd hardly want him to help, would you?" she giggled.

Maggie was staring at her with a mixture of annoyance and perplexity, trying to make some sense of her babbling. Her manner now was more the one Maggie had expected, but her contradictory behavior was weird in the extreme. "Just a moment, Win. You distinctly said that the *reason* I was going to slay you was because you had disgraced us all and that your baby was going to be a gypsy."

Amberwine had hung the flame-colored gown back behind the screen and extracted a pale gold one. "Not your color, I think. It would look better on me." She patted her abdomen. "Fortunately, these gowns were tailored by a brownie seamstress, and alter themselves to fit even me."

"Still—now then, I said—what did you say? Oh, yes? Now that's astounding. I should hardly think I'd say that, Maggie.

165

Really, dear, how could my baby be a gypsy? Unless something happened as I slept, and as I distinctly recall I was already becoming extremely plump around the middle and doing unladylike things in the morning before I left Castle Rowan. I just was on my way to consult Cook about it when I heard him singing. Lovely voice for such a slimy sort of boy. Don't know what put me up to it, I'm sure."

"You are being inconsistent, you know." Maggie was beginning to feel disoriented.

"Part of my charm, so I've been told. Oh, Magpie, I'm so very glad to see you. Do please stop being dreary about my silly nightmares and try on this topaz gown. I'll fix your hair, and you fix mine, and there are even jewels to match—darling, I tell you, this is the first time I've felt cheerful in MONTHS, and I'm absolutely giddy!"

"I can tell."

"Master Brown is quite the gay blade, you know, really. There's a siren who comes to visit—I've seen him talking to her from the battlements when I take my walks. Also, I have been informed by Hugo that we are privileged to be sharing the wardrobe your uncle provides Princess Pegeen when she comes to call. She brings her own entourage, of course, but she has them carrying so many scrolls and ink pots they don't have room for dresses. Awfully careless of her appearance, I've been told, but frightfully clever."

"I suspect she wouldn't find it very grand here after the palace," Maggie said, reluctantly allowing herself to be diverted.

"As long as she has her runes, she's fine, so they say. She doesn't live at the palace any more. She has the best-attended hermitage in Argonia, from what I hear. Do you like your hair up like this, or with a little hanging down? Softer that way, do you think?

"I don't care..." Certain that she was losing her mind, Maggie allowed her sister to help her prepare for dinner.

166

16

Colin and Bosun Neddy Pinchpurse, the former pirate, were spending their off-duty time on deck, where they would not disturb the other crew members who slept. Backs propped against the fo'c's'le, they were engaged in swapping ditties. Neddy was teaching Colin variations on the chanties he had learned in school, and Colin was teaching Neddy some new jigs to play on his hornpipe.

The evening was soft and pleasant, and the deck swayed beneath them only a little, in rhythm with the gentle swell of the silvery gulf waters. The cheerful twiddling of their music drifting across the fresh salt air made the men on duty step lightly at their work, disliking to move too quickly or too loudly for fear of missing the tune.

Colin was enjoying himself immensely on this voyage. The only way it could have possibly been better was if he were not bound to leave behind at Dragon Bay the new friends he had made, and the occupation he was learning to love. For the first time since he'd sung a song in his little-boy soprano, or used his aunt's clay pots as a drum, he had discovered something that he was good at, something that came naturally to him. He had fully expected to disappoint the sailors he'd met at the waterfront tavern. He thought that when they were all sober, they'd see that he was no good at sailing, had had no experience. He had been sure he'd be unable to do anything properly. Although he had told them he knew nothing of sailing, he was sure they at least expected him to be able to do unskilled manual work on shipboard without falling over into the sea or becoming ill—and to his surprise, he discovered that he was. And not only that, he did what was required quickly and well, and didn't need to be told twice. If not for his promises to help Zorah and Maggie, nothing would have made him happier than to stay there, learn to be a sailor, and specialize in songs of the sea.

Instead, he was sitting with Neddy now, sharing songs instead of adventures on foreign shores. He was due to leave them on the morrow, when the *Snake's Bane* docked at Dragon Bay, delivering the last kegs of molasses and ale, the last bolts of linen, and the last of the metal farming implements imported from abroad. For over a week now the *Bane* had been making similar stops at the little towns and settlements that punctuated the arms, legs, nooks, and crannies of the Gulf of Gremlins like suckers on an octopus's legs.

"Land ho!" the lookout cried.

"Ah, let's see now. Must be the first of the Dragon Isles," said Neddy, rising to his feet and unfolding the spyglass that hung around his neck. Colin had never seen such a wonderful thing, unless it was Sybil Brown's crystal. Neddy could see almost as far as the lookout, who carried a similar object. These were made, he had been told, by foreign wizards, and cost nearly as much as the ship's entire cargo. Neddy had implied he had not had to pay the full exorbitant amount for his.

"May I see?" Colin asked. Pinchpurse held it up to him and, awkwardly, he hunched down to peer into it over the bosun's shoulder. At length he was able to spy the rough rock silhouetted against the sea and twilight.

"What d'ye see, lad?" joked one of the men who had been at the tavern in Queenston. "Was the lookout right or no?"

"Right enough, Liam," Colin grinned back.

"Then we're almost done paddling about in the bath, and it's time to go for the open sea. One more stop and we're seamen again! Calls for a celebration, if you ask me."

"Journeyman Minstrel Apprentice Seaman Songsmith here and I might just be able to oblige you, boys!" cried Neddy, blowing a note on his hornpipe.

What they lacked in wine and women they made up in song. Some of those who had been sleeping belowdecks came up to join them, and the captain emerged from his chartroom to demonstrate his dance style to Neddy's hornpipe. The lookout's relief stood his watch a bit early, as it was the man sighted the first island who was also the concertina player. Ching came up from the galley, where he had been serving as ship's cat, switching his tail at first as though annoyed to be wakened from his catnap. He soon settled, purring, at Colin's feet, though, as the minstrel and his fiddle led the crewmen in one song after another.

Looking out across the water, Colin watched the waves roll as he sang, and noticed a few fine fingers of mist were beginning to drift across the surface, and also that the island they had sighted with the glass was now quite visible to the naked eye.

As he sang the second chorus, he thought they must be either drifting slowly into a cloud hanging low on the water or else the mist was advancing, a great deal more of it than he'd first thought.

By the twelfth verse of the song, the mist had become a fog, sending soft smoky tendrils dancing up the hull and onto the deck, caressing men and mast alike until, by the end of the song, Colin could scarcely see Neddy, seated right beside him. Also, Neddy wasn't playing or singing any more. Neither was anyone else. Colin had finished the chorus solo. No one now suggested another, or said anything, or moved, for that matter.

After a few minutes of listening to himself breathe and watching the mist, Colin asked, "Unusual weather we're having, isn't it, mates?"

"Quiet, boy," said Ned. "We're listening."

"Listening to what?" He strained his own excellent ear, and perhaps it was from wanting to hear what they did, but he thought he just might be catching something...

"To her, of course."

"Her who? Where?"

Neddy turned to him viciously. "Are you going to shut your craw, or must I shut it for you?" Colin suddenly remembered that the older man had once been a pirate and gulped, flushing hotly. Whatever they were hearing, he certainly couldn't make it...

He heard her then, at first softly, and then as her voice grew louder and he recognized it, his pulse began to race with hope. Maggie! The same husky alto, singing so low he had to exert his full attention to make out the words.

And everyone was listening. He really had never thought her voice all that fine, himself, but as the mist swirled and parted and joined and parted again in flying diaphanous banners, he could see the other men, still where they should

169

be working, spellbound gray-blurred ghosts listening so intently that even the steersman had abandoned the steering, leaning over the wheel, ears straining.

"How sweet she sings!" whispered Neddy.

"Ah, there never was one to sing sweeter," sighed the second officer.

"I'd no idea you all knew her," Colin said with amazement. 'You certainly didn't mention it when I was telling you about her."

"Quiet! Can't you hear Mother singing me favorite nursery rhyme?"

The conversation was violently shushed by the rest of the crew.

Colin's curiosity was at last able to overpower his desire to hear the song with which Maggie called to him. "Your MOTHER? She's young enough to be your grandchild!" They were about to pitch him overboard when he finally made out the words Maggie sang. It was a tender love song, personally addressed to him.

"There's something funny going on here, lads," he said, and for the first time realized how dangerous their posture was to them all. Snatching up his fiddle, he ducked around them and made for the rigging, climbing high enough that they would be unable to interfere with him right away. Maggie's voice continued to cajole in a tone more alluring than even her dance for the gypsy had been.

He felt another weight drag at the rigging, and looked down to see Chingachgook, all four paws entangled in the ropes, trying to reach his pant leg.

He had not time to spare for cats, though, or even tuning, as he began to saw at his fiddle and yell out the loudest, rowdiest, bawdiest, funniest songs he could think of, not quite drowning out that insidious voice Maggie was using, even at that. If not for his training at singing rounds and part-harmonies, he could never have sustained the concentration it took to sing what he was singing and ignore that voice. As it was, he was able to keep it up long enough to provide a suitably maddening distraction for his fellow crew members, who began to try to shake him down, anger contorting their faces, covering up the song themselves now with their own hostile threats.

It was Pinchpurse who first came to his senses and shook off the enchantment, and he wasted no time at wresting the

170

wheel from the spellbound steersman. "Siren, you lubbers! To your stations!" he hollered, every sinew straining as he pulled the wheel hard to the right, away from the rock that suddenly loomed up at them from the sea.

As the *Bane* heaved away from its own bane, it lurched violently. Pinchpurse hung fast to the wheel to keep it from turning back again, and the other two sailors clung to the rails, almost washed overboard. The others held onto whatever seemed stationary. Colin, cat, and fiddle made a somersaulting dive across the decks, over the railing, and into the sea.

17

By now Maggie was unsure of everything, including why she was creeping down the stone staircase in the middle of the night. Earlier, when she'd left her uncle that afternoon, it had all been very clear.

He was a wonderful fellow, cared about her welfare more than Winnie, the bear, her grandmother, Colin, or Aunt Sybil, and possibly more than she cared about herself. She wanted very much to do something nice for him—something grand and special to show how much she appreciated the interest he took in her.

It wasn't until she began casting around for an idea of what to do that it occurred to her she hadn't used her own power since they'd left the inn at Dragon Bay. And that was peculiar. Now that she thought about it, he had never even inquired as to what manner of witch she was. All he'd done, really, was to tell her how very beautiful he thought her, far prettier than Winnie really, and tell her how she deserved better than a post as a village witch. And show her all of those wonderful magic gifts all of those powerful friends of his were constantly showering upon him, like the spells for turning people into bears (which was done chemically, not just from raw power, as Gran did it) and the giant black swans and this castle.

She straightened her shoulders to squeeze the chill from between them, and boldly tiptoed down three more steps. He didn't really need her talent, she knew, for Hugo did all the cooking. Hugo doubtlessly had also long ago informed his master of the magical peculiarities of his niece at Fort Iceworm. She wondered that he hadn't mentioned the death of her mother, as well. But even if he knew about her talent, she was still miffed that her uncle hadn't asked her to do anything, so she thought she would surprise all of them with a lovely feast from whatever raw materials she could find in the kitchen. Which brought her to this point, hovering at the foot of the stairs, trying to remember which direction to take to find the kitchen door. She knew where it *had* been in the clear light of day, but in the darkness her sense of direction had deserted her.

She thought her eyes must be adjusting to the dark, finally, when she saw a faint lightening of the gloom to her right. A moment more and she should be able to continue.

It was odd, too, how once she'd decided she wanted to make Uncle Fearchar a feast, and had excused herself to take a walk along the parapets to ponder her menu, that the mirror in her pocket began to feel uncomfortably warm, even through her skirt. She pulled it out and stared at herself in it, which was all it seemed to be good for since the visions were used up. "If you still worked," she'd mumbled at it, "I'd try to see Aunt Sybil and find out what dishes he likes especially. I do wish it would be something tastier than what we've had so far." To her surprise, the rainbow glow had appeared in the mirror and her aunt's face followed it.

"Maggie, dear! How exciting! I've done it!" she said.

"Aunt Sybil, I thought your visions couldn't talk to you—or rather you couldn't talk to them— how is it that you're talking to me when you're in the mirror?"

"Because you're in the glass as well. Simultaneous sightings! My dear, we may have made a major breakthrough."

"But how did we happen to use glasses at the same time? And why is this one working? Weren't three visions all I got?"

"But you didn't use three, darling, or I'd never have been able to reach you this way. It was because you hadn't used your last one I wanted to try to contact you and see how you were doing. There's some barrier at Castle Rowan, and when I tried to find you there, I met with failure. Have you found Amberwine yet?"

"Oh—yes, I have. And Auntie—I've met Uncle Fearchar. He's a wonderful man and—"

"He is? You mean to say you've met your UNCLE Fearchar., my brother?"

"Yes, I have and he's, as I've said, a wonderful man and—"

"Well, well. Will wonders never cease?" Her aunt said softly.

Maggie was as puzzled as her aunt appeared to be. "What wonders?"

"Never mind, dear. I'm so glad you've found your sister. How's young Colin? Will you be starting for home again soon?"

"I haven't seen Colin lately. But he was quite well when I saw him last—though in a bit of a hurry. I believe we'll probably stay here with Uncle Fearchar until Winnie's baby is born. Aunt Sybil?"

"Yes, child?"

"I wanted to ask you about something. What does Uncle Fearchar like to eat? He hasn't but one servant, and the man can't cook at all. Everything is flat and bland. I thought I'd fix something nice . . . "

Her aunt's pleasant, candid features took on a stiff mask of reserve. "I really don't recall, Maggie, what your uncle likes. It used to be that he didn't like any of us well enough to mention the matter."

"Sorry I asked. He's changed, though, since then. I'm sure. Did you know he's to be one of the nominees for the crown?"

Sybil looked startled. "No! Who told you that?"

"He did."

Her aunt laughed so hard she began to fade from the glass till at last there were only her bright brown eyes twinkling in among the rainbow lights, saying, "Maggie, dear, you really must take Fearchar with a grain of salt."

Salt. That was what made the food so bad, of course. The lack of salt. It must be that Hugo, like the woman at the inn, upheld some local prejudice against salt, and would not use it. Everything had been so exciting since she'd gotten here that she hadn't really been that aware of what she was putting in her mouth, except that it might have been sand for all the impression it made. Poor Uncle Fearchar, who was not raised in these parts, doubtless had accustomed himself to the saltlessness of the region.

Shuffling slowly towards the light patch she'd noticed before, Maggie barked her shin on one of the low decorative tables her uncle kept beside the ornate stove. This was like playing pin the tail on the cart horse! She wished she'd brought Winnie along for company, if not security, but Winnie acted oddly about Uncle Fearchar. Though she always said he had been good and kind to her, she certainly persisted in looking quaking and weepy in his company, though she reverted to almost her normal sunny self again with Maggie,

174

and never again mentioned their first conversation. Maggie thought her sister probably secretly disliked Uncle Fearchar, but hated to say so after all he had done for her. She ought to have asked her to come, after all. Even if Winnie didn't like him, she wouldn't have minded helping—then the darkness would have been less intimidating—and Winnie would have insisted they bring a candle.

As she was considering how much noise it would raise if she should cause the fire in the tile stove to kindle, thus getting both warmth and light, the patch of light to her right began to glow brighter, and to grow. First the legs, then the body, and finally the arms—shimmering pale and eerie they were—but certainly legs, body and arms of a once-human entity. Maggie waited for the head to form as well, but it failed to appear.

A headless ghost then. All too common in a land where bounty on an enemy had been awarded the dispatcher of that enemy on receipt by interested parties of the head of said enemy. Or something like that. Bounties had been outlawed since Maggie was a child, but she'd come across one of the scrolls government officials used to read aloud. At the time she'd been disappointed there were no famous outlaws mentioned, but her father explained it was the custom to save expensive scribed parchment by having the name added orally at the time the scroll was publicly read.

She was very curious to know if this headless ghost was that of some notorious bandit or other, but could hardly expect it to speak without a head. Raising an armload of ghostly clanking chains, the spectre floated towards her. For chains that appeared as insubstantial as the wraith itself, they made an awful racket.

"Do be quiet," she whispered. "I appreciate the light, but I'd rather not wake everybody. It's a—" she broke off, shivering, as the ghost brushed her gown. It was hovering before her now, in the opposite direction from where it had been. Slowly, it beckoned.

Maggie followed hopefully. Perhaps, since it was easier for ghosts to find their way in the dark, it would lead her to the kitchen. Although she couldn't imagine what a ghost would want with a kitchen, particularly a decapitated ghost.

As the ghost passed through the room's furnishings, the cold light it shed illuminated them, so that if Maggie kept very close behind the spectre she was able to miss most of the obstacles in her path. Unfortunately, she did not see the outline of the door when the ghost passed through it, and got quite a nasty jolt when she did not pass through it as easily. It was as she was recovering from this that she heard the voices on the other side of the door, slightly raised to make themselves heard above the clanking of the chains.

"Damn, Hugo!" her uncle's voice said. "There it is again. I do wish you had heeded me when I told you that murdering a man in his own home invariably leads to an impossible tenacious haunting—shoo, you! Get away!" The last, Maggie imagined, was not spoken to Hugo.

"I know you told me, but you talk so much I have to give my ears a break once in a while. Besides, I thought if the dragon disposed of the body he'd have no reason to come back and haunt this hall."

"No reason, indeed! What about that head you hung on a stake at the threshold to greet me when I took possession? You have a grisly sense of humor, my friend."

"Don't go getting all lordly on me, Fearchar Brown. If your magic hadn't give out on you, you'd have talked that spook into moving to a sunnier climate and there'd have been no work for me to do."

"Give out on me indeed! Watch what you say or I'll convince you to go for a stroll on the Feeding Grounds yourself."

"Your wizardy wiles don't work on me, as well you know, Master Brown."

Maggie thought she heard a chuckle. Fearchar's?

"No, Hugo, you're too salty for me—just like poor Seagram here—oh, get out of here, I tell you! I haven't got your bloody head."

More clankings and an agitated rattling drowned out any conversation for a time. Maggie didn't think this ghost was one of the nasty sort who could actually do physical harm, but she worried for a moment. Even if he was a murderer, she didn't want her uncle slain by a ghost just when they were getting acquainted. The thought surprised her—she didn't quite understand why she felt it was alright for Uncle Fearchar to kill someone named Seagram but not alright for Seagram's ghost to kill Fearchar.

"Lucky for us at least some of the townsfolk follow your restriction on salt. Little Miss Maggie can be a regular terror.

I hate to think what would have happened if your magic hadn't worked on her and the bear."

"It did, though. My lovely niece, far from being a regular terror, has been gentle as a dove. Though it gave me pause, I'll admit, to see her and that so-called sister of hers reunited barely an hour after she was in the castle. And after all that wonderful speech I made the stupid faery cow about how little Maggie was out to kill her. If it wasn't for their red eyes and sniffles at the dinner table, I'd never have known how they found me out. I had Amberwine so terrified of Maggie I'd have sworn she'd jump out the window when she first saw her."

"Window's not big enough."

"Unfortunately. But as I was saying, I am pleased with my little niece. She'll make a beautiful queen, don't you think?"

Maggie pulled her earlobe. Surely she hadn't heard that bit correctly. Queen? Could her great-uncle be thinking to marry her if he won the throne of Argonia?

"Don't count your chickens till they're in the nest, Brown. That bear can't sign nothin' proper till the gypsy gets here so you can turn him back into a man again. Then could be you'll have a problem with both of 'em. You can't make no sweet little bride out of Miss Maggie Brown neither. She'll be more queen than you or Davey, either one, can handle once she's away from you and on the throne of Ablemarle."

"Nonsense. She trusts me. Once you've finished your job—I say, you DID tell Lorelei what to do with that ship the swans saw Songsmith on, didn't you?"

"Lorelei does as she pleases, too, but she'll do it. And she wanted to know when you were going to keep that promise you made her when she gave you the song to charm her ladyship with. One of these days, Brown, you'll have to dry her out from all that salt water long enough to convince her she'd rather have some nice merman for a mate or else you'll be needin' a salt pool at the palace. Princess Pegeen wouldn't like that now, would she?"

"Never mind Lorelei and Princess Pegeen. They are my business. Yours is to redeem yourself for bungling that job you started on William Hood. Once you've done that, and removed my sister's subversive influence . . ."

"And I'll want half your bloody kingdom for that, I can tell you . . ."

"And when, once enthroned, my niece learns of the tragic loss of her lady sister, and the baby, of course, she'll naturally turn to her only relative for advice and assistance."

"And good old King Fearchar will be there with bells on to help the little witch out, eh?"

"Yes, I will. How I envy young Davey such a beautiful bride!"

"You only think she's good-looking because she's brown as a bear, just like you," Hugo said spitefully.

A long silence, then Fearchar saying, "Ahhh, yes, that's what I like about you, Hugo. You're so perceptive. Shall we retire?"

"Aye, I'm tired with all that fetching and carrying for you and the women and that bloody bear. And I expect you must be too, Master Brown. Becoming king of two countries on such short notice is bound to be tiring."

Maggie backed away from the door, hoping to hide in the darkness of the far corners of the room where their candlelight would not penetrate. She kept on backing, long after she ought to have reached a wall. The door creaked open and candlelight spilled into the room, lighting the men who bore the lamps with sinister shadows redundantly in keeping with their conversation.

They didn't see her, but ascended the stairs with no further conversation. When their lights had completely disappeared, Maggie whistled with relief, lowered herself to the floor, and sat there shaking with a delayed reaction to being nearly caught, to hearing so much derogatory information about her uncle while she was still technically spellbound, and to the alarming contents of the conversation. From all that they said, she had at least gathered the reason for lack of salt in their diet. It appeared to be some sort of antidote for Fearchar's magic, whose nature was still not entirely clear. She could stop her reaction to the aborted enchantment by finishing it off in the prescribed manner, now that she knew what it was. She ordered a fire to light in the nearest lamp. For a moment she saw the glow of the light, but didn't see the lamp, then realized it was behind and above her. Turning to fetch it down where she could use it to explore her medicine pouch, she found herself staring into two shining feral eyes.

"Hullo, gurrrl."

Maggie caught her breath again and took the candle from

178

the table to sit beside her on the floor. "Your Highness, you frightened me out of a year's growth."

"Sorry." He lumbered over and sat opposite her in the candlelight. "I don't like to look gluttonous at the dinner table, but I'm afraid that though I now think and talk as a man, I'm still hungry as a bear."

"Here, have some." She held out a palm full of salt she had taken from her medicine pouch. He licked her palm clean in one large slurp and she was very glad that he, at least, was her friend. Taking some salt herself, she began to feel better, and replied to his last remark. "Well, I hope you're feeling ferocious as a bear, too, then. We are in deep trouble."

When Maggie told him what she had learned, His Highness was all for charging upstairs and tearing Fearchar and Hugo to pieces. After hearing her uncle's plans for the demise of everyone near and dear to her, Maggie was by no means unconvinced of the merit of the plan. She did suggest that perhaps he could just restrain them while she either flayed them or set fire to their underclothes, she hadn't made up her mind which, perhaps a combination of both.

"The only problem is Colin."

"Why's Colin a problem, gurrl? We'll save him a piece!"

"They said someone named Lorelei was supposed to know what to do about Colin and a ship he's on, but that was really all they said."

"Likely unpleasant," said His Highness.

"Likely," Maggie agreed, sitting back down and unashamedly chewing a fingernail.

"We could force them to tell, then tear 'em to pieces."

"We could."

"How long does the salt help after your uncle starts his razzlin' and dazzlin'?"

"I don't know. Maybe it only helps afterwards. And there's the matter of Davey's heart too, Prince. Uncle Fearchar said that after Davey gets here he was going to change you back into a man so you could sign something."

"Writ of abdication."

"What?"

"It's a document, gurrl, says I give up all title and claim to the throne. Of course, by being absent more than seven years, I've done that. But if, as you say, Brother Worthless is having a hard time at the kinging, Fearchar probably has a few of my old supporters lined up to accept me back as

179

king—with his quick tongue, your uncle will have no problem substituting my son. Especially with a writ of abdication signed by me, naming Davey as my successor."

"And Xenobia and Davey are in his power."

"Too right. And he plans that you'll be as well. I still say we tear 'em to pieces. I can get out of them what's happened to young Colin, and we'll search the castle for the heart at our leisure..."

"But after we find it, what if it doesn't work, and my uncle is dead. Then what will we do?"

The bear narrowed his little eyes at her. "Doesn't sound to me, gurrrl, as though you want to tear 'em to pieces any more."

"I suppose not. I just think we could find out more if he thinks we can't use anything he tells us. I'll expand my salt for the three of us till we can find out where the heart is, and what's happened to Colin, and how to get off this island with no boat. I doubt Uncle Fearchar's familiar swans would pull us."

"You understand more about these witching things than I do, but I still think we should tear 'em to pieces."

"Afterwards," Maggie said.

"Afterwards, then," the bear agreed.

18

When Colin surfaced, realizing with equal degrees of pleasure and surprise that he was not, dead, the first thing he saw was his fiddle floating on the water beside him. He grabbed it and held it aloft as he swam for the rock that had nearly wrecked the *Snake's Bane*.

The second thing he saw was the *Snake's Bane* sailing safely away. In all the confusion they probably hadn't even noticed when he went overboard.

The third thing he saw, as he hoisted himself up onto the rock, was a green-haired girl frantically scooting backwards on her scaly tail, being stalked farther and farther back onto land by a cat. Ching, furious at his recent dunking, was bent on having that tail for his supper.

The mermaid implored Colin with her sea-green eyes. Feeling damp and slippery and fresh out of gallantry, he took advantage of her status as a captive audience to lecture her sternly. "Madam," he said, "do you realize that you very nearly caused the wreck of a fine sailing vessel complete with a stout and hearty crew?" She was unimpressed. Wrecking ships was, after all, what mermaids did. "Not only that, but you have given my cat a bath, to which he has an aversion, and very nearly ruined one of the finest fiddles ever made, if I do say so myself. If you have anything to say in your own defense, I advise you to do so before I allow my cat to eat you up."

She started to cry. Colin realized, as he was supposed to, that he was being a beast, but he was really very upset about his fiddle. The tone would never be the same. Seeing she showed no sign of relenting, he stood and glared, hoping he would be in time to catch Ching should the cat decide to take a bite out of the mermaid.

"How can you be so cruel to me? You could be my own

181

great-great-grandson all grown up and gone to land, and come back with nasty cats to torment me."

"I didn't come back here to torment you at all. I was sailing along with my friends, minding my own business, when you start singing to us in all your different voices, and before I know it I'm floating around in the sea, my best fiddle ruined. So I ask you, who's tormenting whom?"

"You are being impertinent, young man," she said severely, under the circumstances. It sounded odd for her to call him young man, too, but Colin did realize that these creatures lived to great age. She might be anywhere from the eighteen years she looked to seven hundred and sixty, for all he could tell. It was typical of a creature who survived on the strength of her youthful beauty to try to pull the rank of age when confronted with difficulties.

She must have read his face, for she tossed back her long green hair from her shoulders and said, with a fetching pout, "You don't like me."

Colin could hardly avoid looking at what her new coiffure revealed about her stunning upper half. He blushed deeply and stammered, "Oh, no, really, I like you. I'm just annoyed with you."

She arranged the seashell combs in her hair. "Annoyed?"

"Only a little. Less all the time, in fact."

"I thought so. You can call your monster off, you know. I couldn't drown you, whatever Fearchar says. You wouldn't drown anyway, being one of us."

He hardly knew what to ask first, but the moon was nice, the stars were bright, and the night was young. He gathered Ching onto his lap, got slapped smartly on the hand for his trouble, and settled down for conversation.

The mermaid appeared poised to dive for a moment, but after a warning look from Colin she, too, made herself comfortable on the rock, flipping her tail in the water now and then as they talked.

"Now then," said the minstrel, staring determinedly into her eyes. "I am Colin Songsmith, Journeyman Minstrel."

"Of course you are. Fearchar told me that."

"And who are you? And who is Fearchar? Is he by any chance related to a family named Brown? And why do you keep saying I'm one of you?"

"I'm Lorelei, silly. Fearchar is my friend at Evil Island, and some day he will find a spell to grow a tail and come join me, he says. I think I *have* heard that terrible man who works for him call him by the name of Brown, but I'm not certain. And I keep saying you're one of us because you are. Oh, not recently, and not directly—but you had an ancestress among us, you may be as sure of it as you are of your voice and the way you swim."

Colin refused to let himself wonder how he with legs, fair hair, and no scales, had been descended of a woman with scales, tail, and green hair. It was beside the point, and stranger things happened in Argonia. It would explain his musical talent, considered by his masters to be exceptional, though he naturally wasn't supposed to know that. It would explain how he, raised in East Headpenney with nothing but streams all around and no knowledge of water, had been able to swim just now, and perhaps it also explained why he was so frightfully clumsy on land, but perfectly at home at sea in spite of previous inexperience. Slowly he nodded, and she dimpled at him prettily.

"You could stay here and play with me, and I'll teach you the loveliest songs! I get so lonely here. I think I'm the only mermaid in the Gulf right now—Fearchar wanted me to come, and he's so handsome and clever I couldn't wait to get here. But he doesn't come to talk to me as much as I'd like, and he can't swim properly, and there's not much sport in wrecking ships with all this calm water and help so close by. A girl can't have any fun. He's promised me a sea serpent to liven things up, but it hasn't been delivered yet. Oh, Colin, do stay, please. We could have the most wonderful times—" she gazed at Ching with a distinctly jaundiced eye. "We'd have to drown *that*, of course."

The water did look very inviting, and she was very attractive in a green-haired sort of way, but Colin realized that though she was unable to drown him she was not above trying her other lures, and he refused to be tempted. Reluctantly, he shook his head. "It's very kind of you to ask me, Lorelei, but I have other obligations. I think they may even include your friend. Would you show me where he lives?"

Her tail splashed the water in agitation, showering them both. "Oh, no, Colin Songsmith! Oh, no, you mustn't. Fearchar doesn't like men. He will rob you of your will, and surely have that awful Hugo kill you, and then you could never come back to play with me either."

Colin couldn't help smiling. "I can't see why that would bother you. After all, you were about to drown not only me, but all my friends as well."

Lorelei gave him another pretty pout. "That's different. It was nothing personal, you know. It's what I do. Think how dull it would be for sailors if there were no perils like me to make things interesting for them—and so entertainingly too! The poor things would just always be sailing aimlessly around with nothing more dangerous or intriguing than a little weather to amuse them."

As a poet, Colin could understand this from her point of view, and nodded.

"But you're one of us. I can't let you swim into certain doom now that we're getting to know each other better—though I'd be glad to see the end of *that!*" She flipped her tail in Ching's direction and got spat at.

"I have to go see him. If you know him so well, maybe you'd tell me how to protect myself from his power. Isn't there some plant or religious medal or something he particularly dislikes?"

"Like wolfbane, or garlic, or something like that?" she asked, cocking her head and touching her sweetly webbed middle finger to the dimple in her chin. "We-ell, yes. Come to think of it, you probably are at least partially immune. I am. I don't really believe that story about the fishtail, you know, except that I do love him and I hope it's true."

"What *is* his power, exactly, other than changing people into bears and stealing hearts and that sort of thing?"

"Ooooh, did he do that?" the sea green eyes widened and she shook her hair again, distractingly. "I didn't hear about that! He's just so powerful it gives me frogbumps all *over* sometimes."

Colin surmised that frogbumps were undoubtedly the aquatic equivalent of goosebumps and asked again, "But what is his *main* power. Like, I have this friend who—she uh—" he searched for a way to explain Maggie's hearthcraft to a mermaid with no fire to keep or doorstep to sweep, found none, and gave up, continuing, "Her grandmother, for instance, can change people into animals, and she has an aunt who can see into the present and—"

The mermaid was regarding him with a critical expression. "Strange company you keep, dearie. Don't you think you'd

184

be better off staying with me? Oh, well, then, if you insist. Fearchar's source of power is that he is very convincing."

"What kind of a magical power is being convincing?" Colin digested the information, scratching his head.

"A very great one. He could convince a tuna to take up tree climbing, if a tuna wasn't a sea creature."

"It doesn't work on sea creatures then?"

"Only me," she said ruefully. "But really no. It's something to do with us swimming in the salt sea all the time. It's salt that confounds him, I think."

"Thank you very much, Lorelei," Colin said slowly. "You've been a great help. Now could you show me how to find him."

"We'll have to swim, of course," she said.

Colin found the prospect oddly inviting, but glanced at Ching. "What of my cat?"

"What of him?" With a movement so swift his eyes couldn't follow she leapt high in the air and dived below the surface, rising again to float on her back, tail flapping leisurely at the moonlit water. "Come on, if you want to find Fearchar."

Colin shrugged, stripped off his shirt, and apologized to Ching before he jumped into the water. He felt the cat would be safe enough on the rock until he could fetch him.

Ching, however, had other ideas. Colin was only a stone's throw from the rock, swimming easily in tandem with Lorelei, when a killer whale, crowned with color-coordinated cat, flashed merrily past them.

19

Maggie's jaws and neck felt tight and stiff from all the unnatural nodding and smiling she was doing, listening to her uncle's voice drone on. Without the benefit of his magical credulity he was something of an overblown, pompous bore, she decided.

Amberwine had pleaded the weariness of pregnancy to retire to the relative seclusion of the tower room for a midday nap. She had been more than a little shocked and upset to discover that instead of the sanctuary it had promised to be while she was under Fearchar's spell, the ancient castle was her prison, and intended to be her tomb. Maggie regretted the necessity of having to upset Amberwine with the frightening truth of their situation so far in advance of their escape, but then could scarcely risk not telling her. She might insist on an explanation of their behavior at some crucial moment, and spoil the whole plan. At least she had looked legitimately pale and wan when she retired.

His Highness was also conserving his strength for their escape by giving in to the demands of his bear's body and getting lots of sleep. He, at least, was available if she needed him. Claiming the chamber upstairs was too warm in daylight hours for his fur-bearing form, he was curled up on the cool flagstone floor of the study, beneath Fearchar's alchemist's bench. The wizard had not carpeted that area of his study, for safety's sake. Molten metal accidentally spilled on the furs could set the entire interior of the castle on fire.

Her uncle lay the scroll he had been showing her on the table and was casting a critical glance over her. Her mouth went dry and she wet her lips with her tongue and smiled harder than ever, trying to look innocent and trusting. Was he able to detect when someone had eaten salt?

"Maggie, dear, you are not your usual radiant self. I had

186

hoped you would abandon those old rags and attire yourself in the pretty things I provided as more befitting a lady of your station."

"I'm sorry, Uncle," she replied demurely. She had worn her woolen costume today in preparation for their escape. It was sturdier and more comfortable than any of the gowns, and had pockets to conceal her medicine bundle, the remaining bottle of love potion, and the dagger Rowan lent her. "Winnie and I were going to try to plant you a little garden in the courtyard later this afternoon, and I didn't want to get your nice things dirty. With my craft I can grow you lovely giant melons and cabbages long before anyone else has them—then you'll have fresh food, and some to dry for winter."

"Your craft? Oh, yes, I believe Hugo mentioned. Hearth-crafting, is that right? That's very considerate of you, I'm sure, to try to plant me a garden. But I would like for you to stop doing vulgar things like digging in the dirt and those other menial jobs hearthcrafting implies. I hardly think hearthcrafting, other than a little needlework, perhaps, is a fitting occupation for a queen."

Here it comes, Maggie groaned inwardly. She tried to make her shrewd brown eyes go all wide and dewy as she asked, "Queen, Uncle Fearchar?"

"Yes, dear girl. I had planned to surprise you when your bridegroom arrives, but now seems as good a time as any."

"Whatever are you talking about, Uncle? How can a simple village witch like me become a queen?"

"How indeed, my dear! How did a simple village wizard such as myself become the man of power and influence you see before you today? With the help of the princess, when she makes the nomination in the tribunal in a few months, I shall become king of our fair Argonia. How? Because I've had the foresight to anticipate my opportunities, and the courage and determination to seize them. Coupled, naturally, with a deep and abiding compassion for my fellow man.

"As king I shall change the face of this country. No longer will we bow down to foreign oppressors, accepting their emissaries or making concessions to our inferiors! And that ridiculous law claiming magical personages should be prosecuted for the same dreary offenses as the non-magical rabble will be abolished. No longer, when I am king, will the vulgar hordes be able to associate with us on equal footing—and they most certainly will not be able to intermarry with us and taint our

187

sacred blood, sullying it so that the resulting descendants of fine old families are as relatively powerless as you are. No offense, dear girl, but it's true.

"No longer will any of their kind be allowed to call themselves noble, or be in positions of authority which they can dare to abuse by using our womenfolk as William Hood did when he betrayed your mother's love to marry that foreign faery hussy." He took a deep breath, for he was becoming overwrought and flushed beneath his dark complexion. His eyes had a look about them wilder than the bear's had ever been. Gradually he calmed, and said, "You won't have to go to all the trouble of being the resourceful crusader I am, of course, my dear, since you're related to me. In order to be queen, all that's required of you is to marry Davey."

"But, Uncle," she protested just enough for effect. "I think I should dislike being queen of the gypsies. And Xenobia is rather fierce."

"I'll worry about Xenobia. You are obviously not going to be Queen of the Gypsies. That is not my idea of wealth and nobility. You are to be Queen of Ablemarle."

"Ablemarle has a queen."

"Ablemarle has for a queen only the wife of Worthyman the Worthless. Believe me, they'll be delighted to have the niece of Fearchar the First instead."

"I'm afraid I don't understand."

"You don't have to understand, dear girl. Just leave everything to Uncle Fearchar and don't worry your pretty little head about it. His Highness Prince Worthyman the Bear," he jerked a thumb at the sleeping noble, "has privately expressed to me a desire to retire permanently from court life. He fears it would disagree with him after all the fresh air he has recently enjoyed. Pegeen and I just happened to research the laws of Ablemarle quite recently, and I've come across a convenient writ he may sign, once he is in human form, to allow him to abdicate his rightful place as crown prince to young Davey."

"But doesn't he have to give the heart back to Davey first?" Maggie asked.

"That's what the spell says."

"How can His Highness change back, then, to sign your paper, with the gypsies miles away?"

Her uncle smiled fondly at her. "Dear, dear, so many questions. Didn't I tell you to trust your uncle, child? The swans were dispatched early this morning to fetch Davey and Xenobia."

So soon, then. Maggie had to get Davey's heart so that she and the bear would have a bargaining point, in case they were overwhelmed by the sheer number of their foes after the gypsies arrived. "It seems to me," she said, "that if I am to marry the gypsy, I ought to have his heart. He's far too fickle for my taste as he is, and we didn't part on exactly cordial terms. In fact, I think he quite dislikes me."

"Impossible!" said her uncle indulgently, "What young man in his right mind could despise such a ravishing creature? He'll be overcome with joy."

She followed him as he went to the ladder he kept in the study for fetching scrolls from the topmost compartments. "All the same," she said, "I would still feel better . . ."

He looked at her sharply. "You are unusually argumentative today, Maggie. Didn't I tell you to trust me?" He moved the ladder to one of the high, deepset windows above the tapestry that told of a sea serpent hunt in the middle of a map of the Sea of Smokings.

"Oh, of course I do, Uncle! Forgive me. I guess any girl is apt to be a little silly when she is first engaged." "Ugh," she thought, "if he believes that one . . ."

He cupped her chin between his thumb and forefinger and looked deeply into her eyes. Again she wondered if he could smell salt on her breath—or perhaps the fishiness of her excuse—but he said, "Naturally you would be, my child. And I can deny you nothing." He climbed the ladder and Maggie nearly swooned with the effort it cost her to keep from pushing it out from under him.

Light danced around the stone walls, sparking bright new colors onto the worn tapestries, encrusting Maggie's worn woolen garments with gems of luminescence, and skipping around on the bear's closed eyes till he turned over on his other side to sleep.

From the wizard's hand dangled a crystal prism. "If you look deeply into it, you will see his heart," he told her. Maggie examined the prism, which seemed to be made of solid light itself. There, framed by a thousand glittering facets, was a tiny rose, the color of heart's blood.

"*That* came out of *him*?" she asked, in spite of herself. Her uncle jerked it back abruptly and Maggie struggled to resume her docile niece pose. It was no easy task to deceive such a professional sneak as her uncle. "I mean to say," she said, "now that I know his heart, how can I help but love him?"

Mollified, her uncle set it into one of the pigeon holes of his desk. "How indeed?" He turned to the door the ghost had passed through the night before. "Ah, Lady Amberwine, refreshed from your nap, I trust?"

Winnie, pale as the proverbial lily, inclined her head, which was about all the communication she was capable of now that she knew the wizard's villainous nature.

"You may as well know, too. Your gypsy friend, Davey, and his charming mother, are on their way here in order for Davey to marry your sister. We have just been discussing wedding plans. Perhaps you'll persuade him to sing that song you're so fond of." He hummed a few bars of the tune for which Colin had so often fashioned lyrics, though somehow on his lips it sounded strange, and Winnie went rigid. If she was pale before, Maggie thought her ashen now.

This time Maggie was unable to control the anger that pounded in her ears and she had her hand on her dagger when there was a ringing of footsteps in the corridor without. "Brown!" Hugo shouted, "Come here and see what I've brought you!"

They turned to the doorway. The peddler was a burly fellow when he wasn't all bent over pretending to be humble and holding his hat in his hand. Now it was Colin he held, a shirtless and disheveled Colin with his face contorted from the pain of the grip Hugo held on his arms, which were forced up behind his back.

Uncle Fearchar crossed to them. "Hugo, old friend, you're so uncouth! Where are your manners? Is this how you treat a friend of my niece?" He made as if to dust Colin off, after Hugo released him, but it was difficult to straighten the collar of a shirtless man. So he settled for giving him his best sincerely convincing smile. "Minstrel Songsmith, I presume? But what has become of your raiment?"

"I never wear my shirt when I go swimming," Colin said.

It was all Maggie could do to keep from rushing over to hug him. She had been terribly afraid that whatever end they were plotting for him had already come about, and an imaginative revenge would be all she would be able to do about it.

"I think my sister and I would probably prefer to hear Colin sing at my wedding," Maggie said. "Colin, it's too

190

wonderful," she winked from behind her uncle's back. Hugo had gone to poke up the fire that was kept burning in the drafty hall to keep out the chill. "Uncle has arranged for me to marry Gypsy Davey and be a queen and everything."

"Oh—er—how nice," he said, not quite sure what the wink was meant to convey.

"Mrrow?" asked Ching, sauntering through the door left open when Hugo had forced Colin into the study.

"Animals in the house. Disgusting," said Uncle Fearchar, moving to shoo the cat.

"I beg your pardon?" said His Highness the bear, rising from his nap.

"Er—present company excepted of course, Your Highness," amended the wizard, crossing to his desk, where he began rummaging in the papers.

Ching triumphantly leaped to Maggie's shoulder and began to purr.

"Now that we're all together again," said Fearchar jovially, "I thought you might like to see the writ of abdication I found for Your Highness that you may sign to leave your throne to young Davey and Maggie."

"There was another item involved, wasn't there, Wizard?" asked the bear, lumbering over to the desk.

"Ah, yes, of course. Davey's heart." He picked up the crystal, waved it around a bit, and laid it on the desk, out of the bear's reach. "Have it right here, so when the boy comes all you'll have to do is hand it over to him and—poof—there you are, good as new, in all your regal splendour!"

"Let's see," said the bear, putting his forepaws on the desk and extending himself to where he could sniff at the crystal. "Yes, I guess that about does it. There's the heart, the boy's on the way, here we all are, and there's young Colin. I think the time has come." He rose to his full height and roared deeply. "Run along, now, children, unless you want to see me tear him to pieces," he told Maggie and Colin. "I'll meet you at the boat."

"Watch out, prince!" cried Maggie as her uncle snatched a phial from the desk and flung it at the bear's face. But it was too late, for no sooner had the white powder been released from the phial to float into the bear's nostrils than the huge, menacing prince subsided into a sleeping roly-poly heap of fur at the sorcerer's feet.

"Maggie, I am seriously shocked at you," said her uncle, as

he tried to fix her with his expression of sincerely, seriously, shocked injury.

"Oh, dry up, you conceited ass!" she cried, unable to control herself and maintain the charade any longer.

"What a way to talk to your only uncle! You'll watch your nasty mouth when you're queen, my girl."

"I'll do nothing of the sort, and I'm not your girl!" Maggie informed him, anxiously watching at the same time as Winnie and Colin bent over the fallen bear.

"Is he dead, then?" murmured Winnie.

"Not yet," snapped Fearchar. "I just happened to have laid that dragon-strength sleeping powder there. You'll be meeting the dragon soon."

Colin had straightened, having wit enough to retain his bewitched expression. "Oh, Master Fearchar, sir, do you think that's safe? I understand dragons can be hazardous to one's health."

Maggie knew she would explode if she heard one more syrupy answer from the lying wizard. Facing him squarely, she threatened. "Tell him the truth now. Go on, tell us all the truth if it's in you. I'm sick to death of your hokery pokery."

Her uncle seized her wrists and glared at her. Hugo had twisted Winnie's arms behind her now, and had a dagger at Colin's throat, in case he wasn't so enchanted as he seemed to be. "You will not refer to my magical powers as hokery pokery, niece. Hereafter you will be respectful and will do precisely as you are told." He smiled unpleasantly, "Too bad you didn't array yourself as I asked so you would be pretty for your bridegroom. As it is, there will just be enough time for you to accompany us to the feeding grounds to give the dragon his evening meal. You will shortly see, while my scaly friend feasts on Lady Amberwine's tender flesh and that of the minstrel, that I am to be reckoned with. Your little deceits have cost you their lives. You understand that you are responsible for this unfortunate turn of events, not I. You force me into violent action. By the time the gypsies arrive, the effects of your salt will have worn off, and you'll once more be docile, if somewhat subdued by the loss of your friends. You and the bear will do my bidding, and when he has signed the writ, you will be married and he will be removed to the dungeon till the next feeding."

"And you really think I'm going to go along with all this?" she asked, fingering the dagger in her pocket.

"Oh, my dear child, I'm afraid you have no choice. It is not actually you who will be queen at all once you marry Davey. Your charming appearance will remind the Ablemarlonians who really rules them, but you will work no more tricks, make no more unwise decisions. You will be quite subdued—permanently. I think I have just the spell to do it."

Ching's ears had been flattening as Fearchar's voice rose higher and higher while he leaned into Maggie's face to emphasize his point. He had been so intent on making his effect, he failed to notice the laid-back ears of the cat on his niece's shoulders, and the lashing tail. He could not, however, fail to notice the lightning slash of claws that ripped across his face, catching the corner of his eye.

Screaming with pain and clutching his eye with one hand, the enchanter slapped Maggie to the floor with the other hand as he grabbed the cat by the head and flung him into the fireplace.

Maggie recovered quickly enough to shriek at the fire to stifle itself. With a terrible yowl, Ching leaped out of the coals and streaked out the door.

"Catch that beast, Hugo!" ordered Fearchar. But Amberwine took advantage of her proximity to the peddler to stretch out a dainty foot and neatly trip him. By the time he recovered his composure, the cat had disappeared.

Fearchar, still clutching at his injured eye, was stalking towards Maggie, who lay sprawled by the fireplace watching his advance. His uninjured eye tried to skewer her where she lay.

The pulses in her throat were throbbing so that she kept swallowing, and her hands trembled as she drew the dagger from her skirt pocket. Colin leapt forward to help her but was checked by Hugo's knife. Maggie lost her balance once and had to support herself on the mantle as she stood to meet the wizard. Her eyes felt dry as paper and fastened on him with awe and an odd loathing respect. His was the first real malevolence she had ever encountered, and she found it shamefully attractive. It crossed her mind that all she would have to do to be back to their relationship of yesterday would be to smile, apologize, offer repentance, marry someone she hated, and sit idly by and watch her friends murdered. Not so attractive after all. When she took a backward step, he didn't rush her, but followed her with a corresponding step. The silence made her nervous.

"You have a lot of nerve abusing Ching," she said. "I don't know what Gran will turn you into for that—a weasel perhaps. I don't think there is an animal suitably vile enough to hold your form. You've injured my father, disgraced my sister, and threatened your own sisters and my friends. I don't think we want you in our family, Uncle."

"I resigned from your family a long time ago, niece," he snarled. "But I was willing to adopt you into mine."

"Only when you thought I could be useful. You didn't even want to use me for my own power—just because I look like you. But my magic is all my own, not stolen, like your castle, or gotten by lies, like the spell for Davey's heart and probably, if you could tell the truth, the one for changing His Highness to a bear. I can do an honest month's work in a half an hour if I'm pressed. That's not very grand by your standards, but all you seem to be able to do is convince people of things that make fools of them and cause their food to spoil, and play a few parlor tricks you've begged or stolen from your betters. You're not even a decently magicked village wizard and you think you should be king on a magical supremacy platform!"

He kept coming after her, but she was drawing courage from her own speech. She stood, dagger poised to meet him, in the middle study. Her voice quavered, and to her annoyance hot tears began to flood her eyes.

"You ought to have listened to me, Maggie. It will be very hard on you now. You don't know the extent of my power," the smile he wore as he stalked her was not pleasant. "I can control you completely—so completely you will have to have my permission to bathe or dress yourself in the morning."

"Not if I keep salt on my tongue at all times, and I will if it dries and cracks it in my head, rather than submit to you." She shook her head slowly from side to side, raising the dagger slightly. "I won't be your creature. You cannot injure my cat, murder my friends, and expect to take over my body before I'm done with it. I may be a dilute witch, as you think, but I am powerful enough to prevent your doing that. You can have no power over me that I don't cede to you. You're a wretched wizard, and a villain, and I think you may be a coward as well."

He let drop the hand that held the swollen, bloody eye and stepped as close to her as possible to still be out of striking range of the dagger. "Perhaps. Shall we see . . ."

"Maggie!" Winnie cried, "The gypsy's behind you!"

She swiveled to see Xenobia flying towards her, skirts like bat wings flapping as she ran. Maggie threw the dagger and missed. She plunged a hand into her pocket and flung the next heavy object she found, the vial of love potion. Her aim was better this time, and the vial struck the gypsy woman squarely on the forehead, where it broke, its contents mingling with her blood as she fell to the ground.

For a moment Maggie and the others were frozen as Davey, handsome and cool-seeming with only his bolero covering his chest and a dark curl falling over his forehead, turned to his mother. "Are you alright, mum?" he asked. The woman's head lolled backwards, but even from where she stood, Maggie could see the battered bulging bodice of the green silk gown that had been Winnie's rise and fall.

She was spun around and her teeth knocked together, bright spots exploding behind her eyelids as her uncle slapped her hard twice across the face. She kicked him as hard as she could with her old boots, but had not gotten her head clear from the slapping when his fist slammed into her jaw and she fell crashing into darkness.

20

Lady Amberwine cradled Maggie's head in her lap as the swan-propelled boat sped them near to their doom. "When will you ever learn to be still?" she murmured tenderly to her sister. "If only you had kept your tongue, he would have spared *you*." Maggie said nothing, nor had she done more than breathe since being knocked senseless.

Colin scowled and struggled with the ropes that bound him. The bear, too, starting to recover from the effects of the sleeping potion, was bound. In the far end of the boat sat the sorcerer, looking appropriately sinister now that he had covered his eye with a black patch. Xenobia's usually sour expression was fragmented with what Amberwine, had she not known the gypsy queen better, might have called emotion. The gypsy was wearing her kerchief as a bandage for the wound made by Maggie's missile. Davey looked sleek, attractive, and bored, swinging his feet restlessly against the equipment storage box he sat upon.

The little boat stopped, and Hugo lumbered over the side to tie her up.

"Ladies first, Hugo. Show Lady Amberwine to the stake of honor. The others will have to make do with lying on the rock till the dragon notices them."

"Right." Hugo took Maggie from Winnie's lap and dumped her unceremoniously onto the beach. From the corner of her eye, Winnie saw Colin's mouth tighten and the bear gave a feeble, sleepy growl. Hugo handed Winnie out of the boat, and the smell of the animals and remnants of animals who had been left there all week for the dragon to feed upon nearly knocked her over.

"Come along, milady," mocked the peddler. "We have an excellent viewpoint reserved just for you." He pushed her off the beach into the throng of milling animals. The island rose

196

to a central mound and in the center of this was a metal stake driven into the sheer rock. To this pole Hugo lashed Amberwine's wrists, ankles, neck, and middle. "This is reserved for Master Brown's special guests, milady. You might say it's the dragon's rotisserie." He went on to describe in great detail, as he finished tightening the knots, in what condition they had found the remains, if any, of former occupants of the stake. Winnie was not listening, having conveniently fainted after the initial explanation of the pole's purpose.

Colin raged at his inability to do anything to help Maggie and Amberwine, but was unable to do more than shuffle off the boat and onto the island. His Highness was rolled off a miniature gangplank by Davey and the sorcerer, flopping to the beach in an excellent imitation of a stuffed nursery bear.

Hugo returned and the wizard gestured at the bear. "Skin him out here. He's too dangerous to have running amok. I can control Ablemarle without him through that spineless brother of his, if need be. The dragon may have his meat, but I want that handsome hide for my floor." Before Colin could decide whether to butt him with his head or bite him on the leg, Hugo had grasped His Highness by the furry throat. Before the bear could wake enough to do anything, the peddler was knocked off his victim by a rampaging Xenobia, who practically flayed Hugo with her fingernails before her son and the sorcerer could pull her away from him. "No! You can't! I will not allow it!" she cried as they strove to subdue her strong, squirming body. The sorcerer, who was beginning to like that sort of thing, slapped her hard across the face.

"Whatever is the matter with you now?" he demanded, shaking her roughly. "The dragon will come to feed at any time now, and when he's ready to eat he isn't going to stop for a chat, even with me. Nor will he be selective about who he eats. I suggest we finish our business and depart."

The bear groaned and rolled over.

"You can't skin him alive and use him for a rug, Great Sorcerer," begged Xenobia, "He's the father of my son—"

"What?" Davey actually looked up from the inspection he was making of his fingernails.

"—and his hide has enormous sentimental value to me."

"Perhaps I shall just concentrate on my conquest of Argonia right now, and forget about Ablemarle altogether until some arrangement can be worked out with the present ruler. I can surely find more reliable allies later." His back was rigid with contempt as he reboarded his swan powered vessel. "Come, Hugo, if we hurry I can reach the princess's palace by morning, in time to compose my acceptance speech. You may all stay here and be eaten if you so desire." Hugo didn't desire, and leapt aboard. Before the others could express further preference, the boat was gliding wakelessly through the tossing sea. Xenobia began to shriek curses after it, and Davey ceased to look bored. If he hadn't pulled her back, she would have drowned as she tried to wade off into the sea after the boat.

Colin thought he detected streaming green hair and a flashing tail now and then showing above the surface as it followed the wizard's boat. He screamed to Lorelei, but received no answer.

His Highness yawned cavernously and attempted to sit up. "I say, what's all this?" he asked. Xenobia hovered possessively above him, casting accusing glances out to the uncaring gray sea.

"We are about to become dragon fodder," Davey answered.

"Why is young Maggie napping, then?" the bear asked. The situation was explained to him, and since they were all in the same situation and all would be needed if they were to successfully fend off the dragon for any length of time, Davey and Xenobia were prevailed upon to loosen the bonds of the bear and Colin.

Wasting no time, Colin threaded his way through the animal bodies. He tried not to slip and fall on the rock as he climbed the hillock that held Lady Amberwine. She was beautiful, fragile, and not a great deal of help as he tried to untie the knots that held her with her full unconscious weight dragging against them. "I do wish," he grumbled to himself, "that people would try to remain alert around here. After all, there IS supposed to be a dragon in the vicinity." He caught Amberwine just above her abdomen as she slipped down the pole when he untied the last knot.

Failing to wake her by chafing her wrist, shaking her, or shouting in her ear, he first tried to carry her in his arms, but she failed to bend sufficiently through the middle and he slipped, while attempting to climb down the hill, when one of his well-manured boots slid out from under him. He sat down abruptly, barely keeping the lady aloft. Finally he managed to haul her onto his back and began to wend his way through the animals to where the others waited. He hardly struck the romantic pose he had seen in tapestries, but his novel method of carrying pregnant ladies served quite well to allow him to guide them safely through the meandering livestock.

He had almost reached their companions when he heard it. The beat of the wings sounded like a giant playing a drum, and the sky was overcast from the shadow of the great airborne beast, flame-colored, soaring directly overhead. The wind created by the movement of his wings tore at Colin's hair and he slid on through the animals, who were now running in as much room as they had to run in, some of them plunging into the sea. One or two of these the dragon boiled with his flame before he swooped down to pick first a cow and then a pig up into his mighty jaws. Colin forgot about swimming as a means of escape. His hair had stood on end as the dragon flew within inches of him, returning to the hillock to eat his prey.

"Get down!" screamed His Highness, rearing on his hind legs. Colin bent over and down as far as he was able without spilling her ladyship over his head. He then plunged, goatlike, across the remaining area until he managed with one final thrust to clear the beasts, nearly tumbling, Amberwine and all, into Xenobia's lap. His Highness was clawing the air, roaring his challenge to divert the dragon and to give Colin time to rejoin them.

The dragon, having finished the boiled pig, noted the bear with a casual burst of flame. He was apparently surprised at any form of opposition from his meals here, and circled around to pick up a bleating sheep to devour while considering the bear's novel behavior.

"Sit down, Prince darling," hissed Xenobia. "Perhaps he's in the mood for mutton today."

The bear sat, but it was difficult to sit still with the poor sheep bleating so piteously. Colin almost fainted himself, thinking what might have become of Amberwine had he not gone straight to the rock to release her.

"Maggie does all those little tricks with fire," suggested His Highness, whose brain was functioning at its best now, in time of peril. "Perhaps if we could wake her, she could put out the dragon's flame, then we'd only have claws and teeth to deal with."

They both tried to rouse her, but to no avail, though they

199

shook her and tickled her and called her name. Amberwine started to cry again, holding her sister's head and shoulders in her arms as she began to rock and keen and mourn like a banshee. "Here, here," said Colin severely, "she's not dead—not yet, anyway. If you're going to sing, sing waking-up songs, like this." He began to whistle the spritely Argonian Army Reveille. Maggie sat up and rubbed her jaw. "I think Uncle's side of the family must be part mule," she said.

"Leave off the genealogy for the moment, Maggie, please, and see if you can do something about the flame on yon beastie," said Colin.

"I can't do anything till he's closer," she said, after considering the matter for a moment. "I'll have to be able to look at the fire to order it around."

"Splendid," said Colin grimly.

The bear got to his feet in order to resume his fighting stance once more. Colin tapped Davey on the shoulder. "Hey, you. If you're going to let your father do all the fighting, give me your dagger." He held out his hand but the gypsy man stood up, shaking his head. The sheep had stopped bleating.

Xenobia and Maggie stood as well. Colin was discouraged, but he stood beside them. He didn't really know what they could do against a dragon except make themselves a little tenderer eating by battering themselves fighting him. The creature in the center of their island prison spread his sundown-colored wings and sprang from the rock to circle the little island again.

The bear roared another challenge to the soaring beast. Davey and Xenobia stood with daggers poised, beneath the bear's mighty arms. Maggie crouched before them, as if she planned to physically spring upon the dragon. Oh well, thought Colin, as he picked up a rock. When the dragon flew low enough to singe His Highness's fur, Colin hurled the rock as hard as he could, straight into the beast's flaming mouth.

The dragon back-flapped out of Maggie's range and sat down amid the hysterical animals. Baffled anew by this curious spice his food was tossing into his mouth, he thoughtfully munched a few chickens, which he caught in midair with his long tongue as they flapped frenziedly around him.

"Sorry," Maggie said, "that blow to my jaw must have slowed my reaction time. Let's try again, shall we?"

"We haven't much choice," Colin said.

Amberwine shuddered, and said in a small, sick voice, "He's even more horrid than I'd imagined."

That was the last comment there was time for as the dragon now flew in, preparing to dine on whole roast bear with a side order of gypsies on the rocks. This time Maggie was ready, almost scorching herself as she leapt up crying to the dragon's fire to stifle itself.

Miraculously, it worked, the torch from the creature's craw sputtering and dwindling into a sulfurous belch.

Colin embraced her, competing for the privilege with Amberwine and a genuine bear hug from the prince.

It was not over yet, however, for the dragon disliked being deprived of his cooking apparatus, and streaked back toward them, the great translucent orange wings fanning, if not fire, then at least a very foul fetid breath, into all their lungs. The bear slashed out with his claws, the gypsies with their daggers, and Colin and Maggie both hurled rocks.

This time, however, the dragon was undeterred by the rocks, which bounced harmlessly off his scales. His claws stretched to graze the bear, who missed a swipe with his claws and fell to the rock, carrying his two gypsy guardians with him.

Suddenly a whirlwind spun the beast snout to tail to wingtip and Colin, following the funnel, found Maggie's finger at the source of the vortex. His friend was every inch the powerful, commanding enchantress as she compelled the very elements about her, intoning in her throaty alto, "I wish to make a very *large* souffle—whip me twelve dozen eggwhites—at once—there!" The whirlwind, he could see now, was flecked with the broken and separated eggs of the chickens still squawking on the island as well as those of the ones just devoured by the dizzy dragon.

"We're saved!" cried Amberwine. She'd been looking out to sea, since her gentle nature made it too painful for her to watch her sister get gobbled alive.

"Not yet," said Colin, "she's hardly used to this, you know. I don't know how long she can hold out." He did not yet see, as Winnie did, the longboat full of warriors rowing swiftly to their aid.

"Will-you-all-just-be-still," said Maggie from between gritted teeth. After his initial confusion, the dragon had begun to find the whirlwind amusing, and forgot feeding long enough to make repeated dives in and out of it.

"But we are saved, laddie!" cried Prince Worthyman, who by now was waving vigorously at the boat. "Unless I miss my guess, that redheaded chap is set for dragon-slaying, and the young lady is bound to save my neck again. I don't know who the other chaps are, but they appear to mean business."

"Look out!" cried Winnie, turning back to her companions just in time to see the dragon swoop again, but she was too late, for the dragon's tail had caught the bear on the side of the head and knocked him down. "Oh, Rowan, my love!" she cried to the boat. "Do hurry, else we're all slain!"

Not waiting for the longboat to land, with one mighty bound from deck to shore, Rowan leaped among them brandishing sword and shield, which he instantly employed in skilled anti-dragon maneuvers. He protected Amberwine and Maggie and as many of the others as he could with the shield, while wielding the sword in their defense.

By then the boat had landed and beside him stepped Neddy Pinchpurse. Colin recognized the boat they came in as the longboat from the *Snake's Bane*. "You get down in the bottom of the boat, lass," Neddy instructed a flashing-eyed Zorah before he set to work covering Rowan's back with his cutlass. The second officer from the *Bane* relieved the redheaded noble of his shield and, keeping Amberwine and the gypsies covered with it, herded them back down to join Zorah on the deck of the longboat.

Maggie had refused to leave the island, and while the beast was circling again, Rowan cast an eye upon her, saying, "Go on now, be a good lass. You've done your share and I can finish it. We Rowans have made short work of many a dragon."

She continued to watch the creature do loop-the-loops on the far side of the island. Turning to Colin, she said suddenly, "I have it now, Colin. Where have you heard of a dragon of that particular description before?"

"I—er—" he said, a bit tired for guessing names or repartee.

"That's right. Grizel. That must be Grimley up there." Urgently, she turned back to Rowan, who shook her from his sword arm. Still she persisted. "Lord Rowan, you mustn't slay this dragon."

"What? Not slay him? After he's nearly done in the lot of you? What a lot of rubbish you're talking to me now, lassie. Terror must have taken your wits."

He had no other chance to speak for several minutes, as he and Ned Pinchpurse and Colin, with the second officer's saber, slashed away in the general direction of the dragon. The bear recovered from his fall and defended them with his claws.

"See, he's tiring," Maggie insisted of the dragon, as the creature abandoned them for a measly pair of geese. "I think he must be getting full, too. Can't you just cover our escape?"

"Gurrrl," said the bear, "it's a menace he is to the community. Would you have him devour us and the townfolk too? For too long he's done the wizard's bidding."

"If we kill him, we'll have to kill Grizel eventually, too," she pleaded. "She's our friend now, but if we kill Grimley she'll be a more remorseless enemy than ever he was. She never wanted him to accept this arrangement in the first place."

"Look out!" yelled Pinchpurse, but it was too late, for this time it was he who was knocked down by the sweep of the dragon's tail. The beast was apparently enjoying himself now, playing with them, and they slashed till their arms were weary. With one last mocking swoop, the dragon picked up Maggie from behind. Rowan lunged to pierce him, but Maggie, in spite of the pain in her shoulders from the claws of the dragon, screamed "Don't!"

Colin caught one of her ankles and His Lordship grabbed a knee, then abruptly the beast retracted his claws, and Maggie would have dropped to the rock if her friends hadn't cushioned her fall.

Amberwine screamed suddenly, piercingly, and Xenobia wailed, "We're lost!"

"Not quite yet, we're not," said Rowan, steeling himself for another onslaught.

"Alas, it's true!" wailed Davey. "There's another one!"

The red and gold dragon had been charging them again, but abruptly did another backflap, using his tail as a rudder, and flew off at top speed to meet the blue and green dragon whose wingbeats were now as distinct as their own. Colin cried out, "It's Grizel!"

Maggie raised her face from the rock and broke out in an ear-to-ear grin. "Thank goodness Grimley's safe. I hope my shoulders didn't dull his claws or anything, or we're in trouble."

"I just hope she'll remember us."

The female dragon paid them no attention, however, and they all watched with varying degrees of trepidation and wonder as both dragons alighted on a central hillock of the island. A black and white streak flew from the neck of the aquamarine dragon just as she and the red and gold dragon twined necks, he shyly offering her a cow.

"Ching!" Maggie greeted the cat as he lept over the backs of the farm animals, who were now completely prostrate with terror. He sprang onto her chest and she cradled him against her shoulder, stroking his fur, immaculately black and white even after his flight. "How in the world...?"

Even Colin could hear the smugness in the purr, but what the cat told Maggie was, "I really do broadcast very well when I'm sufficiently outraged. When that *person* tried to murder me and you helped me escape, I ran straight out the side door and over to the most isolated spot I could find and yowled my head off for revenge. Grizel's quite fond of revenge herself, and just happened to be on her way back to Grimley, so she was only a few leagues off and..."

"A few leagues?" said Maggie, impressed.

The others were regarding the girl and cat's apparently one-sided conversation strangely. Colin grinned apologetically. "They go on like that all the time," he said.

"And here we are," finished Ching.

As they all piled into the longboat, Davey asked, "Will someone please explain to me why with one dragon we are in mortal danger, but with two we're supposed to be safe?"

21

When the innkeeper's wife, thrilled almost beyond words to have a great lord like Rowan stopping at her inn, had finished bandaging Maggie's shoulders and various other amazingly minor wounds, she served them all a fine supper. Maggie pulled out her medicine pouch and with a wicked grin at the woman, sprinkled a generous amount of salt into everything.

It wasn't until they had finished eating that the crew of the *Snake's Bane*, led by Bosun Pinchpurse, arrived. Ned touched Colin on the shoulder as he took a place on the bench beside him. "Sorry, lad. We tried to give chase in the *Bane* but he were long gone. Some fisherman said he saw the blackguard trying to dock at his island, but a mermaid was screaming at him and wouldn't give him a chance to unhitch his swans so he could fly away on them. That's what the fisherman said, leastways. Too much ale, I'm thinkin'."

"Believe it or not, Ned, he was probably cold sober," said Colin, who was not, and was very weary besides.

"Anyway," said Ned, "this fisherman says the last he seen of the wizard 'e was headin' out to sea."

"He did say he was going to see the princess," Maggie said.

"Yes, ma'am, and he'll have a bit of a trip in that little boat of his. But them giant swans the lad here told us of will be makin' their own wind, and it's too calm for the *Bane* to make much headway, so we lost him, as I said."

"No matter," said Lord Rowan. "Now that we know how to break his spells we can supply everyone, including Princess Pegeen, with liberal amounts of salt. I doubt he'll stand much chance of being nominated on his personal integrity alone. Especially not after I lodge my complaint with the council."

"You know," said Maggie, "I'm not so sure this country and

our magic folk are deteriorating at all. Your ancestors Rowan the Rampaging and Rowan the Reckless would never have thought to lodge a complaint with the council over a wizard-induced misunderstanding."

Rowan laughed. "No, more likely they'd have slaughtered every available wizard and gypsy in the land." He hugged Amberwine, who sat at his side sipping tea from a pottery cup. "Not to mention the lady."

"We're lucky you came when you did," Colin said.

"Well—yes. It would have been better if I'd come with you at once, but I'm still Rowan enough that I listened to my pride for awhile before I set out to follow you. I'd decided by the time I met Zorah that I was no fit king, or even much of a hero, if I let my sister-in-law do all the rescuing in the family. And when Zorah told me the mess you'd got into..." He glared across the table at Xenobia and Davey.

"How did you know where we were, though?" Maggie asked.

"Zorah said you were off to find the Sorcerer of Dragon Bay, since she'd extracted Colin's promise to get that scamp's heart." He indicated Davey, who studied the food he was carefully masticating twenty chews to the mouthful, "And the last day, your Aunt Sybil's budgie bird come bringing us a message that you're up t' the sorcerer's place and something was amiss."

"We was about to leave port when 'is lor'ship come askin' for you, lad," said Neddy. "We didn't like leavin' you, after you'd saved the ship and all, but when we went back to the rock, you was gone. So as I say, we was just lucky he come when 'e did."

"Whew," said Maggie. "*You* were lucky!"

"I have some unfinished business," said Rowan, rising to his feet. "It pains me, sir," he said to Davey, "for His Highness of Ablemarle is a fine man, or bear, depending on how you look at him, and he tells me you're his son and acquitted yourself nobly in the dragon affair. But you've offended the honor of m' lady and for that you'll have to answer."

"No!" Zorah lept to her feet as well. "Do you think I brought you here so you could kill him?"

Rowan looked bewildered. He was honor-bound to Zorah as much as he was to avenging the insult. While he was trying to decide if it was more important to avenge a reputa-

206

tion lost than to reward a life saved, Amberwine tugged on his sleeve till he sat down.

"I only regret we let the villain get away before we got that heart for Davey," said His Highness. "He was such a good boy once."

"Is this it?" asked Amberwine, pulling it from her pocket. Its jeweled light danced across their eyes.

"Winnie," said Maggie, "How ever did you . . . ?"

"When your uncle put the bear to sleep, Maggie, I saw it sitting about, and dropped it in my pocket while they were all watching you. I wasn't sure what it was, but it seemed important to you," she said the last to the bear as she gently set it in his paws.

His Highness rose and made Amberwine a bow. "Madam, if I wouldn't wet you to the elbow in so doing I'd kiss your hand." He climbed heavily over the bench and waddled on his hind legs to where Davey sat beside his mother. The cynical smile on Davey's lips as the bear pressed the crystal against his empty beast underwent a subtle change. "Be a man, my son," said the bear as the light gradually was absorbed into Davey. While everybody was busy feeling touched, the bear changed back into human form and embraced his son.

The innkeeper's wife screamed at the naked prince as she had not screamed to see a bear at her table. Rowan hastily handed the prince a cloak. Enchantments were sometimes careless about details.

"Ah, yes," sighed Xenobia. "I believe I do like you better in that form."

"Can you forgive me my callousness, dear lady?" asked the prince, who, if not young and handsome, was, as they all knew, brave and kind and intelligent, which was the same thing, only better. Actually, Maggie thought he still looked like a bear. His hair and beard were dark and curly, and before Rowan had produced the cloak his body hair had seemed equally copious—and he was a short, stocky, sturdy-built man. But the little dim eyes were chocolate-drop brown and looked at the gypsy woman kindly. "Had it not been for you I'd now be a hearthrug for that murderous magician."

"Had it not been for me, you wouldn't have been in such a condition. Of course I forgive you, Worthy . . ." and they went on in that vein for some time, until they too finally stopped to watch the long, passionate clench that Davey and Zorah were

207

indulging in, much to the general edification of the crew of the *Bane*, who had filled up the rest of the inn and were cheering and laughing and taking bets on how long the couple could hold out without coming up for air.

Finally they did, however, and Davey, handing Zorah the empty prism that had once imprisoned the best part of him, sighed. "Ah, Zorah, darling. And to think I didn't know I cared!"

It was altogether an extremely long night. If matters had been left strictly up to the initial participants in the situation, everyone would have retired early. But the crew of the *Bane* had seized the occasion as one suitable for celebration and a great deal of drinking, singing, and lying ensued on the part of all and sundry.

At one point in the festivities, Colin returned to the *Bane* to pick up his kit, guitar, and Obtruncator, plus the soggy remnants of his beloved fiddle, rescued by Neddy from the rock. He returned the sword to Rowan. "I thank you for its use, sir, but it didn't suit me like my fiddle did. That's ruined now, but I can make merry enough with my guitar, if Neddy and his hornpipe and Tom on the concertina give a hand."

"Suit yourself, lad," said Rowan. "But I have a wish that you'd hold on to Obtruncator a spell longer. I'd the feeling there was something following us in the wood almost until we approached the Bay."

Colin groaned, as he had had more adventure than he expected ever to want to see again. "Of course you needn't go back with us," Rowan said quickly. "The captain tells me he'll be delighted to have you on the *Snake's Bane*. Say the word, and I'll ask him to 'prentice you as an officer trainee so that you can accept an admiralty I'd like to offer you in the King's Navy—if I'm the king, that is."

Colin nodded, but said, "That's kind of you, my Lord, but I'm afraid my new friends might be put off a little at such grand promotions not obtained—er—in the line of duty. I'll see you safely to the castle, and perhaps you could use my services till you're ready to return to Queenston for the election? I've never been to court before, other than as a student. Perhaps then I might wait there till the *Bane* returns, to sail with her next time around."

No sooner had the *Bane* put to sea than the gypsy band came tumbling into the town. Rowan was saddling his horse when Prince Worthyman and Davey came to tell him that they wouldn't be going along back to Castle Rowan after all. "I've decided not to return to Ablemarle for now," the prince explained. "I want to spend some time with Xenobia and my son here, and now that I'm not in a cage I rather enjoy the gypsy life."

"Will you let your brother know you're alive then, Highness?" asked Rowan.

"Only if he gives you any trouble when you take over rule of Argonia. Perhaps then I could be a bargaining point..."

"Spoken like a born statesman, Prince." Rowan's huge hands engulfed Worthyman's as he said goodbye. "I hope I may count on you for advice, in case I'm elected."

The coming of the gypsies to Dragon Bay was not to be the last event that morning to ruffle the town's composure. People ran screaming in an orgy of frenzied terror as Grizel and Grimley flew low over the streets, as though they were looking for someone.

"Eeeeeek!" shrieked the innkeeper's wife. "'Tis the sorcerer's revenge! They've returned to murder us all in our beds!"

"You're not *in* your bed," pointed out his lordship, "But Mistress Maggie and her cat are. I suggest you fetch them here."

A tangle-haired Maggie was rubbing the sleep from her eyes as she came downstairs, and Ching had to pause to wash a paw, having yet to complete his toilet.

After good-morning-did-you-sleep-wells all around, Rowan told her what he had in mind. "You talk to the cat, lass, do you not?"

She yawned and nodded.

"Do you think he'd serve as me recruitment officer for a moment or two?"

When Maggie had secured Ching's agreement, he walked out a short way from them, and in one or two flips of his tail he was joined by both dragons, right there in the middle of the corner at Bayshore and Second Avenue.

In a moment he came sauntering back to Maggie and Rowan. "You can tell him," Ching said, "that the dragons will be happy to move out to his place in exchange for their own sheep and cattle herds and all the enemy bandits they can eat. I think they'd go for anything that involves eating and flying about, but Grizel says they were thinking of moving to a better neighborhood anyway, with more room, as there may be little dragonets along in another year or two."

Maggie told Rowan, who gave the dragons the universal sign for victory.

Ching continued. "And if you don't mind very much, witch, Grimley would like to know if the Mighty Enchantress—I suppose that's you, as you're the only one answering a description anything like that—would very much mind restoring his fire. Grizel is delighted to cook for him, naturally, but he says he misses the warm feeling in the pit of his stomach."

22

It was still chilly early morning when Winnie hugged Maggie one more time, carefully, with one arm only, for the other cradled little Bronwyn. They had breakfasted in the kitchen, to save time, and Rowan and his lady had risen early to say goodbye.

"I wish you could stay longer," Winnie said. "It's been so much brighter here with you about."

"It certainly has," said Cook, handing Rowan a lidded basket. "After you shined the brass, polished all the silver, cleaned the chimneys, swept the entire keep from top to bottom, waxed all the floors, and washed the walls and windows, not to mention laundering the carpets and draperies, it's very bright around here indeed. Tell me, is your sort of witchcraft common? I hope not, or you'll put the entire servant class on the streets to beg..."

"At least she's earned her ride out of the rowan groves by polishing all the diamonds in Grizel's new nest," Rowan laughed.

"Ching did say Grizel greatly appreciated my little housewarming present," Maggie admitted.

"I wish you'd let her take you all the way, or at least let me provide you an escort, if you won't wait until after the coronation when we all come north for the christening," said Rowan, who was now officially king-elect. Maggie had stayed to help and keep Winnie company while Rowan was in the capitol for the tribunal and for the many other government conclaves that eventually led to his selection as king. She had spent the last six weeks helping Winnie pack what she wished to take to Queenston and make arrangements for the management of the estates in their absence.

In a day or two, the soon-to-be royal family would be leaving for the capitol, and Maggie really did need to return now to

Fort Iceworm. Aunt Sybil's budgie, flying high above the rowan trees, had brought word that while Sir William's health had vastly improved, his temper had not. Granny Brown had not Maggie's management abilities, and had already turned Sir William's solicitor into a weasel and one of the local merchants into a raccoon. So it was time for her to return home, but she was in no great hurry to get back to what awaited her. "I'll have escort soon enough," she reminded Rowan. "I'll be traveling in your lands almost the entire two days' journey till I'm to meet Xenobia's caravan, and that whole way I'll be in plain view of Grizel and Grimley's patrol flights."

"Very well, lass, I know you've your own mind, and that's been to my benefit. Are you sure there's no royal boon I can grant you in parting?" Maggie shook her head and occupied herself with undoing her pack to check it one more time.

"Never," said Cook, standing at the window with her hands fisted at the waist of her apron, "will I get used to seeing dragons land in *my* courtyard."

Maggie's eyes raked the kitchen. "Where's Ching?"

"There he is, coming across the coutyard. I suspect he went to say farewell to the barn cats," said Winnie.

"It's good-bye then, I suppose, till after the coronation," Maggie said, shouldering the pack that contained the magic mirror her Aunt Sybil had given her, a new hand spindle carved for her by Colin, a dress, formerly underwear, which she planned to wear while in the company of the gypsies, her medicine pouch, a few staples for her magic to transform into meals, plus a small bag of gold from Rowan—she had had to insist on small. The amount he had tried to lavish on her would have been far too heavy for her to carry. There was also, carefully wrapped in velvet, a miniature portrait of the infant Princess Bronwyn, a gift for her maternal grandfather from the new king and queen, plus a few dried herbs and flowers peculiar to the area around Castle Rowan. Winnie, in the last stages of her pregnancy, had picked these for Granny Brown while Maggie was occupied with repairing the Rowan family tapestry showing Rowan the Rampaging single-handedly defeating the entire Brazorian army.

Rowan and Amberwine saw Maggie out to where Grizel sat waiting. They knew good-byes had to be quick, for even though the rowan trees in the courtyard had been transplanted to save Maggie the discomfort of her witch's allergy to them, still their essence wafted up from the groves that surrounded the castle.

She hugged Winnie again, and kissed baby Bronwyn. Then Rowan, too, stepped forward to embrace her. "Take care of our loved ones, my liege," she mumbled into his massive chest, "and your reign be blest."

He backed away from her with a sweeping bow and, before she could mount, snatched up her hand and kissed it soundly. "I can hardly fail with a mighty sorceress in the family, now can I?" he teased.

"Shall we get ON with it?" Ching said, "I'd rather not hear the minstrel's bitter complaints ringing in my ears the first five miles of our journey about how we made him stand a night and a day holding your horses."

Maggie mounted quickly and Ching sprang to her shoulders. Grizel spread her wings and puffed up a take-off.

For a long time Maggie made a point of not looking down. Ching butted his head against her cheek. "I know how you feel, witch. I will certainly be glad to be home riding nothing more spirited than my hearthrug. Dragons, whales, and horses are all very well in themselves, but hardly suitable cat accommodations."

"Hush, you'll hurt Grizel's feelings," scolded Maggie, looking down and quickly back up again. The trees were passing below them in a dizzying dazzle of green, and the road whipped along like a dusty brown serpent. Perhaps she ought to have risked the trees after all.

"She doesn't understand our conversations unless I choose for her to," said Ching. "Since I am your temporary familiar, we share privileged communication."

"That's nice," said Maggie. "Will you still talk to me sometimes back at Fort Iceworm?" The cat said nothing. "Well, will you?" she repeated.

"There will be no need, will there?" he asked, not at all in his usual bantering tone. "And Granny must be very lonely—she's causing all that trouble again too. She needs my help again—I suspect I shall be very busy with one witch. Sorry. I shall say cat remarks to you occasionally, and rub against you to be petted, and listen to you when I have nothing better to do, but our relationship will have to be pretty much as it was before."

213

Maggie said nothing else, as Grizel was circling in for a landing, and the witch was busy keeping her stomach in order.

Colin rode a dapple gray mare and held a pretty chestnut for Maggie. He had ridden out from the castle the afternoon before, to be on the path beyond the rowans when Grizel arrived.

Seeing that all was in order, Grizel made her good-byes and flew off to meet Grimley to discuss her new rear firewall for their lair.

"That's quite a dragon," said Colin. He looked rather undressed without his guitar slung over his shoulder, Maggie thought.

"Yes, she is."

"I trust her reconciliation went well with Grimley? In all the excitement of the coronation preparations and the tribunals and all you never told me what the cat said about that. I've meant all these months to get around to asking. He wasn't angry or anything, because she went off like that?"

Maggie knew they were making conversation to keep from facing the moment when they'd part, and she strove for a light touch. "Oh, no, Ching said Grimley admired her spirit. Called her his 'little spitfire'."

"Oh no. He didn't?"

"That's what she told Ching. I—I suppose as soon as you get to Queenston you'll be sailing off on the *Bane*?" Maggie put her back upon her saddle horn with deliberate precision, put her foot in the stirrup, then took it out again to stand waiting for his reply.

Colin had squatted down and was mauling some clover. "No—not right away, at least. Actually, the king asked me to delay that for a while. As soon as he's taken office and the coronation's over, he's planning a little voyage to Ablemarle."

"Round the horn?"

"Yes, and he wants me there to record the whole event and make a song of it so the taxpayers will know what he's doing with their funds."

"You'll be coming up for the christening, then?"

"I suppose so, if you promise me I can keep my own shape."

Maggie grinned. "I can promise that, I think."

"Good. I say, your basket is making noises." It was too, squeaking, odd noises. Maggie lifted the lid. A tiny kitten

214

replica of Ching put a white paw on the edge of the basket and tried to scramble out.

"I can't talk to you, Maggie, but you'll have your hands full with Sonnyboy, when he learns to talk," said Ching, the fur on his snow-white chest puffing with fatherly pride. "Rowan thought a powerful witch like you ought to have your own familiar. He told me to tell you that, and you can't know what it cost him. You ought to have seen him, down there in the hayloft, not knowing if I understood or not while he talked to that charming calico mother of Sonny's and me, and us mewing back ever so innocently."

"Well, he won't have as interesting a job, being my familiar, as you did," she said, chucking Ching under the chin while stroking the kitten with one finger between his ears. "No more dragons or wizards for us now, kitty, just scrubbing that year's worth of pots Gran won't have done, and finding another one hundred and one ways to prepare ground venison."

"I wish you wouldn't talk that way about your magic," said Colin. "It's demeaning. It's absolutely wonderful the way you can control fire and food supply and all, *I* think."

She looked at him curiously. "You really think so?"

"I do—it may not seem like much when you're safe and sound in your own castle, but Rowan says it's an enormous tactical asset."

"Rowan—the king—said that?"

Colin nodded. "He called you our secret weapon. Of course, from him, being called a weapon is a compliment. He said a siege would never take a castle with you in it. And look how you provided for us on the road and kept us comfortable in all that bad weather, not to mention holding off Grimley till Rowan could arrive with Neddy."

"I had a little help," she reminded him.

"It doesn't matter."

"It's just that it's so everlastingly dull up there, Colin, with the winters so long and everyone at me to do this and that."

"Well," Colin said slyly. "You'll have help with all that at least."

"He's a bit small. We can't even talk together yet."

"But we can, dear Maggie," said a familiar voice in the back of her mind.

"Moonshine?" she asked.

Colin smiled. "He's been waiting here outside the rowan

215

trees for six months, ever since he followed us back from Dragon Bay. He's followed everywhere you've gone, always within the woods. But he can't stand the rowans either, bewitching creature that he is. The shepherdesses saw him and . . ."

He broke off, for she was no longer there. She was running to the edge of the woods, which seemed to break to show a bit of pearly morning sky.

Colin thought that nothing would be quite ordinary, ever again, for any of them.

ABOUT THE AUTHOR

ELIZABETH SCARBOROUGH was born in Kansas City, KS. She served as a nurse in the U.S. Army for five years, including a year in Viet Nam. Her interests include weaving and spinning, and playing the guitar and dulcimer. She has previously published light verse. She presently makes her home in Alaska. Her other novels include THE UNICORN CREED, BRONWYN'S BANE and THE HAREM OF AMAN AKBAR.

BANTAM
SHOP-AT-HOME
C·A·T·A·L·O·G

Special Offer
Buy a Bantam Book
for only 50¢.

Now you can have an up-to-date listing of Bantam's hundreds of titles plus take advantage of our unique and exciting bonus book offer. A special offer which gives you the opportunity to purchase a Bantam book for only 50¢. Here's how!

By ordering any five books at the regular price per order, you can also choose any other single book listed (up to a $4.95 value) for just 50¢. Some restrictions do apply, but for further details why not send for Bantam's listing of titles today!

Just send us your name and address and we will send you a catalog!